Other Angie Amalfi Mysteries by
Joanne Pence

IF COOKS COULD KILL
BELL, COOK, AND CANDLE
TO CATCH A COOK
A COOK IN TIME
COOKS OVERBOARD
COOKS NIGHT OUT
COOKING MOST DEADLY
COOKING UP TROUBLE
TOO MANY COOKS
SOMETHING'S COOKING

JOANNE PENCE

Two Cooks A-Killing

AN ANGIE AMALFI MYSTERY

AVON BOOKS
An Imprint of HarperCollinsPublishers

This is a work of fiction. Names, characters, places, and incidents are products of the author's imagination or are used fictitiously and are not to be construed as real. Any resemblance to actual events, locales, organizations, or persons, living or dead, is entirely coincidental.

AVON BOOKS
An Imprint of HarperCollins*Publishers*
10 East 53rd Street
New York, New York 10022-5299

First Avon Books paperback printing: November 2003

Avon Trademark Reg. U.S. Pat. Off. and in Other Countries, Marca Registrada, Hecho en U.S.A.
HarperCollins® is a registered trademark of HarperCollins Publishers Inc.

Printed in the U.S.A.

10 9 8 7 6 5 4 3 2 1

This book is dedicated to
Aaron and Zach

━━━━

With acknowledgments for her Napa Valley and winery advice (the changes and omissions are mine) to my old college roommate, Dinah Duffy–Martini, Ph.D., and with thanks for their support, ideas, and encouragement, to my agent, Sue Yuen, and my editor, Sarah Durand.

"What's Christmas time to you but a time for paying bills without money; a time for finding yourself a year older and not an hour richer . . . If I could work my will," said Scrooge indignantly, "every idiot who goes about with 'Merry Christmas' on his lips should be boiled with his own pudding, and buried with a stake of holly through his heart."

Dickens, "A Christmas Carol"

Eagle Crest

═══════

Cast of Major Characters and Actors

CHARACTER	ACTOR
Cliff Roxbury Primary owner of Eagle Crest Winery	*Bart Farrell*
Natalie Parker Roxbury Cliff's second wife, former Ice Follies queen	*Rhonda Mulholland*
Adrian Roxbury Cliff's half-brother, formerly sole owner of the winery	*Kyle O'Rourke*
Leona Roxbury Adrian's wife, and Cliff's step- daughter from his first marriage	*Gwen Hagen*
Julia Parker Natalie's sex-kitten niece	*Brittany Keegan*

Directed by Emery Tarleton

*Two Cooks
A-Killing*

Chapter 1

California State Highway 29 cuts through the heart of the Napa Valley, linking wineries and towns. On weekends, traffic stops almost completely as people jam cars, vans, and tour buses to "wine taste" from one establishment to the next. At the center is St. Helena, home to a number of the most famous wineries in the state—Beringer Brothers, Charles Krug, St. Clement, Sutter Home, and Louis Martini.

Just past the town, Angie Amalfi turned off the highway and drove for another twenty minutes along narrow, winding roads. She was a small woman with wavy brown hair with red highlights, big brown eyes, and long silk-wrapped fingernails in her current favorite shade, coconut cream. The color complemented and drew attention to her hard-won, long-in-coming engagement ring. She drove with one eye on the road, the other on the diamond, as she neared the Waterfield estate.

Winery ownership was the sideline of choice

1

for California's nouveau riche such as Dr. Sterling Waterfield, plastic surgeon to the stars, with offices in Los Angeles and San Francisco. In Angie's opinion, Waterfield wines were worse than mediocre, with a bouquet of rancid oil that caused the tongue to shrivel and the mouth to pucker.

The estate had once been known for its grandeur and beauty, but all that was overshadowed when Waterfield allowed the producers of the most popular evening soap opera of all time, *Eagle Crest*, to use it as the estate of the Roxbury family of wine magnates. Their overwrought lives, loves, and wheeling-and-dealing provided weekly proof that money and power couldn't elevate the disreputable to anything other than glitzy sleaze. Viewers loved them.

As a young teen, Angie had watched the show devotedly, not only every episode, but also reruns during the summer months. The early years, which she had been too young to follow when they were first aired, were shown repeatedly on cable networks. She had faithfully watched them several times over. She loved the program and knew several of the episodes by heart.

Eagle Crest had ended ten years earlier after a run of eight years when its two main stars, Bart Farrell and Rhonda Manning, who played Cliff Roxbury and his wife, Natalie, quit out of fear of being typecast. Unfortunately for them, they hadn't quit soon enough. Never again did either have a part quite so dominating or so challenging (or so much to type, according to Hollywood gossip) as that of a member of the Roxbury dynasty.

Rhonda "Natalie" Manning retired from public

life, while Bart "Cliff" Farrell made infrequent and ill-tempered appearances to talk to *Eagle Crest* fans about his starring role. The fans remembered every iota of information ever put on the screen— throwaway lines, jokes, even story angles that didn't work and were dropped. Farrell's inability to remember, let alone explain, such minutiae usually triggered those outbursts of grumpiness.

Now the cast was being reassembled for a ten-year reunion show, a Christmas reunion, and she, Angelina Rosaria Maria Amalfi, had been asked to be a part of it.

A major part, if she said so herself. She was so anxious to get to Eagle Crest, it was all she could do to stick to the speed limit.

Her father had phoned the day before. He'd gotten a call from his old friend Dr. Waterfield: the woman who was to prepare the important center-piece meal of the show had broken her leg. Dr. Waterfield wanted to know if Angie could handle it.

Could she ever!

She made sure her fiancé, San Francisco Homicide Inspector Paavo Smith, had no problem with her going away for a few days. Dr. Waterfield was a widower who lived with his two sons, Junior and Silver. Junior had once dated Angie's sister, Frannie, but things hadn't worked out between them.

Paavo had encouraged her to take the job if she wanted it. *If?* Was he joking? She'd crawl through ground-up Christmas ornaments for this job.

Actually, she couldn't help but suspect he was glad to have her think about something other than their wedding plans. Not to mention engagement parties, bridal showers, and everything that went with them, from dresses to music to napkin rings. They were already making her a little crazy.

Her thoughts sprang back to the Christmas reunion show. The thought that she would be the first true-blue fan to find out what the next step would be in the lives of the cast gave her goosebumps.

The story had begun with Cliff Roxbury. Married and living in Australia, one day he was struck by lightning. He ended up with amnesia, in California. There, he met Ice Follies queen Natalie Parker, who was engaged to winery owner Adrian Roxbury.

Cliff fell wildly in lust with Natalie and her ice skates, stole her from Adrian, and married her. He then swindled Adrian out of half the winery. Adrian was about to shoot Cliff, when—lo and behold!—the two discovered they had the same last name because they had the same father.

From Australia, Cliff's older first wife sent her daughter, Leona, to find her missing husband. Because of his amnesia, Cliff didn't recognize her.

Seeing a chance for wealth, Leona married the still rich but emotionally wrecked Adrian.

Into the mix came Natalie's niece, the wild and man-hungry Julia Parker.

The catfights between Julia and Leona had garnered some of the highest TV ratings on record and set the standards for primetime soap fights. Angie recalled one such remarkable fight which included several tons of grapes, broken vats of aging wine, and evening gowns that left little to the imagination when soaked in wine.

Angie sighed. Yes, those were the days of real television before the invasion of talk shows, reality specials, and Court TV.

Her mind swirled thinking about what might come next. Would Cliff's memory return? Would his first wife come to America? Was Leona's baby her husband's or (gasp) stepfather Cliff's? And would the killer of Natalie's sex-kitten niece, Julia, ever be found?

The storyline had been hastily rewritten after Brittany Keegan, the young actress who'd played Julia Parker, was killed in an accident.

As a young teen, hearing about the death, Angie couldn't believe it. It was the first time she'd experienced the demise of a beloved celebrity. The memory of what she'd been doing when she heard the news—going to gym class—would always be with her.

She'd cried for days and worn nothing but black, head to toe. She'd pored over her *Seventeen* magazines, reading and rereading stories about the pretty, vivacious Brittany, and she even bought a copy of *Newsweek* when it ran a tiny article and photo of the funeral.

Angie had been one distraught kid.

The thought of now meeting the remaining Roxbury clan brought back all the emotions she'd held about them over the years. Cliff Roxbury was her favorite, even though he was devilish and sneaky. Despite his errant ways, deep, deep down, she knew he loved his family. He simply hadn't learned it yet.

She liked Natalie, too, and understood why she was a neurotic basket case with a husband like

Cliff. Leona, she hated; and Adrian was a wuss—albeit a handsome and charming one.

The thought of being with them made her tingle with anticipation. She'd have to do a little work, of course, but for her, the so-called work would be more play than anything.

She reached the entrance to the Waterfield estate. In the center of the massive gate was a cast-iron eagle. Even the owner must have succumbed to its being known as "Eagle Crest" by one and all.

The gate stood open, beckoning. As if in a dream, she entered. The driveway led through vineyards for nearly a quarter mile before it reached the mansion. She stopped the car and simply stared at it a moment.

Eagle Crest, aglow in a winter wonderland . . .

The land around the mansion was covered with snow, even though it almost never snowed in the Napa Valley. The twelve-thousand-square-foot home was outlined with lights, from its Sonoma red rock foundation and first floor, to the rustic wooden French chalet design of the upper two stories. Lights lined the rooftop, the four rock chimneys, the eaves, the windows, the roof of the veranda, and the columns surrounding the front door. Even the separate twelve-car garage was lit. Lighted deer pranced on the snow-covered lawn. Floodlights illuminated a snowman. A decorated tree glowed golden on the edge of the large, graceful walk-around front porch. So many lights had been used that they seemed to brighten the sky on this overcast spring day.

On television, it had looked like a fine house.

Here, it was so awesome the hairs on her arms stood on end.

Ignoring the huge array of cars, trucks, trailers, and equipment parked in front of the house, she imagined the long gravel driveway filled with limos, Cadillacs, custom-painted Porsches, and the Roxbury family and their friends, dressed in the latest Parisian fashions . . .

A horn broke her reverie. A delivery truck was stuck behind her car, the driver scowling.

She drove on and pulled into a space between a Chevy Suburban and a Honda Civic. Lots of people were rushing about, faces scowling and serious, materials in hand, as if they knew exactly what they were doing.

A twinge of self-doubt struck her. Although her father had assured her that Dr. Waterfield had been given the task of finding a gourmet cook to prepare the Christmas dinner, what if the director didn't like her style of cooking? Or didn't like her? Or choked on one of her meals?

She took a deep breath and got out of the car. This was nothing to get worked up about, she told herself, as she checked her black Oscar de la Renta suit for lint and smoothed its wrinkles. She also wore black Ferragamo pumps and carried a black Coach briefcase. For color, she'd added a teal blue Hermès scarf. Dressing like this, as if she were going to a funeral rather than a job interview, meant the director should be assured of how seriously she took the opportunity to display her cooking skills to Hollywood. Maybe Julia Child had begun this way.

She'd already decided on a scrumptious gourmet meal that would look fabulous under bright television lights on the Roxbury Christmas table.

She'd begin with an array of colorful, interesting appetizers such as sautéed trout meunière with pecan sauce, a salad of duck confit with Stilton cheese, arugula and raspberry-shallot vinaigrette, wild mushroom soup with spinach and ginger broth, smoked quail with black truffle sauce, a beautifully presented pistachio-crusted rack of lamb, goat cheese-and-garlic potatoes with an Espagnole sauce, and a side of eggplant and portabello ratatouille. She'd fill a table with desserts, from pears poached in Cabernet Sauvignon (not Waterfield Cabernet, since she wanted one that would taste good) to a simple strawberry flambé. If the fire was a problem on the set, she'd make a St. Honoré cake. A cake named for a saint would be appropriate for Christmas, she should think.

She could hardly wait to start. She was going to make her papà proud of her, proud that his friend sought his daughter's help and that she cooked a meal more pleasing, eye-catching, and mouthwatering than anyone could have imagined.

None of the people bustling about seemed the least interested in who she was or in helping with her luggage. This wasn't a hotel, she reminded herself; she was here to work. And work she would, beginning with her suitcases. She'd probably overpacked for a four- or at most, five-day visit, but she'd had no idea if the dress here would be casual or business attire.

She tugged the Pullman out of the trunk, set it on its wheels, and slid out the handle, then hefted the carryall onto her shoulder and tossed the garment bag over her arm. She grabbed the make-up case with one hand, the Pullman's handle with the other, and somehow managed to wheel, reel, and lurch her way toward the front door.

The walkway looked wet and had a few snowflakes on it, while the lawn was white. She stepped gingerly, afraid the walk was icy. It wasn't.

She bent over and picked up a snowflake. It was plastic.

Despite her struggle to lift the luggage up three steps to the wide veranda, the realization that it was Eagle Crest's veranda made her almost giddy. The double doors had lush wreaths with bows and pinecones and had been draped with ornament-covered fir garlands. Beside them, planter boxes of star jasmine twinkled with Christmas lights. She felt as if she'd just been given a giant Christmas present eight months early.

She knocked on the door. After waiting and knocking a couple more times, she tried the handle. The door opened.

She pushed it wide, and before her stretched the elegant Roxbury entryway. The floor was marble, the walls white, the staircase graceful and gently curved. She knew it every bit as well as her own parents' home. To think she was actually here!

Thick garlands of silver and gold cascaded along the banister and edged the ceiling. Festive wreaths hung on the walls, and a tiny silver tree rotated, playing "We Wish You a Merry Christmas" as it turned. A small table was covered with candles, boxwood plants, and a three-tiered stand of sugared fruit, nuts, and candy. Heavy cables and wires crisscrossed the floor.

She was awestruck.

"Come on in," a young woman called out as she bounded down the stairs to the foyer, rounded the banister, and headed down the hallway to the back of the house. Her yellow shift stopped at mid-thigh and she wore Birkenstock sandals. Angie stared after her. With oversized horn-rimmed glasses—the kind nobody wore anymore except as a prop on a TV show—and brown hair with fluffy bangs pulled into pigtails low on the sides of her head, she looked like a character out of *The Beverly Hillbillies*.

"Wait! Can you tell me where . . ." Angie stopped. No sense wasting her breath. The foyer was empty. To the right, just as on the television show, was the living room with white walls, a white fireplace and mantel, and ecru and ruby red furniture. Before her was the very sofa on which Cliff had seduced his stepdaughter Leona, right after her wedding to his brother Adrian! Angie's heart palpitated. The scene had been so hot that if her TV had spontaneously combusted she wouldn't have been surprised.

In front of the windows stood a fourteen-foot-tall fake Douglas fir covered with white and silver ornaments, angels, and starbursts. The ornaments were hand-blown and painted, fragile, and expensive. Colorfully wrapped presents were stacked under the tree, and bowls of fruits, nuts, and flowers adorned the table. A pear-green and yellow garland of hypericum sprigs lined the mantel, with scalloped embroidered Christmas stockings. The only jarring spot was the mound of television equipment piled against a wall.

A beautiful hand-painted porcelain figurine of the Little Drummer Boy atop a music box held the place of honor in the center of the mantel. Its beauty drew Angie close. She didn't remember it from the *Eagle Crest* shows.

A crystal bowl of delicious-looking miniature chocolate truffles sat on an end table. Angie plopped one in her mouth—and promptly spit it out. Plastic.

She was sure the Little Drummer Boy must be laughing at her. She had to laugh as well. Props, she thought. They were all props.

To the left of the foyer, the dining room was bright with an enormous crystal chandelier over a traditional Chippendale mahogany dining room set. A centerpiece of roses, anemones, and dusty millers filled the tabletop. The buffet was a mass of poinsettias and candles, and a garland of pepperberry leaves. She sniffed. All of it was fabric and plastic.

Adrian Roxbury, the suave, sophisticated, duped-out-of-half-the-winery-and-love-of-his-life brother, often held court in this room, nibbling at insubstantial foods, drinking fine wines, and plotting his revenge on Cliff.

It was all a bit overwhelming.

Angie dragged her luggage into the foyer. Now what? Still beyond belief at her good fortune to be here and actually to be part of the Christmas show, she went down the hallway to an enormous wood-paneled family room. Many a tryst, and many a war of words, had taken place there. Her gaze wandered over the honey brown leather furniture, the Kilim rugs, the moosehead over the massive river rock fireplace, and the full bar, where Cliff Roxbury often got sloshed while coming up with a devilish plan.

Here, too, another grandiose tree, this one filled with colorful rustic hand-made ornaments of wood, glass, and china filled a corner. She could hardly take in all the wreaths, holly, candy, candles, lights, and other knickknacks that covered the room. A bowl full of luscious grapes sat on a table. She reached for one to cleanse her mouth of the plastic taste from the candy, then stopped.

Fooled again.

Just beyond the family room was a breakfast room with more decorations. On TV, the kitchen was connected to it, which she assumed was the case here. The door, however was closed.

Three sets of French doors led to a courtyard enclosed within a four-foot adobe wall, and a bougainvillea-covered archway over a carved gate. It had always been great fun to watch a Roxbury sneak into or out of that gate late at night.

Yet another Christmas tree stood in the courtyard. Blinking lights had been strung through all the plants and over the adobe wall. Plastic snow covered the tiled floor, gated archway, and even the bougainvillea.

In the courtyard were three men and one woman, all seeming to be talking at once. The pig-tailed woman wasn't among them.

Angie joined the group. They were obviously part of the crew, judging from clipboards, tape, and lighting equipment, and their generally bad dispositions.

They ignored her.

"Hi. I'm here to help with the show," she said brightly, interrupting a pudgy, balding fellow who was waving his arms and complaining about lights and cantilevers, whatever they were. In his hand was a blue lava lamp.

"Oh! I can't believe it!" Angie squealed, pointing. "That's the very lamp Leona convinced Cliff that Natalie would love, to make up for his sleeping with Leona, of course. It was so funny when Natalie hit him with it! I'm surprised it's not broken."

All talking ceased as four heads swiveled her way and regarded her as if she'd just dropped in from the *Jerry Springer Show*. "It *is* broken," one man said.

At the same moment, another fellow ran up to them holding a jeweled hand mirror. Angie's breathing quickened. It was Natalie's very own—the one she always used to check her makeup before doing some particularly dastardly deed.

The mirror was cracked. "Oh, no!" Angie wailed.

"It's got to be sabotage," the man holding it said. The others swore profusely.

"Well, you folks are busy, so maybe you can tell me if Mr. Waterfield is around?" Angie asked. "I know the family."

"Not here, as you can see," the woman snapped.

"Just what *do* you want?" A bushy-haired man with a clipboard and a belt filled with measuring tapes and carpenter tools gave her a harsh glare.

"I'm trying to find out who's in charge. I'm here to see about handling the food preparation."

"Food preparation? The food is down by the trailers." The woman sniffed and turned back to the others.

"I'll be working on the show. Who should I report to?" Angie asked in a friendly voice, despite the irritation building inside. She supposed she'd have to work with these people.

"How should I know?" the woman said. She and two men walked in one direction, while the other two men went the opposite way.

"Merry Christmas to you, too," Angie muttered, hands on hips. This did not bode well.

"They don't talk to anyone who isn't a star. Or their boss," a male voice explained.

She turned to see a young man standing in the doorway. He was movie-star handsome, with black hair and green eyes and a perfectly sculpted face. His tailored green plaid shirt was unbuttoned at the neckline, the sleeves rolled to the elbows displaying a Patek Philippe gold watch on a tanned wrist. Sliding his hands in his pockets, he strolled toward her, his gaze devouring her in a way that told her he liked what he saw.

"Welcome to Eagle Crest," he said with a cocky smile. "I'm one of the unfortunates who lives here."

Angie gawked. "You're a Waterfield?" She never imagined anyone with his good looks would be part of the family.

"Silver."

"Junior's little brother! Somehow, I never got a chance to meet you."

His smile dissolved. "Sounds like you do know the family. I thought you were just trying a bit of one-upmanship with the crew. I expect they thought the same."

"Perhaps they weren't completely wrong," she admitted with a sly grin, "although our parents are old friends. My father is Sal Amalfi. My name's Angie. I met your brother a couple of times when he dated my sister, Frannie."

"Francesca Amalfi. Yes, I remember." He slowly circled Angie as he spoke. Little puffs of plastic flew into the air and landed on his shoes. "Junior was quite gone over her. Didn't last long, did it?" He stopped moving, his words more a statement than a question.

"No, it didn't." Angie hesitated to say more. Her sister Frannie wasn't easy to get along with, but Junior must have been even more difficult, because Frannie broke it off after a couple of dates. In college, Frannie had hung around with the "in" sorority crowd and tried to go out as often as the most popular girls when she could find boys brave, daring, or desperate enough to date her. Young Waterfield was rich, and his family's house had been on television. Her sorority sisters would have been "so totally" impressed, Angie would have sworn Frannie would continue to date him even if he looked like the Incredible Hulk and had the personality of Hannibal Lecter. Strangely, she didn't. "Is Junior here as well?" Angie asked.

"He still lives at home. Like me."

She glanced over the enormous house. The back of it was also festooned in Christmas lights. "I'm not surprised."

He followed her gaze, then placed his hand on the top rail of a wrought-iron chair, disturbing the fake snow. "This is a hard spot to leave," he admitted. "Especially since my mother passed away, and Dad spends so much time in Los Angeles. Junior and I are the ones who look after the place. It's probably the one thing we're suited to do." He gave a small smile, but his eyes held bitterness. "So, you're here to work with this menagerie, are you?"

She clasped her hands. "I'm looking forward to it."

"That'll change. If you found the crew rude, just wait until the cast shows up. I was a kid when they first swooped down on the house. They aren't exactly here to win friends. They'd fight and backbite their way to winning a Miss Congeniality award."

She wasn't surprised. "Who's in charge?"

"Emery Tarleton is the director. I guess he's as close to running things as anyone. The producers never have shown up. I think they're a conglomerate of suits, not human at all."

"Is Bart Farrell around?" Angie asked, looking from side to side in hopes the actor who played Cliff Roxbury, one of the favorite dream men of her teenage years, would materialize.

"None of the stars are here yet. Just the set-up crew. The talent will arrive in a couple of days. They're too big to sit around and wait. Not to mention, they can't stand each other."

"What's he like?" she asked, unable to hide her interest.

"Bart Farrell?" He sounded surprised at her question.

"Of course!"

"Angie?" called a voice behind her.

Stunned that anyone was acknowledging her let alone knew her name, she turned to find the perky pigtailed one approaching.

"I'm Mariah," the woman said, her voice soft. "Em told me to get you and show you to your room and all that stuff."

" 'Em'?" Angie asked.

"Emery Tarleton. The director."

"Of course." Angie smiled. "And a clever throwback to James Bond movies, too."

Mariah gaped blankly at her. "Whatever. Follow me."

As Angie moved closer to Mariah she saw that the young woman was wearing a wig. She wondered what had happened, if she'd lost her hair because of chemotherapy or some horrible accident.

Angie glanced over her shoulder to say goodbye to Silver, but he had gone.

She faced Mariah again. "Have you worked with Mr. Tarleton long?"

"I worked on other projects with him. Nothing much panned out, so we're eager to get started with this."

"Really? Have you met Bart Farrell or the other stars?"

"Sure. They're no big deal. This way." Mariah led her through the family room and foyer.

"My bags . . ." Angie wanted to ask more about Farrell, but she needed some help.

"Let me get one." Mariah picked up the little make-up case, then climbed the stairs to the second floor.

The suitcase wheels did no good on those stairs. Angie slung the carryall back onto her shoulder, the garment bag over her arm, and lifted the Pullman by its grip. She could barely manage to clear the stairs with it, but had to walk sideways, like a crab-turned-stevedore. Someday, somehow, she would learn not to pack so many clothes.

She was panting and perspiring onto her Oscar de la Renta by the time she reached the landing. To her horror, she saw that Mariah had continued up another flight to the third floor.

Angie took a big breath and this time tossed the garment bag onto the suitcase and hefted both into her arms. Wordlessly, her knees splayed outward and her legs bowed under the weight, she followed. Nice group here. Friendly. Helpful. Really knew how to make a person feel welcome.

Mariah walked to the end of the third-floor hallway, unlocked the door, and stepped aside.

Angie nearly toppled over as she dropped her suitcase and garment bag onto the landing and struggled to find her breath. She set the Pullman back onto its wheels, piled the other bags on top, and steered everything into the bedroom. This part of the house had never been shown on TV. No wonder. Her room was little larger than a closet. A single bed covered one wall, a dresser the wall opposite, and straight ahead was a window overlooking the courtyard and hills beyond. "How tiny," she exclaimed. The room was dark, depressing, and cold. Unnaturally cold. A chill rippled down her spine.

Mariah leaned against the doorjamb. "This floor was remodeled to add some bedrooms as the cast grew. Since we aren't going to have a big cast for the reunion special, nobodies like you and me get to stay in the big house."

Thoughts of all the actors Angie had hope to meet clutched her. "They won't all be here?" she asked, her voice strangled.

"Nope. Just the big four—Bart Farrell, Rhonda Manning, Kyle O'Rourke, and Gwen Hagen."

Angie breathed again. Cliff, Natalie, Adrian, and Leona. They were the ones who mattered most. "Why not the others?" she asked.

"Nobody's saying, but salaries for O'Rourke and Hagen probably nearly busted their budget. And Em apparently has a very special idea about the script as well. He swore they were the only ones needed."

"Interesting," Angie murmured, more curious than ever about what the script would reveal.

Suddenly, she shivered. "Why is it so cold? It feels as if all the air-conditioning in the house is concentrated in this room."

"I don't know," Mariah answered. "It's always this way."

"It's much warmer in the hallway." Angie stepped out. "Whose child was that?" she asked, pointing toward the stairs.

Mariah joined her. "There's no child in this house."

"But I saw . . ." What had she seen? It was a child, wasn't it? Perhaps carrying the luggage up two flights of stairs had been harder on her than she'd thought. "My mistake."

"Your key's on the bureau." Mariah pointed to the bathroom, third door on the right, as she crossed the hall.

Chapter 2

The block-long Hall of Justice dominated that section of San Francisco where the rough, rundown South of Market district butted up against the ugliness of the Central Freeway. A utilitarian gray concrete slab with all the artistry of an old Soviet government building, the Hall did nothing to beautify the area.

Inside, the Homicide bureau on the fourth floor was even shabbier, with mismatched desks, file cabinets, bookcases and shelves, antique computers, and (some swore) even a rotary dial phone or two. As part of the Bureau of Inspections, the homicide inspector had a jurisdiction which covered the entire city and county, all forty-nine square miles, with its population of two million people by day and about eight hundred thousand at night when the commuters went home. An ever-present number of tourists helped fill the sudden void of humanity on evenings and weekends.

Despite the hundreds of thousands of additional

21

bodies that routinely descended on the city, it was usually the residents themselves who kept the homicide inspectors, like Paavo Smith, busy.

He hit the print command on his computer. The report he'd just finished would send the murderer of a young gas station attendant to San Quentin for life. Paavo and his partner, Toshiro Yoshiwara, had been on the case for three weeks. When they found the killer, a druggie out of his mind from methamphetamine, they made sure they did everything by the book, taking no chance the guy would walk. Paavo had talked with the D.A. that morning and confirmed that the case was clean and solid.

He reached for the phone, then stopped. Normally, he would have called Angie and gone out tonight to celebrate. This case deserved it. His hand dropped to the desk. She was probably already on her way to Napa County.

Leave it to Angie to end up working on a Christmas show in April! It didn't make any sense to him. Hollywood and what went on there were as foreign to him as Bangladesh. When he thought about television and movie portrayal of police work, he knew the people involved understood him as little as he understood them.

Still, to him, Angie and Christmas went hand-in-hand—both full of warmth, hope, and love.

He only wished Sal Amalfi hadn't been involved in getting her the job.

Although Angie hadn't picked up on it at all, he understood why her father had urged her to spend time living in a rich man's house, with eligible bachelors close by.

Sal Amalfi didn't know his daughter well if he imagined an opulent setting could influence her or affect her heart. At the same time, he didn't blame Sal for trying. If he were Angie's father, he wasn't sure how happy he'd be about her engagement to a poor homicide cop. As that poor cop, he was ecstatic.

"Can I help you?" Inspector Bo Benson stood at the doorway and spoke to an unseen person. Benson was the fashion plate of Homicide, today in a light gray Armani suit, white shirt, and striped gray silk tie. He once said he was sorry the term African-American had come into popularity because he much preferred the alliteration of being Bo Benson, black and beautiful.

Women flocked to be near him, no matter how he said it.

"I'm looking for Paavo Smith," came the curt reply.

The woman's sharp voice cut through Paavo's elation at watching his twelve-page report spit out of the printer. He glanced up, but couldn't see who Bo was talking to.

A moment later, the mystery was solved.

Stepping around the file cabinet that had hidden her, head held high—or as high as it could be held—and marching steadfastly down an aisle crowded with desks, law books, case histories, and folders, came one of the tiniest women Paavo had ever seen.

She was at most four feet tall. She wore a full-length dress of pink satin with ruffles on the bodice, and a wide-brimmed straw hat with a row of white daisies circling the crown. Paavo almost rubbed his eyes to make sure he hadn't fallen asleep. One look at the faces of the other inspectors, and he knew they were seeing the same thing.

In the past, Angie had whimsically sent a leprechaun and even an Italian tenor bellowing "O Sole Mio" his way. He stood, a smile on his face. He knew Angie was busy, yet she'd taken the time—

"Paavo Smith?" the woman demanded. She stared up at him, tilting her head nearly all the way back to take in his full six-foot, two-inch height, clasping her hat to her dyed blond hair as she did so. Her face was round as a pancake with large, watery blue eyes, an upturned nose, and lips smeared with ruby red lipstick. She reminded him of Miss Piggy. Her frowning face did not give the impression that she was about to burst into song.

The sinking feeling that this visit had nothing to do with Angie struck. He tried to ignore his disappointment.

On the other hand . . .

He glanced at his colleagues. Ever since his engagement he'd been the brunt of so many gags he felt he was living a skit out of *Saturday Night Live*. The others weren't smiling, either.

"Won't you have a seat?" He pointed to the guest chair by his desk. She hoisted herself onto it. "What can I do for you?" he asked, also sitting.

"I heard that you're a damn good cop. I don't want the butterbrains they've been sending me to mess up this case any more than they already have." Her strident voice was ear-splitting. "We have an acquaintance in common, Connie Rogers. I live nearby and shop in her store, or go inside to say hello when it's empty, which is most of the time. Anyway, I told her I needed a cop with brains. She said you're engaged to her best friend. That I should talk to you. She also said if you didn't do right by me, she'd tell your fiancée, and that one would set you straight."

Paavo's eyebrows rose. He could feel the amusement of the other inspectors.

"You're involved in a homicide?" he asked.

Her big eyes blinked rapidly and she lifted her shoulders in a woeful shrug. "I hope that pissant fool hasn't gone and gotten his effing brains blown out, but he might have." She appeared on the verge of tears. "I'm worried about him."

"Are you saying someone has disappeared? Have you checked with Missing Persons?" Paavo asked, his voice calm and soothing.

"Of course I did! What kind of birdbrain do you take me for?" She folded her little arms. She was round and well padded, without a discernible shape under all her skirts and ruffles. "They haven't done anything. I'm sure Fred's out there, lying in some ditch, hopefully still alive. Who knows, with all the time they've wasted? What the hell's wrong with that department?"

"Let's start at the beginning," Paavo said, keeping his tone placid as he pulled out a notepad and pen. "Tell me your name."

"Minnie Petite."

His hand froze. He'd ask what her real name was after he talked to Missing Persons. "Age?"

"Do you need that?"

"Yes."

She glowered. "Fifty-nine."

"Residence?"

She gave him the information he needed about her home in San Francisco, plus mentioned her work in movies and on television whenever they had a role for someone "extremely vertically challenged."

"Now," Paavo said, "tell me about the missing person."

She folded her hands. "His name is Fred Demitasse, age sixty-four. Gray hair, brown eyes, one hundred ten pounds, and four feet three inches tall."

Paavo put down his pen and looked hard at his partner.

If Yosh's family had stayed in Japan, he might have become rich and famous as a sumo wrestler because he was tall, stocky, and muscular. Instead, he was a third-generation poor American cop. Such was life, and Paavo knew few people who enjoyed life more than Yosh.

His partner had been openly eavesdropping ever since Minnie had first strolled between their desks. Yosh's face was an open book. If this was a practical joke, Paavo would know it. Either Yosh wasn't in on the joke, or the woman was legitimate.

"All right, copper." Minnie thrust out her jaw. "I'll explain this once, and once only. Fred is a dwarf. He has achondroplasia, a not uncommon condition that results in short arms and legs, and a slightly enlarged head. It's not life threatening or anything else. He was, in every way except limb size, quite normal. On the other hand, I'm all in proportion"—she sat a little straighter—"just small. People used to call those of us who are ultra petite 'midgets.' These days, you call me that and I'll deck you. Got it now? Can we get on with finding Fred?"

Paavo cleared his throat. "Yes, ma'am." Yosh buried his head in his papers.

"Now, ask your questions," Minnie demanded.

"What is your relationship to Mr. Demitasse?" he began.

"We're just friends, good enough to . . . you know. But marriage isn't our thing. We often work together, so we share a house with two other little people, also actors. They're both out of town with gigs. One with Ringling Brothers. The other is part of a show in Vegas."

"When did you last see Mr. Demitasse?"

"Three days ago."

"Has he ever gone off without telling you?"

"He has, but this time I'm worried." She opened her handbag, pulled out a lace handkerchief—he thought everyone used tissues these days—and dabbed her eyes.

"Why is that, Ms. Petite?" he asked.

She looked heavenward. "I have a feeling about it."

A feeling, Paavo thought. Great. *Thank you, Connie Rogers, for sending Ms. Petite this way.* "When Mr. Demitasse left in the past, how long did he stay away?"

"A week, sometimes a little longer. But usually the other boys would be home. He never left me alone before."

"When will the others be back?"

She blew her nose with a loud honk, then daintily put her handkerchief back in her purse. "Not for a month"—she sighed despondently—"maybe longer."

"I see. Well, Ms. Petite, I'll look into this situation and let you know as soon as I find out something."

"What the hell kind of brush-off is that?" she brayed, to his amazement. "You don't believe me, either!"

"I believe you, but you're letting your imagination run amok," he said. "There's no reason to think anything bad has happened to Mr. Demitasse. I'm sure he'll come home soon, and you'll find it was a simple mistake."

She slid off the chair, held her purse in front of her with two tiny hands, and cast a steely eye at him. "I'll be back, Inspector Smith. I won't stop until I find Fred, so don't try to blow me off. I may be little in size, but I have a big mouth, and I'll use it if anyone tries to push me around."

The threat didn't sit well with Paavo, but he held his displeasure in check. "We'll do our best to find him, Ms. Petite."

She put a hand on her hip. "You damn well better!" With that, she strode out of the room.

Paavo sank back in his chair, feeling like he'd been run over by a Mack truck. Yosh glanced at him and grinned. "Looks to me, pal, like that's the long and short of it."

Paavo wadded a piece of paper and threw it at him.

Chapter 3

Bart Farrell stared at the empty suitcase on the bed of his six-million-dollar Bel Air home—the house that Cliff Roxbury bought. It was a stately white mansion on Stone Canyon Road, the kind of place that looked more imposing, Farrell had to admit, from the outside. The rooms were small, the walls had spidery cracks from numerous earthquakes, there was no view to speak of, and the plumbing needed to be torn out and replaced, if he had the money to do it.

The time had come to pack. He sucked in his gut and looked at himself in the mirror. Not bad. He'd only gained a bit over fifteen pounds . . . maybe twenty . . . at most twenty-five, over the past ten years, and stretched out over a six-foot frame, it was barely noticeable. Anyway, many megastars wore girdles from time to time.

From the top of the closet he pulled down a hatbox and lifted out a tan Australian bush hat with one side tied against the crown—the Crocodile Dundee look. He never quite understood why

Cliff Roxbury, who had left the Outback with amnesia, wore an Aussie hat since supposedly he couldn't remember he *was* Australian. Farrell was a bit ashamed that it took him four years into the show before he thought to question the hat, but since nobody else brought it up, he kept that little discrepancy to himself. He guessed he was simply more clever than most.

Before the mirror again, Farrell placed the hat on his head, cocked it to one side, and viewed his left profile, then the right. He adjusted the hat a little lower on the brow and tried again. That was it. Dashing. Rakish. And, if he did say so himself, sexy as hell.

That was the real reason he didn't question Cliff wearing the hat.

He leaned closer to the mirror and stroked his cheeks. The wrinkles hadn't been there in the past. Soon it would be time for another facelift. The last one wasn't half bad. He especially liked the way it pulled his eyebrows up and outward, as if they were wings, ready to fly away. He'd be seeing Dr. Waterfield in St. Helena. Maybe they could work out a deal.

Too bad the skin tuck couldn't remedy the bushiness of his brows. He'd tried plucking the stray hairs out, but they grew back thicker and more corkscrew-like than ever. When he trimmed them, they protruded like needles on a porcupine. He forced himself to ignore them, or, if absolutely necessary, to slick them down with pomade.

He studied the lines on his face more critically this time. No problem, he'd simply ask for a heavy filter on the camera lens. Who'd ever know, besides the crew and cast?

The cast . . .

He shut his eyes. How could he go through it all again?

Bring it all back to the surface after all these years? He should have been able to put it behind him by now, to move on. But he hadn't.

Somehow, from early on, he knew he'd be forever stuck in the *Eagle Crest* world, unable to break away. Not *wanting* to break away.

And he'd been right.

If it was his career he was thinking of, it wouldn't have mattered so much. If it was only his career, he'd be glad. Instead, it was much, much more.

Don't think about the past, he ordered himself, not Rhonda, or Gwen, or Kyle . . . or Brittany. Especially not poor, dead Brittany. *Put it out of your mind and stop. Right now. Just stop!*

He let himself drop onto the edge of the bed, the hat shadowing his eyes, and stared at the Persian carpet covering the floor.

Rhonda Manning entered the bedroom of her suite in San Francisco's Fairmont Hotel feeling pampered and beautiful. Three days ago she'd left her home in Beverly Hills and traveled north. Here, she was only a couple of hours from St. Helena.

In miles, the distance involved wasn't bad, but in years, it felt as if centuries had passed.

She took off her gloves and tossed them onto

the bed, followed by her coat. The chilliness of San Francisco as compared to Los Angeles never ceased to surprise her.

Today, she'd gone to Elizabeth Arden for "the works." For the past ten years, she'd been a tall, slender, sleek-haired blonde, but now she was back to Natalie's flaming red color and bouffant, Ice Follies–queen style. Her blue eyes, always enormous, appeared even more spherical and wide with the carefully applied make-up, and her high, round cheekbones were made more pronounced by the dark, coppery blush in the hollows of her cheeks.

The cosmeticians had told her she was even more gorgeous than she'd been in the past, that she was more "mature" and more elegant. Her face had more character, more finesse.

She spun toward the mirror. Her jaws clenched, the joint below the ear working as she ground her teeth. She hated the way she looked.

It was one thing to look at her transformation at Elizabeth Arden, quite another to see Natalie here, in her hotel suite.

The past rushed at her.

With her hand on her chest, in a breathy, little girl voice with a heavy hint of the Southern belle, she said, "It's all yo-ah fault, Cliff dahling. Ah know you! How day-ah you talk to me lahk thay-at!"

Her face fell and she stared, hard, at her reflection. "And I know you, Natalie. What you are. What you have the power to make me. How I hate you! I hate you!"

She threw a hairbrush at the mirror. It hit with a clatter, but the glass didn't break.

She flung herself into a chair and covered her mouth with shaking hands. Soon her whole body trembled.

Playing Natalie again was the last thing she wanted to do. She didn't know if she could bear it. A Christmas special, no less. Brittany had died while taping a Christmas special. What an ironic coincidence.

She began to laugh aloud, then stopped.

Or was it?

What if it wasn't a coincidence?

What if it was on purpose, all of this was on purpose? What if someone wanted to resurrect the horror after all these years?

Her initial reaction had been to prevent the Christmas special from going forward. Now she was more convinced than ever.

She clenched her fists. The show must *not* go on.

Angie dashed down the two flights of stairs to the main floor of the house. She hadn't bothered to unpack, but had simply freshened up before going in search of the director or someone in charge. It'd be prudent to make sure she had the job before she moved in.

Also, she didn't like being in that oppressive bedroom any longer than necessary.

In the family room, Dr. Sterling Waterfield sat at a bar outlined in Christmas tree lights, with a Rudolph the Red-nosed Reindeer figure on one end. Rudolph's nose glowed as he bucked up and down—which looked like he was either "prancing" awkwardly . . . or humping the bar top.

It had been several years since Angie had last

seen Waterfield. He appeared younger than ever—which, she supposed, was the way it should be for someone in the plastic surgery business. With thick gray hair and dark eyes, his face was sun-baked to a bronzed hue and looked as shiny as polished leather. No sags, though. Not around the eyes, not even beneath the chin. He was of medium height, and bony, as if in his quest to keep his skin firm, he'd forgotten to eat. He wore a maroon velvet smoking jacket and black slacks. On the bar at his elbow was a drink. It wasn't wine.

"Dr. Waterfield." She walked toward him, her hands outstretched.

He jumped up. They air-kissed, then he took one hand, stepping back to look at her. "Angelina! How you've grown. You're beautiful! Simply beautiful!"

"Thank you," she murmured. His hair no longer receded as far as it used to. She studied his hairline for plugs. Sure enough, the little devils were there. When she was young she'd had a doll with washable hair. The hair had been attached by punching tufts of it into the doll's scalp.

It wasn't too ugly on a doll.

"Look at that face." He lifted her chin, running his hands along her cheekbones. "Usually, I can find something to improve upon. I'm very skilled, you know. But not with you. You're beautiful enough to be a part of the *cast*, not just the crew . . ." His words trailed off as tiny eyes scrutinized her face.

She caught her breath, waiting.

Something was wrong.

He coughed slightly, then turned and walked around to the back of the bar. "Won't you join me in a drink? I'm having a little Scotch. I treat myself to my own wine at dinner." He made a small smile. She was afraid the skin on his face would split open if he stretched it any more broadly. "I don't like to sit here and drink alone, but when I see so many people descend on my home, I feel the need."

From the little she'd already seen and heard, Angie could understand needing liquor to deal with these people. Perhaps vast quantities of it— as long as it wasn't Waterfield wine.

Joining him was the only sociable thing to do. She sat down on a barstool and switched off Rudolph. The reindeer was too distracting. "I'll have some sherry." She glanced toward the Christian Brothers on a shelf and prayed the Waterfield winery didn't make sherry. Luckily, he reached for the bottle on display. As he poured, she said, "I'd like to thank you for giving me the opportunity to come here and take part in all this."

"It was nothing. I was just lucky that I happened to be in the city and ran into your dad at our favorite watering hole in North Beach."

"You ran into him?" she asked, trying to hide her surprise. That wasn't what Salvatore had told her.

"Yes. We started talking. I told him about the show, and how a big scene would take place around the Christmas dinner table. He suggested you cook the meal for us."

Angie was shocked. "I didn't realize that."

"He didn't tell you? I wonder why not?"

Her mind was racing. Why would her father lie? Did he think she would be offended that it was his idea and not Waterfield's? "I don't know," she admitted. "But it's fine. I appreciate your faith in me."

"You're most welcome. I think you'll do much better than the caterer we were going to use—"

Caterer? She was horrified. Visions of huge metal bins of overcooked spaghetti and undercooked pot roast assaulted her. *I should hope so!*

"—And, we love having you here. When your dad said you could use some time out of the city, I was glad to offer my place. You remember Junior, I hope. Sal and I were always sorry things didn't work out for Junior and Frannie. I've always wanted you to meet Silver."

"I see." Angie's lips pursed as her father's possible motive took an ugly turn. "This is all most interesting."

"Not telling tales out of school, am I?"

"Not at all." She gave a weak smile, then tried to come up with a diplomatic way to ask her question. "With this large house, I'm surprised you don't have your own cook, not to mention a housekeeper and gardener."

"I do, but when the TV crew shows up, they take care of everything. My people are on vacation."

"They take care of the food as well?"

"It's all catered, but Tarleton also brought along his own cook, who's staying in the house, in fact. He takes care of anything special Tarleton might want."

Angie didn't need to hear that. "I don't understand. Tarleton has his own cook, yet he wants someone else to prepare the Christmas dinner?"

"I don't understand it either."

Angie's brow furrowed.

"Don't worry. I've been told the special is all yours. At most, he'll provide an extra pair of hands for preparing your Christmas feast." He raised his glass in a toast. "Here's to a wonderful meal—good tidings and good wassailing."

"Thank you. *Salute.*"

Feeling somewhat appeased as to her prospects for the job, she had a pressing question. "Earlier, you said that with my looks I could be in the cast. Then you stopped. I was wondering why. Did you notice some problem?"

"Oh, my dear girl!" He chuckled self-consciously. "How could you think such a thing?"

He didn't deny it. She steeled herself. "I can take it."

"Why do you care? Are you interested in acting? If so, I'm sure I can introduce you to some important people. You can't be a plastic surgeon in Los Angeles for as many years as I have without meeting lots of the right people."

"I've never thought about acting." *Much.* "At least not until I came here." *And started thinking about it full time.*

"Looks like the acting bug may be nibbling at you already." He chuckled. "Have you ever acted, Angie?"

Completely flustered, she could only murmur, "I've been in a couple of plays." High school plays, but he hadn't asked for specifics. "I had a lead role in *Damn Yankees.*"

She took a deep breath and belted out, "Whatever Lola Wants," complete with well-practiced hand gestures.

When she got to the part where she sang, "Little man, little Lola wants you!" and pointed at Waterfield, he stopped her.

"That's enough!" he cried, rubbing his ear. "You have a very strong voice. Rumor has it Tarleton will be directing a musical next. They're making something of a comeback, you know."

"Really?" Was this fate? Kismet? Is this why she'd never found a job that satisfied her creativity and paid a decent wage? Because she was cut out for stardom?

"Thank you," she beamed.

"Won't Salvatore be proud to see his very own daughter in the movies! You'll have riches and a glamorous way of life beyond your wildest dreams! And many rich, handsome men after you . . ."

Her heart hammered. "I'm sure, but . . ."

"But?"

"I'm engaged. I'm going to be married."

His face fell. "Oh, Angelina, I'm so very sorry." With that, he took his Scotch and left the room.

Chapter 4

 Paavo hung up the phone. Angie had used a landline in the house since she couldn't get her cell phone to work. The location was too remote, the hills too high. They'd barely begun to talk when someone else picked up and began dialing. They cut the conversation short.

She'd sounded overjoyed to be at Eagle Crest and babbled on about all kinds of things and people that made no sense.

Plastic chocolates? Lava lamps? And who in the world was Lola?

Then she hung up, and his world seemed even emptier than before they'd talked.

Yosh came in to the bureau. He immediately searched all the table and desktops, and practically stood on his head looking under them when he found nothing on top.

"What's up?" Paavo asked.

"Oh, nothing. I was just thinking how, when you and Angie were first engaged, she kept sending food down here. Remember the cream puffs, and how they had so much powdered sugar, it sprinkled out of the bottom of the box and the whole hazardous materials team, in their suits, followed it up the elevator, down the hall, then came in here and quarantined us?"

"Yeah . . . I remember," Paavo said glumly.

"Or," Yosh chuckled—"when she sent the angel food cake covered with little balloons, and how we were all having such a good time popping them? Who knew someone would report gun-fire?"

"I remember." Paavo grew impatient.

"Or the ten-foot-long mortadella, and how we said it must remind her—"

"Stop! I remember, all right?"

"It was kinda cute, you know." Yosh sounded wistful. "Not that I'm missing it, or anything. Hey, it couldn't go on forever. She's got a life, after all."

"Yeah, she's got a life," Paavo said, feeling more morose than he had in a long time. Yosh wasn't the only one who missed Angie's attention.

Angie downed her sherry and squared her shoulders. Time to get to work. As she headed for the kitchen, a sense of peace and purpose settled over her for the first time today. She had a job to do on a popular TV show. With a skip of joy, she sang to herself—quietly this time—"This Could Be the Start of Something Big."

To Angie, kitchens were oases of comfort, of warm aromas and friendly memories. Of child-hood and family, dinner parties and holidays. Of times when you're feeling sick and need some-thing soothing like hot soup. Or joyful, and want to splurge with a bowl of Häagen-Dazs topped with whipped cream and a maraschino cherry. Or troubled, and you sit at the counter or table with a cup of latte and a biscotti or two. Or simply feeling good about cooking a meal that is nourishing and tasty for those you love.

Eagle Crest's kitchen was situated in the center of the house between the breakfast room on one side and a butler's pantry leading to the dining room on the other. The door was propped halfway open. One step inside, and she stopped, amazed.

It was a gourmet cook's delight—roomy, with lots of counter space, a massive center island, and filled with professional-quality Viking appliances. As she compared it to the small, well-packed kitchen in her apartment, she gave a little "Ah" and walked further into the room.

"Ouch! What the hell!" A red-faced chef dropped his knife onto the onion he'd been slicing. He stuck a finger in his mouth as he glared over his shoulder at her.

Angie froze. He was scarcely taller than she was, with what seemed to be a muscular physique under a long-sleeved white chef's smock and an apron that reached past his knees. His hair was the yellow-white color that comes only from bleach, and atop it was a tall chef's cap. His eyebrows were similarly bleached. She hadn't noticed him because the half-opened door had blocked her view of his part of the kitchen. She was horrified that she'd caused him to cut himself. "I'm sorry!"

He remained flushed with anger. "Who are you coming in here and scaring the vits out of a person?"

"I didn't mean to . . . *vits?*"

"Vits! Vits!" He stabbed at his forehead with his cut finger. It left no blood. The cut was obviously miniscule. No doubt, he was being a baby. Typical chef. He seemed to have acquired an accent much like Sergeant Schultz in *Hogan's Heroes*. She didn't remember any accent when he cut himself.

"Who the hell are you?" he ranted. "Who let you into my kitchen? Nobody is supposed to come in here. Vhat's wrong vit you people? Get out!"

And she did. She supposed a man who'd just cut himself was allowed to be in a bad mood. This was not the time to introduce herself as the person who'd be giving him recipes and expecting him to help her cook—*if* the director agreed to give her the job.

She needed to find Tarleton. Once she had the job, she didn't care how much the cook yelled. He wasn't keeping her out of *her* kitchen.

As Angie passed by the dining room in her search, she stopped and entered. In this room, TV cameras would film the food she'd prepare, her creations, her delectable joys—she ran her fingers over the solid mahogany table—here, for millions and millions of people to see.

Her gaze stopped at the ornate mirror over the buffet, and an earlier, troublesome conversation rushed back at her. She looked over her shoulders, even stuck her head into the entry hall. No one was around. This was as good a time as any.

She darted to the mirror and studied her image.

Up close, back further. What did Dr. Waterfield think was so wrong with it?

She remembered reading that a lot of movie stars were putting collagen in their lips to make them thicker. Maybe that was the problem. Her lips, though, weren't thin. In fact, her mouth was usually described as "full," although possibly not full enough. Not Warner Brothers full.

She stuck her tongue under her top lip to see if that might give her an idea of what she'd look like with a puffier mouth.

It told her what a fat lip looked like in a boxing ring.

She protruded her lips and tried folding back the upper one. All it did was hit her nose and make her gums show.

"Miss Amalfi? Is something wrong?"

In the mirror, she saw another tall, tanned, thin Hollywood-type heading her way. Did everyone have a tan who lived in that part of the state? Hadn't they ever heard of sun block?

This man was L.A. personified with a short-sleeved tangerine shirt that had the first three buttons open. His gray chest hair was a lot fuller than the few similarly colored strands that stretched across the top of his head. A gold-chain necklace winked at her. It seemed so dated, the costume of an over-the-hill, only-in-his-own-mind swinger.

She frowned. "Who are you?"

Voice icy, words clipped, he replied, "Emery Tarleton."

The director! She spun around, blushing furiously. "Oh! I'm so sorry. I . . . I just wanted to make sure there was no food stuck between my teeth. I hate it when that happens." If the floor had opened up, she would have gladly sunk into it.

Tarleton adjusted his thick black-framed glasses, studying her as she did him. "I wish to talk to you about your role," he said. "The *Eagle Crest Christmas Reunion* will be aired during the December sweeps. Already, the buzz is that it will be the most watched show of the year—if not the decade. Inspiration got the cast together again." An eyebrow arched. "Inspiration and genius."

His genius was clearly what he was thinking. His good luck, she thought, that the two members of the cast who'd gone on to become popular movie stars—Kyle O'Rourke and Gwen Hagen, aka Adrian and Leona Roxbury—were available and still affordable.

"Yes, sir," she murmured.

"You will present the Christmas dinner— mouthwatering, somewhat-traditional-but-not- overly, entrées and desserts," he declared. "The Roxburys put on airs to show off their money. They might serve frogs' legs, but none of them would actually eat one. Same for escargots. You get the picture. That's the kind of food I want."

"No problem." A few tweaks here and there in the dinner she'd planned, perhaps by adding sea urchins, sweetbreads, eel, or other equally gourmet-but-squeamish foods, and she'd have it.

"You will serve a different wine with each course. Waterfield wine."

"Waterfield?" The word fell from her lips. Did the man have no taste? Could she tell the director, on their first meeting, that Waterfield wine was only useful for clearing clogged drains? She tried for diplomacy. "Are you sure we don't want to showcase other great Napa Valley wines?"

He frowned. "This is the Waterfield winery. Dr. Waterfield allows us to use his home, and as a favor, we use his wine on the show. The man's rich, but he's got to get some compensation. Don't you agree?"

It wasn't a question that required anything more than an "Of course," which she immediately gave him.

"Keep in mind," Tarleton said, "the menu must be exact."

"Yes, sir," she replied, as if she knew what he meant. *Exact what?*

"If you aren't able to do something so simple, speak up now." He turned sharp eyes on her. "Don't waste my time later saying you can't do this or that. I'll refuse to hear it. Refuse! Absolutely. No backing out. Got it?"

"I've got it." He was making her more nervous by the second. She hated being spoken to like a backward child.

"You'll have a budget; I expect you to stay within it, give or take a few grand. All I want is to see the results, not to hear about them. Is that clear?"

"It's not that difficult," she protested when he stopped barking orders.

He scowled derisively. "Have you ever worked in television before?"

"No."

With pursed lips, he smirked. "It figures."

"I can do it," she said. "I'm already thinking of a meal—"

"Quiet!" His eyes narrowed as he put his fingers to his lips and began to stroll around the dining room table. "The more I think about it . . . yes!" He waved his arms. "Forget everything I just said! We're going to use the same menu as on an earlier Christmas show."

She prayed she'd misunderstood. "I can come up with a wonderful holiday menu. Something elegant, true haute cuisine. How much is my budget, by the way?"

"Forget it. My idea is much better. Perfection. I even surprise myself sometimes!"

"What are you saying?" She felt tears threatening. She wanted to create a fabulous meal and show the world—or the *Eagle Crest*-watching part of it—what she could do. Launch a television career, make a name for herself . . .

With his hands flat on the tabletop, he leaned toward her, dropping his voice. "We're going to re-create the meal that was served on the night Julia Parker was murdered. I don't suppose you know what I'm talking about."

"Of course I do," Angie said, puzzled. "She was Natalie's sister's daughter, the result of the sister going to a sperm bank and getting sperm that, in fact, might have been Cliff and Adrian's fathers, making her their half-sister. And, if so, part owner of the winery. Then, she was mysteriously killed. After that, there were hints that Julia was haunting the family. In fact, everything inexplicable that happened after she died was blamed on Julia's ghost. Frankly, I always suspected it was just a cop-out when the writers couldn't come up with a halfway decent rationale . . ."

She snapped her mouth shut. As director, Tarleton had to have approved the scripts. "If so," she said with a broad smile, "it was clever. Extremely clever."

Tarleton stared at her. "You really do know your *Eagle Crest* history."

"Of course," Angie said proudly. "But what does that have to do with the dinner?"

"Haven't you ever wondered who killed her?"

"I know Cliff was accused. Of course, he was innocent." She remembered her disappointment with the storyline. "Big surprise! As if the public would continue watching if the show's sexiest star was cooped up in jail instead of out flirting and making mischief. As I understand it, the whole problem came about because the actress who played Julia died. I remember the press trying to hint that drugs or something more was involved, but the police said no, that it was just a terrible accident. Am I right?"

"Exactly." Tarleton said. "She was a beautiful young woman named Brittany Keegan." His jaw clenched. "But everyone has forgotten her. Everyone! She died right here at Eagle Crest."

Angie's eyes widened. "In this house? I didn't know that. How could I have missed hearing such a thing?"

"After the initial reports," Tarleton said, lifting his chin, "the follow-up stories were worded so that the fans would assume her death took place in Los Angeles, not on location. We did it for the sake of the Waterfield family, of course."

"Of course," Angie replied. Not to mention for the sake of the show, although it continued only one more season after that.

When Bart Farrell and Rhonda Manning refused to renew their contracts, the show was as dead as Brittany Keegan.

"I'm telling you this simply because you'll be working here, and everyone else knows it." His gaze was severe. "I trust you'll keep it quiet."

"Yes," Angie promised. Not only was it unbelievable that she had this job, now she was privy to insider-only Hollywood gossip. Wait until she told Paavo!

"Miss Keegan was only twenty-three years old." Tarleton walked over to the poinsettias on the buffet and stroked the red leaves. He brushed off his fingertips against his slacks, grimacing with disgust at forgetting they were fake. He spun toward Angie.

"Everyone kept a stiff upper lip and continued on as if nothing had happened, except, of course, coming up with the new plot about Julia's murder." His voice softened. "It was almost as if Brittany had never lived and hadn't died right under their noses. The show grew ever more popular—even after it was cancelled. The younger stars—O'Rourke and Hagen—went on to bigger things. Their salaries soared. Brittany should have been one of them."

His gaze turned inward and hollow.

"She died from a fall, right?" Angie asked. "Horseback riding. Or was that also a lie?"

"Not a lie, exactly. A rumor given to the tabloids." His toothy smile was close to a grimace.

"It was more . . . glamorous . . . than to say she was found dead in the courtyard."

"The courtyard?" Angie shuddered. "What do you mean? How did she die there?"

He didn't answer for a long while. "She was *found* in the courtyard. Her bedroom was on the third floor. She fell from her window."

"Oh, no!" Angie was horrified to think of a young woman dying that way. "Suicide was ruled out, I take it?"

"Yes, definitely. She was happy, a fine actress, her whole life ahead of her."

Another possibility filled Angie's mind. "My fiancé is a homicide detective, so maybe that's why I'm asking, but did anyone suspect she might have been helped out that window?"

He nodded. "It was suspected, of course. However, the door to her room was locked with a metal slide bolt. There was no way anyone could have gotten in or out. We had to break it away from the door jamb to get into the room."

"Her room was on the third floor"—Angie's voice became very tiny—"facing the courtyard?"

"That's right."

She didn't know what made her ask, she only knew the answer she was expecting. "Which room up there was hers?"

"I'll never forget. It was the last one on the left."

Why, why, why did Angie know he was going to say that?

It was the room she'd been given. The room that, frankly, gave her the creeps.

Chapter 5

Paavo sat at his desk in Homicide, looking out at the dreary, foggy day, and listened while Angie excitedly rambled on and on about her new job. She'd finally met the director and the only problem was that he wanted to use an old show's menu rather than hers. Disappointed but undeterred, she planned to make it the best version of the meal he'd ever had, to use exquisite recipes that would make him and the other actors take notice.

Suddenly, she gave him a quick "I love you" and said she had to hang up. Someone was nearby that she wanted to talk to.

"I love you, too," he said as the dial tone sounded in his ear.

He was glad she was enjoying herself. Glad she wasn't up there miserable and missing him . . . he supposed.

Finally, he put down the receiver.

As Angie had been talking to Paavo on the extension phone in her room, she'd heard a door close.

She stuck her head out into the hall and saw Mariah heading for the stairs.

"Mariah, wait!" Angie quickly hung up and hurried after her. "What's this about Brittany Keegan? I heard she had the same room as me. And that she died here at Eagle Crest!"

"How should I know? I wasn't here at the time. I'm going to dinner." Mariah walked down the stairs, her perky pigtails swinging.

"You must have heard something," Angie said at her heels. "Didn't you? I don't know that I want to be in that room. Who else is on our floor?"

Mariah reached the foyer and spun around. "Who cares about Brittany Keegan? Isn't it enough Em talks about her all the time? What was it with her? Look, I've got a room up there, too. So does Em's chef and the scriptwriter—when she shows. It's better than you going into town or living in a trailer because believe me, the one you'd be given would be several steps down from the lush homes-away-from-home the stars live in. Get over it!"

Angie stepped back, her mouth agape.

"If you want to eat, you'd better get your butt down to craft services before it's all gone. The caterer's truck left a half hour ago." Mariah left, slamming the door behind her.

How rude! Angie had only asked a few simple questions.

Her stomach rumbled.

Outside, floodlights and lanterns strung across the field a short distance from the house illuminated the area filled with technicians, tents, and massive pieces of equipment. Lights and shadows created a busier and more chaotic appearance than it had by day.

Angie's spirits buoyed and she crossed the fake snow-filled lawn and lighted angels and snowmen to the tents. Her nose led to the food, a spread of ham, chicken, roast beef, green salad, macaroni salad, fresh fruits and vegetables, and a variety of breads and spreads for sandwich making. Junk food reigned supreme with a variety of chips, candy bars, sunflower seeds, bags of peanuts and cashews, packets of cookies, crackers, and sodas, fruit juice, coffee, tea, and milk galore.

Angie made herself a plate, then introduced herself to the crew. Most were newcomers to the set.

Except one.

Donna Heinz had worked as a costume designer on the original show. She was celery-stalk thin, with dull coal-black hair combed straight back close to the head, and with thin, penciled-in charcoal eyebrows. Even though she was now retired, she'd agreed to come back and help dress the stars in the haughty, self-confident style for which *Eagle Crest* had become known. Much older than the others and apparently ignored by them, she sat alone, a glass of wine in one hand, a Virginia Slims in the other.

Angie sat on a folding chair beside her and chatted about *Eagle Crest*. For Angie, hearing the inside secrets was fascinating. Finally she asked if Ms. Heinz remembered Brittany Keegan.

"She was genuinely cheerful," Donna said. "And ambitious. I knew it would get her into trouble one day. I didn't think it would be so soon, though."

"Get her into trouble?" Angie asked, munching on a strawberry. "So, you think she committed suicide because she was troubled?"

Heinz grimaced. "Brittany would never have killed herself."

Angie ate, waiting for an explanation.

"It had to have been an accident," Donna said. "A horrible accident. There's no way anyone could have entered her room."

Angie pushed the strawberries and melon cubes to one side and took a bite of fresh peach cobbler. "Did the rest of the cast get along with Brittany?" Angie asked.

Donna eyed her coldly. "Why so interested?"

"I was a big fan, and now I've been given her room. It's made me curious."

"I should imagine!" A shudder rippled through her. "Did she get along with others? Who knows? All these people are jealous of each other no matter what they say or how they act. Hollywood is the only place where people can literally kill you with kindness."

With that, she finished her wine and went into her trailer. Angie joined some young audio engineers. They were polite, but might have been speaking in tongues, for all she understood of their conversation.

Going back to her cold little room held no appeal. Instead, she slowly walked around the house to the courtyard and entered through the gate. Twinkling Christmas lights gave it a magical air.

The smell of cigarette smoke told her she wasn't alone.

"Hello?" she called.

"Hello."

Silver was at a table hidden behind a miniature orange tree. The lights and fake snow at his feet were incongruous with his rolled shirtsleeves.

"What are you doing out here all by yourself?" she asked.

"I should ask you the same thing," he replied, gesturing for her to join him. "Lonely?"

"A little. I miss my fiancé," she admitted, sitting across the table.

"Fiancé?"

She showed him her ring.

"Tell me about him," Silver said.

She liked to talk about Paavo. How brave and strong and smart he was; how many cases he'd solved; how handsome he was with his dark wavy hair, large blue eyes, and high cheekbones; how gentle and kind he was with her despite making crooks and killers quake by his mere glance.

Silver was soon chuckling as she described her and Paavo's differences, and how, even after knowing him for some time, she was still amazed that they decided to get married.

"He's a lucky man, Angie," Silver said. "I'd give anything to find a woman who'd talk about me the way you do about him."

"I'm sure you will someday."

"Not out here, though."

"If you don't like it, why do you stay?"

"Contacts. It doesn't hurt to make them. I could use some if I ever get to Hollywood. I'd like to go. But so far, I haven't had the nerve."

"You want to act?"

"I'd love to. My mother, when she paid attention to such things, used to tell me I'd make a great actor—that I had the looks and the talent."

"Your mother." Angie couldn't help but smile.

"Oh . . . I know what you're thinking. What difference does it make what one's mother says? They always try to uplift one's spirits, don't they? Tell one how great one is?"

"Oh . . . I don't know that I'd say that," Angie admitted. Serefina was more apt to list her shortcomings than her talents. In fact, had Serefina ever mentioned her talents? She couldn't remember. She knew she was loved, but sometimes it seemed she was loved "despite" everything, not as a result of it.

She glanced at Silver. He certainly had the looks to become an actor. She found herself staring at his face, trying to find a flaw. Those she noticed— a slight crookedness to one eyebrow, two laugh lines on the left side of his mouth, and only one on the right—were charming.

"Your mother doesn't praise you? I find that hard to believe," he said.

"I can be a burden to her, I suppose. She isn't as happy about me as she would like to be."

"I can't imagine you being a burden to anyone, Angie. You're a good person."

"That's nice of you to say." Her gaze softened. "I was sorry to hear your mother passed away. I would have liked to have met her."

"No." He shook his head. "You wouldn't have. Trust me."

She didn't know what to say, so she stood. "I

think I'd better retire. Tomorrow, I'm going to have to nail down the details and start preparing an enormous feast."

"Merry Christmas, Angie."

"Good night, Silver," she said. A smile crept to her lips, which she tried hard to suppress.

"Say it!" he ordered.

Her eyes widened and she shook her head, trying harder than ever not to allow the laughter to break out.

"Listen, I've lived with the name all my life," he said. "I know exactly what you're thinking."

She shook her head.

"Hey, it's not so bad. With a father named Sterling, a mother named Crystal, my older brother Sterling, Jr., I'm just lucky I wasn't the third brother. He'd probably have been named Pewter."

She did laugh.

"Say it, please."

She drew in her breath and said, "Hi-yo, Silver."

He just nodded. "Goodnight. Lock your door, Angie. Around here, that's the only sensible thing to do."

The moon was a thin crescent over the vineyards so devoid of illumination that no shadow fell as a dark figure approached the mansion. The alarm system was left off, now that the crew had arrived. If not, the people working late and arriving early would be setting it off continuously. Besides, the house was far too remote for mere thieves to approach.

The only dangers stemmed from those who

knew its layout, its owners, the cast and crew. And knew why everything involving them should be stopped.

All was silent in the house as the front door opened. A penlight lit the way to the living room. Audiovisual equipment filled one corner of the room. Carefully and methodically cables and wires were detached from the sockets in which they belonged and reattached to any plug, slot, or connector they could be forced onto.

The figurine of the Little Drummer Boy stood on the mantel, its lifelike eyes watching every move.

Chapter 6

Paavo marched into Homicide, hurled the morning's *San Francisco Chronicle* on his desk, and slammed himself into his desk chair. Scowling, he took a gulp of his morning coffee.

"Hey, Paav," the boisterous voice of his partner jangled his eardrums, "how you doing? Beautiful morning, isn't it? Good to see that sun after three days of fog. Makes us all little rays of sunshine today."

"Hmmph." Paavo flapped the paper and scanned the front page.

"Uh oh, Angie must be giving you a hard time about something. What's it this time? The color of your tie for her big engagement party? If the invitations should be on ivory colored paper or white with sweet smiling little cupids?" Yosh chuckled.

"Not funny, Yosh," Paavo muttered. He snapped the paper open to page two and stuck his nose closer in a not-so-subtle hint to be left alone. He was bothered by Angie's conversation last evening. First, she'd quizzed him about her face.

Her *face?* To him, it was perfect. He had no idea what was bothering her.

No sooner had she left that topic than she told him about Brittany Keegan having died from a fall on the property. He learned more about the crew and cast than he wanted to know, not to mention Sterling and Silver Waterfield. What names! Why she hadn't yet met "Junior" puzzled him. Something about the entire set-up was off-kilter. And it was a lot more than Christmas in April.

He managed to squeeze in a few words about Connie sending Minnie Petite over to ask him to find her missing "significant other," who happened to be a 62-year-old dwarf and was also an actor.

A strange coincidence, he had to admit, considering that Angie was surrounded by actors.

She found it amusing that instead of a hardened murderer, Connie had him chasing a wedding-shy little person . . . and then she went right back telling him about *Eagle Crest* scenes that took place on the very sofas, chairs, and tables, or by the bar, fireplace, courtyard, and even bathrooms she was using. By the time he hung up, his ears were ringing.

"I know why he's so grumpy." Rebecca Mayfield, Homicide's only female inspector, interrupted his thoughts as she crossed the room to rest an arm on the filing cabinet by his desk. She had long blond hair, worn loose about her shoulders today, and a body that showed the positive effects of many hours at a gym. Her clothes were basic and inexpensive, her shoes sensible, her demeanor serious and logical. To Paavo, she was the anti-Angie—he couldn't imagine two women more different.

Rebecca was half in love with him, or thought she was, and had been since they'd first met. Her lingering gazes and heartfelt sighs made him uncomfortable. There was nothing he could do but ignore them.

"Angie's probably wondering if the guests would prefer aspic or confit as an appetizer," Rebecca said with a smile. "Paavo doesn't want to tell her he doesn't know what the hell she's talking about."

Even Luis Calderon, who rarely cracked a smile, let alone a laugh, snickered at that.

Paavo crumpled the newspaper. "What do you guys know about the old TV series *Eagle Crest*?"

"Hot stuff," Calderon called.

"All I remember," Yosh said, "is my wife used to tell me to be quiet on Friday nights so she could watch it. It was when we were first married, too. I had other things on my mind than some dumb soap on Friday night, let me tell you. I never understood what she saw in it. Some of the women were babes, but the guys were puke-buckets. I tried to watch a couple of times. She'd get mad when I'd laugh and it wasn't supposed to be funny."

"I don't blame her." Rebecca snapped. "If I'd been your wife, that would have ended our relationship. I used to watch every minute of the show. Every second, in fact."

"So that explains your wasted youth," Yosh said.

"Stuff it!" Rebecca turned to Paavo. "Why do you ask?"

"Angie's not in town. She's gone to St. Helena for a few days to work on some Christmas reunion show."

Rebecca gasped. "You're kidding me. They aren't in St. Helena now, are they?"

"Did you tell her it's April, Paavo?" Yosh said with a chuckle.

Paavo ignored him, and answered Rebecca. "Angie's there, so I guess the others are as well."

Rebecca, starry-eyed, murmured, "I can't believe it. Cliff and Adrian, in *Eagle Crest*, again. Dear, sweet, hunka-hunka Adrian."

"Hunka-hunka?" Calderon looked as her as if she'd lost her mind.

Rebecca cleared her throat and turned toward her desk.

"One of the cast died mysteriously while the show was being filmed," Yosh said. "I don't recall the details."

"Angie's curious about that," Paavo said. "Of course."

His words brought Rebecca back. "Julia Parker, Natalie Roxbury's niece. She was a bitch and a troublemaker, but it was really sad when she died. People were in tears all over America."

"Wait a minute," Paavo said, confused, "are you talking about a character or an actress?"

"A character, but the actress died, too," Rebecca replied. "I don't remember her name, though."

"Brittany Keegan," Paavo said.

"That's right!" Yosh exclaimed. "I was living up

in Seattle at the time. My wife was terribly upset. I wasn't working Homicide yet, but it seemed they went out of their way to keep information from the public. The death was ruled an accident, but my wife said she thought one of the other women on the show probably knocked her off."

"It was all strangely hush-hush," Rebecca added. "Not even the tabloids speculated about anything other than it being a sad accident. A riding accident on her Malibu estate, as I recall."

"I vaguely remember that," Paavo said. "The newspapers made it sound like she was in L.A., but Angie swears she actually died in Napa County."

"Weird," Yosh said.

"Maybe I need to find out about the woman's death," Paavo murmured.

"Ever the cop." Rebecca shook her head. "How does Angie feel about you wanting to check up on everybody she associates with?"

He thought about Angie staying at a rich man's house with his two bachelor sons. Maybe Rebecca had the right idea.

"Get me out of this, goddamn it!" Kyle O'Rourke yelled into his cell phone. He lounged on the redwood deck of his split-level Laguna Beach home and stared out at the Pacific. "How many times do I have to say it?"

Once again, his agent gave him all the reasons he was not getting out of it and was going to St. Helena, which boiled down to three reasons that were bull, three that were shit, and one that was real: if he didn't show up to play the elegant albeit shoved-around Adrian Roxbury, he'd be sued for breach of contract, and it could cost him somewhere between five and ten million dollars.

He punched the "End" button on his Nokia, snapped it shut, and tossed it onto the small table at his side. He'd already known it was way too late to get out of the deal, but the closer the time came, the more he felt the need to yell at someone about it. His agent was the easiest target.

Memories of *Eagle Crest* rushed at him. Bad memories, despite the way his career had benefited from the role. He had a good life in southern California now, a beautiful wife, two children, and a contract to star in a Ridley Scott film beginning next month.

He wanted nothing more to do with the Adrian Roxbury role or the people he'd worked with. Not Bart or Rhonda. Not even Gwen. He smiled, remembering her. Since he and Gwen had played the rockily married Adrian and Leona when the cameras rolled, it made sense that when the cameras were off, they'd find time to kiss and make up.

Gwen was cool. He believed she'd never tell his wife, and she didn't.

Still, there were always small-minded people around who used stars like him to find their way into the news. What was said in jest might have more than a little truth to it. He didn't want to take the chance. He'd insisted that his wife stay home with the kids.

Keeping his wife out of the loop was hard enough, but the real trick would be to keep the press out of it. There was too much dirt they could dredge up. Ironically, his new film persona was based on Adrian Roxbury's character, not on Kyle O'Rourke's.

Kyle would never forget the day it dawned on him how to act when fans came up to him with tears and sympathy, saying they thought he was wonderfully nice and sweet and shouldn't have to be made to suffer so much because of his horrible brother, Cliff, and his cheating, shrewish wife, Leona.

Instead of protesting that Adrian was simply a character he played on TV, he began to thank his fans for their concern, and say that somehow, he had the faith that this would all turn out well. The fans loved him for it. They would smile and hug him, pleased by his good nature, forgiveness, and God-loving charity toward others. Adrian Roxbury, candidate for sainthood.

Since that was what his fans wanted, he gave it to them in spades. He began looking for movie roles with Adrian-type, charming, educated good guys. And he got them.

His movies were all big box office hits—not blockbuster films, but ones that women clamored to see, that they bought on videotape, and again on DVD, and rented over and over and over, Kleenex boxes close at hand as they watched.

Someday, he hoped to be the young Robert Redford of his time. He didn't see gambling all that by letting it be known that his personal life was akin to *Return to Peyton Place*.

Negotiations for the *Eagle Crest* reunion had been well along before his agent let him in on what was happening, thrilled at the amount of money the producers had offered, and that the timing of the shoot was pushed all the way up to April so as not to interfere with his and Gwen Hagen's film schedules. As famous as Bart Farrell and Rhonda Manning were when the show first appeared on TV, Kyle O'Rourke and Gwen Hagen were now the big stars—and the storyline for the reunion would reflect that.

How the script would mesh Christmas with the sexy sleaze of the Roxbury clan was another matter.

He had immediately asked to be written out of the story. But the producers refused and threatened a lawsuit.

The usual phone calls began. Quickly, he realized just how stuck he was. The horror was already beginning.

He caught a view of himself in the mirror, and stopped to admire the sight. He wasn't as tall as Bart Farrell, but his physique was definitely better—toned and muscular. He glided his hand against thick, sandy blond hair that reached in back to his collar, studied his cobalt blue eyes, then touched a face that sun, sea, and age had made increasingly craggy.

Robert Redford, all right.

Tomorrow, the private jet he'd chartered would be heading north.

Somehow, he would get past *Eagle Crest* and move on with his life. He could do it. He was a great actor.

Gwen Hagen tossed aside the screenplay she'd been reading. Not funny enough; not enough action. She enjoyed action films, ones that didn't require a lot of retrospection or insight. Ones that didn't force her to delve inside her soul to understand the character she was playing.

Some days, she was convinced she had no soul. Although it bothered her, the possibility of moviegoers seeing the same blackness was positively frightening. What would happen to her career then?

Action films were safer, as was comedy. One had to be careful with comedy, though, as it was often a humorous way to expose the same truths as drama. She was always leery of revelation.

Packets of scripts from her agent were stacked on the coffee table in the living room of her Malibu house. She was lying on the sofa going through them. It was tedious, but she was the best judge of roles she'd consider playing. She would never give that decision-making power to anyone else.

She picked up the next script, read the logline, and saw that it had a Christmas theme. She sat up and slammed it onto the reject pile. No *Miracle on 34th Street* for her, thank you. Not even *The Santa Clause*.

She hated Christmas, and she particularly hated Santa Claus.

Not having seen the script yet for the *Eagle Crest* special upset her. This was the one time she had no control, no choice. It had been written in her original *Eagle Crest* contract. Restless, she stood and paced the room.

She wondered if it'd be so hokey as to have Santa

Claus make an entrance. When she was a child, Santa was the one who'd brought gifts to "good" boys and girls, but never to her. One year when she was six and believed in Santa with all her heart, she tried all year long to be a "good little girl."

That Christmas had come and gone, and there were still no presents. Not even a Christmas tree. She never tried to be good again.

Not until she was fifteen and made some money on her own did she buy herself a Christmas present. A small teddy bear.

She still had it, too. It was the one thing she'd kept with her all these years. The one thing that reminded her of the way her life used to be, and that she'd do anything, anything at all, never to have to go back to that life again.

In her bedroom, she lifted the long, curly black wig she used to play Leona Roxbury from its box. The curls stood out about five inches all the way around her head and cascaded halfway down her back. The long, thick hair made the wig so heavy it gave her a headache.

She placed it over her short, straight black hair and became Leona once again. Years ago, after two arrests for prostitution, and afraid to go back out onto the streets, she felt her life change when she answered a casting call for a television show.

A good whore is nothing but an underpaid actress, she'd reasoned. And she'd been a good one.

She put everything she had into the reading and lied up one side and down the other on the job application. Only her phone number had been real.

To her amazement, she was called for a further audition. After much back-and-forth, she landed the role of Leona Roxbury.

At first the job was heaven. Then it all started to go to hell.

It didn't take her long to learn there was scum on both sides of the tracks. In many ways rich scum was worse than what she'd left behind in Watts. The rich had no reason to be rotten, except for greed, selfishness, and ego. The actors she met had all of that in abundance.

She thought of Bart, Kyle, and Rhonda, and even Emery, and of all that had happened between them.

And Brittany.

She shut her eyes as she thought of Brittany. Then she took a .22 Glock from her nightstand, removed the magazine, carefully took the gun apart and placed it in its traveling case. She'd learned to use a gun when she was growing up in Watts. An occasional trip to the shooting range now and then made sure she never forgot it.

"Merry Christmas, Eagle Crest," she whispered, then tossed the gun and the ammunition into her suitcase.

Chapter 7

An urn of weak Folger's coffee and a platter of store-bought Danish pastry greeted Angie in the breakfast room. Not surprisingly, no one was there. The craft services area seemed more attractive than ever.

Last night as she tried to fall asleep, over two dozen questions for Tarleton popped into her head as all the details involved with a television show began to overwhelm her. She needed to ask if she was responsible for the presentation of the food on platters and bowls, or for the dinner table—plates, silverware, glasses, napkins, even salt shakers, or for anything beyond cooking. She also needed to check out the kitchen supplies and equipment.

This morning, the crew was crawling all over the house, inside and out. Tarleton was with them, red-faced and shouting orders.

She opted for the kitchen, the one main room in the house free of all but overbearing Christmas decorations.

This time she knocked before entering, not

wanting to scare the cook into a repeat of yesterday.

"You again?" he grumped. He sat at the counter
with a cup of coffee and a Marlboro, reading the
Sacramento Bee. A small TV blared ESPN sports
from the corner. "Who are you? Vhy do you insist
on bothering me?"

She inhaled sharply. "My name is Angelina
Amalfi, and I'm considered by many to be a fine
gourmet cook. I studied at the Cordon Bleu in
Paris, I've worked in restaurants, on radio, on
television cooking shows, I've done restaurant reviews, and owned my own business as a chocolatier and cake decorator. I think I'm qualified to
be in this kitchen."

With each word she spoke the chef's face grew
redder. "Vell, bully for you!" He snuffed out his
cigarette, then stood awkwardly, as if his legs
didn't work quite right.

With his hands on his hips, she noticed that his
arms seemed unnaturally short. "So, you come
here vit your hoity and toity vords. Do you think
to take over my kitchen? Is that vhat this is all
about?"

"Not at all. In fact, I'd hoped we could get
along. I didn't catch your name, by the way."

"My name? You vant my name?"

"Yes." She smiled sweetly.

He looked about to explode. "I am Rudolf
Goetring."

She had never heard of him. "Mr. Goetring, I'll
be creating the Christmas dinner for the TV
show." She walked over to the pantry, opened the

door, and stepped inside, checking the shelves. "I thought it would be lovely if we could work together, since I need to test the recipes Mr. Tarleton will be giving me, as well as get to know the equipment."

"So that's vhat you thought, is it? Get out of there!"

She came out, pleased with what she saw, and began opening cupboards.

"No one has said a vord to me about you or any of this! Vhat am I here? Am I some dog barf? You think you can just svoop in and take over? I have vork to do! I vant you out."

She tried to open a door on the far wall, but it was locked. "What's this?"

"The maid's quarters. You can't go in there! You can't stay in here!"

"Making coffee—poorly—and opening packages is hardly work." She checked cabinets under the sink and counters. "I have a real job to do. *You* get out!"

"I must vork on the lunch," he protested.

She was becoming truly irritated, and opened a door that led to a basement. It must be the wine cellar. "Lunch is catered."

"Not for Mr. Tarleton." He lifted his chin.

She shut the door and gave the kitchen another quick once-over. "Fine. It still won't require you to use the entire kitchen. I need it this afternoon. I'm going to talk to Mr. Tarleton. I *will* be back."

"I think he went into town," Mariah said when asked Tarleton's whereabouts. "The equipment is all fouled up. Some fool plugged things into the wrong slots. Em threw a temper tantrum and left."

"Oh, dear!" Angie was glad she hadn't tried to talk to him earlier. They were standing on the front veranda. She eyed the crew filling the fake-snow machine. "You know it doesn't snow in St. Helena, except maybe once in ten years."

"They want snow," Mariah said.

Angie decided not to argue. "Do you expect him back soon?"

"I guess." Mariah turned away.

"But . . . I've got to get started preparing the Christmas dinner."

Mariah looked at her as if she were crazy. "Relax! The dinner scene won't be for a week. Maybe longer."

"A week?" Angie was dumbfounded. "Why was I asked to come here already?"

"Beats me."

Angie couldn't believe it! She liked being at Eagle Crest, meeting celebrities and so on, but she saw no reason to be here a week early twiddling her thumbs when she could be home with Paavo twiddling something a lot more interesting.

As Angie stepped back into the house she was greeted by the foyer Christmas tree whirling and playing "We Wish You A Merry Christmas."

"Bah, humbug!" she said, and entered the dining room. Maybe if she tried to visualize how she'd like to present the food she'd be less upset.

"Angie, excuse me," Mariah called. "Someone's here to see you."

In the doorway stood her sister Bianca, the oldest of the five Amalfi daughters. She looked a lot like Angie, except that she was at least twenty pounds heavier, her hair was straight and chin-length, and she had a preference for polyester slacks over designer outfits.

"I heard you were here. I couldn't believe it!" Bianca shrieked. "I loved this show! I simply adored it! Look at this house! It's like being on TV. Angie, how can you stand it?"

The two laughed and hugged. Finally, Angie thought, someone to share the enthusiasm she had when she first arrived.

"I brought you a gift," Bianca said. "A gold goblet for the dining room. I'm sure you can figure out a way to use it on the table or buffet. It'd be such fun to see it when the Christmas show airs!"

Angie took the heavy goblet. It had been in the family for years. "I can try, but don't get your hopes up."

"Look at all the flowers!" Bianca nearly tripped over cables as she hurried into the living room and stuck her nose into a display on the coffee table. "Phew! They're fake! Too bad, they look so real. Let's see the rest of the house."

Angie walked her through the main floor.

"Where are the actors?" Bianca asked. "Can I meet them? I adore Adrian! He's so suave. I used to say to Johnnie, why can't you be more like him?"

"The actors aren't here yet," Angie said.

"Not here? Oh . . . well, in that case I guess I'd better run." She gave Angie a peck on the cheek and headed for the front door. "One bit of advice—if you get a chance, show off what you can do in the kitchen. I mean, everything! You're a gifted cook, Angie. You never know where that talent might lead you."

And with that, she was gone.

Angie didn't even have a chance to say good-bye.

Chapter 8

The victim was a Latino male, his body riddled with bullet holes. A long white, brown, and black bird's feather was tucked into the neck of his sweatshirt.

Paavo stood over the body in a garbage-strewn alley off Alemany Boulevard. It was in one of the roughest parts of the Ingleside district.

Last week, a nineteen-year-old Guatemalan had been gunned down on Scribner's Street not far from there. A red-tailed hawk feather was left on his chest, tucked into a shirt buttonhole. Luis Calderon and Bo Benson, the on-call inspectors at the time, took the case.

Three days later there'd been a second murder, also in the Ingleside. The Nicaraguan victim had a peregrine falcon feather in his jacket pocket. Calderon and Benson handled that case as well.

This morning, another call came in, similar to the last two. Calderon and Benson were swamped running down leads. With the danger of overlooking something important, Paavo had been assigned to handle the legwork on this latest shooting.

Paavo gave the okay for the coroner's team and CSI to move in. CSI would take the feather and identify it. Judging from the length it was from a huge bird, not the type normally seen flitting around the streets of San Francisco.

Where were the shooters getting these feathers? If he and the other inspectors could figure that out, it might be a major breakthrough. They needed some kind of big lead soon. He had a bad feeling that these murders weren't going to stop without one.

He phoned Information for the number and address of the Audubon Society.

"Angie," Mariah called, her voice filled with outrage. "You have company again!"

"All right, already." Earlier, Angie had marched into the kitchen ready to do battle, only to find it empty. She was carefully going through the spices and condiments checking for freshness. "Is it my fault if people come to visit? Sheesh!"

She marched to the front door, pulled it open, looked at her visitor, and felt her knees go weak. Before her stood Homicide Inspector Rebecca Mayfield. Rebecca held her purse over her head to protect herself from the flying snowflakes.

Angie's heart pounded. Her brain searched for possible reasons for one of Paavo's co-workers to come all this way to talk to her . . . in person. Her fingers tightened on the door. "Paavo?" she whispered.

"Relax, Angie," Rebecca said. "You're white as a sheet. He's fine. I'm here to see you."

Angie's pulse slowly returned to normal. "You want to see *me*?" That made no sense. Rebecca Mayfield hated her, and everyone knew it. "Come in."

"I came bearing a gift."

Where had Angie heard that before? She watched as Rebecca pulled an incense burner from a bag. "I have another at home just like it. It has special significance for me, and *Eagle Crest* is one of my favorite shows. I was wondering if I could just slip it onto a table or someplace where it'd be sure to be filmed?"

Angie's eyes narrowed. She and Paavo had been walking through Chinatown one day when he pointed out a miniature brass temple and told her he'd given one to Rebecca after she'd oohed and aahed over it. "I'm sure I can find an appropriate spot for it."

"Wonderful!" Rebecca cried, fluffing her hair and strolling through the rooms, touching and studying every bit of Eagle Crest minutiae and Christmas paraphernalia as she went. "I have a confession to make. I also came to see the cast. The show was my absolute favorite. I may have even become a cop because of it. I wanted to know who killed Julia Parker and was furious that the dumb cops on the show went after Cliff Roxbury. As if! But you probably have no idea what I'm talking about . . . and I'm babbling . . . but I can't believe I'm actually here, inside the Roxbury house! It's so beautiful."

"I always suspected Leona," Angie said. "The *other woman* and all . . ."

Rebecca peeked in the dining room. "Where's the cast?"

"Not here yet."

Disappointment clouded Rebecca's face. "Bummer!" In the family room, she placed her large purse on a tabletop filled with pictures of the Roxbury family and stood in front of it, lifting and studying each photo.

"Would you like something to drink?" Angie stepped behind the bar and switched off the glowing and bobbing Rudolph. "It's a long trip up here *and back*."

"A Coke's good."

"Diet?"

Rebecca put her hands on her svelte hips. "No."

Angie handed her a can.

"I'll take it with me," Rebecca said as she turned toward the courtyard. "I can still see Julia sneaking into the gate after her romance with the stableboy. He had wavy dark hair and big sky blue eyes just like Paavo. I guess I've always been partial to that combination." She sighed as if she'd been in love with the boy herself. "This is fantastic, Angie. Thank you for letting me see it."

Angie walked her to the door. "Drive safely."

"I'll give Paavo your best. I'm sure I'll see him tonight. By the way, I gave him a screen saver for his computer. A black Corvette. He loves it! He didn't try to give it back, either." She smiled. "Bye!"

Angie hadn't known one could smile and wave with clenched teeth. Somehow she managed to. She'd tried to give Paavo a black Corvette as an engagement present, but he'd refused to accept it. Too expensive he'd said, despite his obvious love for the car. Instead, he drove around in a clunker . . . and looked at Rebecca's present to him at work. Damn!

She glared at the stupid tree and its "We Wish You a Merry Christmas" cacophony. A horrible thought struck her. She detoured to the family room.

There, in front of the photos of the Roxbury family, where millions of TV viewers could see it if the camera panned slowly and they squinted hard, Rebecca had snuck a photo of her and Paavo standing side-by-side and smiling happily.

Angie snatched it up and dropped it in the trash.

The local chapter of the Audubon Society was located near Sigmund Stern Grove. Minnie Petite lived off of West Portal Avenue, right between Paavo's current location and the birdwatchers.

As he drove, he phoned Missing Persons and spoke with Inspector Pamela James for the lowdown on Fred Demitasse.

James had few details. Apparently Minnie had filed a report the evening before going to see Paavo. They had scarcely begun to work on it.

He thought that was strange. Nevertheless, he decided to pay Minnie a visit.

Petite lived in a brown-shingled cottage with white shutters and a green peaked roof. Almost fairy-tale size, it seemed fitting for its occupants.

She was home and invited Paavo in. He felt like Gulliver among the Lilliputians. All the furniture had been cut down, and even the interior door-knobs were level with his knees.

"It's about time you got off your fat ass and tried to help." Petite jutted out her lower lip and glared up at him. "I'm a tax-paying citizen and have rights when my friends go *poof* and aren't heard from again!"

"Yes, ma'am," Paavo said. "That's why I'm here. I'd like to help you find Mr. Demitasse."

"Hmmph!"

Since that was her only retort, Paavo knew he was winning her over. "Why don't you tell me about Fred's last few days at home?"

"I've gone over them in my head, and I don't think you'll get anywhere. You can set yourself on that couch. I'll go through it all again."

He sat. His knees nearly touched his chin while Minnie told him how Fred was working on getting a television role he seemed to think he had coming to him. He hadn't told her much about it, probably because he was afraid she'd tell their roommates of the possible job opening, or maybe that she'd want it herself. Fred was a sneaky bastard, she admitted.

He asked if Minnie knew who Fred had been talking to about the television job. Had she picked up any phone calls or heard him refer to anyone by name on the phone?

"I have no idea. I only know what he told me," Minnie answered. "He mostly used e-mail."

"Have you checked his computer to see if it gives you any information on his whereabouts?"

"I don't like computers." Her eyes narrowed at the mere thought of the loathsome machines.

"The few times I tried to use one, it jammed up and nothing would move. I think computers like me even less than I like them."

"Why don't we take a look at his computer together?" Paavo suggested. "It just might have the answer you need."

She led him through the house. He felt as if he should simply step over the furniture rather than walk around it.

He turned on the computer and waited for it to boot up.

Paavo suggested Minnie take the desk chair. He instructed her to double-click on the AOL icon. If this were a murder investigation, for him to go through Fred's computer without any kind of warrant would be illegal as hell. For one roommate concerned about another's disappearance to look through it, however, was reasonable.

After a minute of loading Minnie hit the sign-on screen. It opened up with the ubiquitous, "You've Got Mail."

"Hot damn! Will you look at that?" she cried.

"He's got his computer set up so that no passwords are needed," Paavo said. He had Minnie open the "Read Mail" window. Five messages were listed, all spam. Typical AOL. "Let's see if he kept old e-mails in his filing cabinet."

Minnie looked around the room. "His what?"

He showed her how to move the mouse to find the cabinet, but it was empty. Familiar with AOL, Paavo had Minnie open the "Old Messages" and "Sent Messages" folders.

The last three messages Fred sent were to someone listed as "Etstar."

"Was he into astrology?" Paavo asked.

"For cryin' out loud!" Minnie snarled. "He was a movie star. Get it now, dummy?"

Paavo bit his tongue. "Hit open, let's see what he said to this Etstar."

Together, they read the most recent message:

The Christmas goose was not kosher.

"What the hell?" was Minnie's reaction.

The second message said:

Aren't you curious about the gander who plucked your goose?

Paavo hoped the earliest message would make sense out of those two. It didn't. It read: *Christmas comes but once a year. Or does it?*

"Fred's gone bonkers!" Minnie cried. "He doesn't even like goose. What does he care about kosher? He's not Jewish. You should see the junk he jams into his fat mouth."

Paavo reread it. "It might be some sort of code."

"A game?" Minnie reread the messages thoughtfully. "Fred didn't like games unless he was making up the rules."

They read through the old incoming messages. All were industry news, Viagra come-ons, how to get out of debt fast, or porn sites.

"Do you have any ideas, or even guesses, who he was writing to?" Paavo asked.

"I have no idea." She glared at the computer as if it might give her an answer. "Maybe you should ask your fiancée if she's heard anything?"

Paavo's head snapped from the computer to Minnie. "My fiancée? Why?"

"Connie told me she was working with some big Hollywood director and that she knew all about what was going on there these days. That's why I went to see you. What did you think? It was because of your big baby blues?"

Paavo mentally rolled his "baby blues." Angie loved to exaggerate, and Connie loved to even more. Before long, he'd probably hear she was up for an Emmy. "You were given the wrong impression, Ms. Petite. I'm sure you have a lot more knowledge of television and movies than Angie."

"Hell! I should have known better than to listen to that gossipy Connie! My so-called knowledge is a damn thirty y—I mean, thirty *months* old. Things move fast there. I need to know what's happening *now*."

Paavo stood. "I'm sorry."

"Get off your high horse and sit back down. Fred's still missing, and you're better than nobody trying to find him." She pointed at the computer. "So, what do you think, Mr. Expert?"

He considered telling her exactly what he thought: no wonder Fred took off. Something might have happened to him, though. He should try to help . . . within reason. He gazed at the e-mails again.

"Etstar. Et. Star. Ets. Tar," he murmured. "E. T. Star—extra-terrestrial! Was Fred involved with the movie *E. T.*, or know any of the stars from it?"

Minnie shook her head. "His only involvement was complaining to ASCAP that they used some animated dummy to play E. T. instead of one of the little people. Namely, him. Cripes, if he'd had his way, *E. T.* would have been a flop."

Paavo grimaced. Maybe Steven Spielberg was behind Fred's disappearance.

Chapter 9

 "There's a man here to see you," Mariah said, after finding Angie in the kitchen. "He said he's your assistant."

"A man!" Angie's eye lit up. Third time's the charm, she thought. It had to be Paavo. He came to be with her after all. He didn't really want to be separated from her for long, lonely days . . . and nights. "How wonderful! Is he in the living room?"

"He's outside the door." Mariah's pigtails swished as she spun rapidly around and stalked off.

Angie was horrified that Paavo had been left standing on the stoop like some door-to-door salesman. "That will never do!" She dashed to the front door and pulled it open, ready to throw herself into her fiancé's arms. She stopped herself just in time.

Standing in the doorway, covered with snow, was her neighbor, Stanfield Bonnette. Stan could have been a decent-looking fellow—early thirties, fairly tall, wiry build, good dresser, with silky light brown hair that flopped boyishly onto his forehead and sappy brown eyes—except that his one fault caused people to overlook everything else about him. Laziness. Those who knew him marveled over the way his father's influence kept him in a cushy job at a bank and a nice apartment right across the hall from Angie.

Somehow, he and Angie had become friends. Not the tell-your-deepest-secrets-to kind of friends, but the I-can-count-on-you-in-a-pinch type.

"Can I come in, Angie?" he asked, teeth chattering. "It's freezing out here."

Freezing? She gawked at the machine shooting a stream of plastic snowflakes over the front of the house and everything on it, including Stan. Some even blasted her. She grabbed Stan's arm and jerked him indoors. "The snow is fake, Stan."

"That's good," he said. "I'm not wearing my thermals." He reached into his pocket. "I brought you something."

"You did?" She was shocked. This was like the Three Wise Men bearing gifts . . . except that Stan was no Magi. Nor, for that matter, was Rebecca Mayfield. Or her sister.

"Your favorite perfume. I was surprised you left it home."

Gold, incense, perfume . . . it fit well enough. What was going on here? This was all too eerie.

He placed the expensive bottle of Fleur in her hand. She stared at it, all thoughts of Wise Men fizzling. "Where did the perfume go?"

He looked at the empty container. "So that's why my car smells so good."

Bah, humbug!

"This house is incredible!" He took off his jacket and shook the snowflakes from it, then brushed his fingers through his hair. More snow fell. "It's like Christmas."

Angie frowned. The small foyer Christmas tree whirled, playing, "We Wish You a Merry Christmas," which was laughable considering Stan, not Paavo, had been at the door.

"What are you doing here?" she asked. "And what do you mean by telling anyone that you're anything to me, let alone my assistant? I don't need any assistance—"

"Calm down, Angie. I just wanted to be helpful. I brought you something you need to know. I had a bunch of the old *Eagle Crest* shows on tape and I transferred them to DVD." He handed her a disk. "Watch and learn."

He darted into the living room and touched all the furniture, piece by piece. "You don't know how demanding these television types are."

"Is that so?" Angie tried to kick the snowflakes under the Christmas tree skirt. The set people were fanatical about the slightest thing out of place. "And you know all about it, I suppose? You still have snowflakes in your hair, by the way." The more she kicked, the more the flakes scattered. She gave up.

"I didn't expect a blizzard." He sat on the sofa, then each chair in the room, practically bouncing on them. "I've watched every episode at least twice. Some even more. If you're part of a reunion show, you need to know what's important to its fans. How many shows have you seen?"

She tapped his disk against her palm. "All of them."

His eyebrows rose. "Really? I had no idea you had such good taste. You don't need this." He took back his gift, then ducked around some dollies and lights and scurried down the hall to the family room. "I love this room! Remember how Julia Parker used to hop up on those barstools? Man, I was madly in love with her. When she died, I actually cried."

Angie shook her head and chuckled. "I had no idea."

"Whatever you need, I can help. Say the word."

"All I need is for you to keep an eye on my apartment while I'm away."

"It'll be like I'm two places at once. Hey, look at that!" He pointed at the bounding Rudolph. Someone had turned it back on. "Man, that dude must be really horny," Stan said.

Angie yanked the plug and stuffed the red-nosed one far in the back of a closet.

When she turned around, Stan was behind the bar, then disappeared to study the contents of the under-counter refrigerator. First, a bottle of Sam Adams was lifted onto the bar top, then a bag of pretzels.

"Want some?" he asked, his mouth full of pretzels as he held the bag toward her.

Angie sat on a barstool. "No, thanks, but I'll have a diet Pepsi. I'm surprised you aren't asking about lunch."

"I don't visit you only to eat." Stan actually looked hurt. He opened a Pepsi and slowly poured it into a glass. "I'm here to help, as you can see."

"This isn't the first time I've had to cook an elegant Christmas dinner. I know how to do it," she said.

"You've never done it for a TV show before." He handed her the glass.

"They won't be filming me. I'll be sweating off-camera, in the kitchen." She took a sip.

"See! You do need me," he said smugly as he walked around the bar and sat beside her. "I can give you cool things to drink and dab your brow with a napkin." Popping another pretzel into his mouth, he looked around the room. "Remember the scene in front of the fireplace where Cliff first seduced Natalie and convinced her to marry him? I was a young teen, and I swear, I'd never seen anything so hot. Man, I can see it right now."

"That's right. When Adrian found out, he tried to melt Natalie's ice skating trophies by putting them in that same fireplace."

Stan sighed wistfully. "I even took up ice skating. I wanted to find a girlfriend like Natalie. Didn't happen. I won a couple of trophies, though."

"You were a skater?" Angie gaped.

"I could have been good, but I got too dizzy when I twirled. Never learned how to stop that. I brought one of my old trophies. It's in the car. No one will notice if we add it to Natalie's"—he pointed to the trophy cabinet—"will they? It'll be such fun to watch the show and see it. Our little secret, Angie."

Stan finished the pretzels, then draped himself over the bar to reach behind it for a jumbo sack of Frito-Lay. He didn't realize that the sack had been opened, and as he lifted it, potato chips tumbled all over the floor. "Oops," Stan said. He went behind the bar and began to pick up chips. He looked around for a wastebasket and found one in the cabinet under the sink.

"Forget the trophy." Angie joined him behind the bar to help. "The crew here is quite picky. Someone's sure to notice, and if they trace it back to me, it wouldn't be good. I plan to impress them. A lot."

"Why are you so uptight about this job? Hey, what's a bottle of wine doing under the sink?" He lifted it onto the bar. "Let's have some. Maybe you'll see things my way."

She smiled. "Not likely. Mainly, though, I want to make my father proud. He asked me to do this for his friend." She stood, having picked up quite enough potato chips for one day.

Stan also stood. "Say, this wine's already been open. I wonder if it was down there because it's bad."

"With Waterfield wines, who could tell?" Angie said.

Stan worked the cork out of the bottle. "How bad can it be?" He sniffed, then coughed and gasped. "It's awful!"

Angie took it from him. "Didn't I warn you?" She made a slight sniff, then sniffed again. "This isn't wine. It's gasoline."

"Gasoline? Under the bar? That's dangerous. Even I know that. And there are a bunch of rags down there, too."

"What was someone thinking? Did they want to start a fire?" Something niggled in the back of her memory. She put the cork back in the bottle. "I'll give all this to Sterling, and warn him about an incompetent worker in the group."

They went around to the front of the bar and sat, Stan with his Sam Adams and an unopened bag of cheese popcorn, which he promptly broke into. "You've got to let me stay, Angie. I even asked the bank for vacation time."

"Vacation time? How can you have any? You're always home."

"Those are sick days. If I don't see my favorite TV stars here, now, *today*, I might get sick."

"I hate to be the one to tell you, but the cast isn't here yet."

Stan gawked. "No cast? You mean Cliff and Natalie and Leona—"

"Not yet."

"How can that be?" He was so upset he stopped eating.

"The crew is filming all the outside shots and getting things ready for them inside. I hear the cast won't be needed for another couple of days."

He stood up. "Well . . . in that case, don't let me take up any more of your time. I'd better head back to the city for now, and try again later. See you soon!"

With that, he grabbed the popcorn and his jacket, then faced the plastic snow, trudging back to his car much like Sir Edmund Hillary braving Mt. Everest.

* * *

The front door slowly opened. Light footsteps crossed the foyer to the living room.

There it was!

Gloved hands reached up and gently lifted the Little Drummer Boy. The temptation to turn the key, to hear the song, was enormous. Instead, the figurine was placed into a large paper bag.

As quietly as the entrance was made, so was the exit.

Chapter 10

Angie hiked a little way into the hills after Stan's visit to get some fresh air, see the scenery, and clear her head. So far, it had been a very strange day.

When she returned, the house was abuzz with activity.

Natalie Roxbury stood in the middle of the room talking to Tarleton. In reality, she was Rhonda Manning, but to Angie she was Natalie come to life. She was taller than Angie had expected and much thinner—skinny, in fact—but looked classy yet fragile, as if she'd suffered a deep hurt. Angie wondered how much of the vulnerability she gave to Natalie's character came from acting, and how much from the woman herself.

Angie glanced down at the jeans, T-shirt, and heavy boots she wore for the hike. She was backing quietly out of the room when Tarleton called her.

"Here's our Christmas cook. Angie, come and meet Miss Manning."

Rhonda flashed a smile as phony as the snow and said, "Hello. How lovely to meet you." It sounded like a child reciting a nursery rhyme— singsong and meaningless.

Before Angie could reply, Rhonda turned back to Tarleton, showing Angie what it felt like to be part of a "crew" and not an individual. She didn't care for the feeling. She reached up to give her hair an arrogant flick, and felt a twig. Nothing like oak leaves and hiking boots to ruin one's image.

At that moment, Bart Farrell swaggered into the room, his head high and his chest puffed out. The years had not been kind to him.

Farrell was wearing a Western-style leather sport coat with a fringe. His brown hair flowed back from his brow, and the gray at the temples was distinguished, but his facelift was so tight she wondered if he could shut his eyes to go to sleep. If he was one of Dr. Waterfield's customers, he wasn't a good advertisement.

His stomach protruded way too far, and his eyes were bloodshot.

So much for the heroes of our youth, she thought with disappointment.

"What are we drinking?" His voice boomed across the room, assuring all attention was on him. Then, he laughed loud, exactly the way Cliff Roxbury would do.

His gaze met Rhonda's and held. A sudden softening gentleness came over his features. Angie wasn't sure whether she was seeing Bart's regard for Rhonda, or Cliff's for Natalie.

"How good to see you, Rhonda." He walked to-ward his TV spouse with his hands extended. She reached out and grasped them. "You look more beautiful than ever." He sounded like a bad movie script even as he kissed her cheek.

"Bart, hello," she replied, in that husky little-girl voice with a twinge of the South that made Natalie such an endearing character—tough, yet vulnerable; bitchy, yet easily hurt. Angie felt a tingle just hearing that particular inflection. Her disappointment vanished and she sighed dreamily. Cliff and Natalie, together again.

"I've missed you," Farrell said, his voice deep and rumbling. Tarleton cleared his throat.

Farrell dropped Rhonda's hands. With a lazy grin, he slapped Tarleton on the back. "But not this slave driver! How ya' doin'?" Tarleton greeted him quietly.

"Doesn't Rhonda look great?" Farrell said. "Why is it she looks younger, and you and I just look older?" His gaze captured Rhonda's again, as if Tarleton had vanished into thin air. "How have you been?"

Her eyes darted from side to side, as if she needed to get away. Not looking at either man, Rhonda replied, "Fine. I've been just fine."

A question marred Farrell's brow. Angie wondered, too, what was wrong with Rhonda.

"Say, you haven't met our cook yet," Tarleton interjected, as if needing to ease the sudden charge in the air. "This is Angie Amalfi."

"Please excuse my appearance, Mr. Farrell," Angie said after introductions. "I took a walk in the hills behind Eagle Crest and managed to slip. I didn't think that was supposed to happen with boots like this."

His gaze slowly drifted over her body, then lifted to meet her eyes. He smiled approvingly, and she felt a "zing," just like when she was a kid watching Cliff Roxbury charm and seduce women on the soap. He might be too old and too overweight and too much work had been done on his face, but still he had that indescribable something that separated sexy stars from mere mortals.

"It's all right, Angie," he said, "as long as you don't get any of that St. Helena clay into our meals, that's all we ask."

She was too tongue-tied to reply. Though she knew she must look like an idiot standing there grinning at the man, she couldn't help herself.

"My God!" Tarleton cried. "Where'd it go?" His eyes raked the group. "Who took it?"

Mariah lightly placed her hand on his back. "What is it?" She moved close, and somehow, her body language wasn't that of an employee.

"There." He pointed toward the mantel—the empty spot where the drummer boy had been.

"We'll find something else to put there," Mariah said. "It's not a problem."

"I want the music box," Tarleton shouted. "It was special!"

"Special? I thought it was a studio prop." Mariah looked from one person to the other, confusion on her face.

"It wasn't." Tarleton shook his head and turned back to Bart and Rhonda. "I'm sorry."

Angie gaped at him, then to Farrell and Manning with equal confusion.

She excused herself and left the room.

* * *

Wearing a simple Vera Wang black sheath and Sergio Rossi heels, Angie glided into the family room.

It was empty.

She hadn't been gone that long, although she had phoned Paavo to tell him all about meeting Bart Farrell—he didn't seem to share her excitement—and about Rebecca's visit. She left out Rebecca's little gifts to the set. She also took a quick shower, practicing "Don't Cry For Me, Argentina" the whole time. It would show off her singing range to Tarleton in case he had any openings in his upcoming musical. All she did after that was to dry her hair, get dressed, and hurry downstairs to join Tarleton and the celebrities.

How had she missed them?

Mariah, her coat on, was on her way out the front door.

"Wait," Angie called. "Where is everyone?"

"Gone," Mariah said.

"What do you mean, gone? I've got to talk to Tarleton about the menu he wants me to cook, and . . . and stuff."

"You can forget about it tonight. He took Farrell and Manning out to dinner." She didn't look happy to have been left behind. "They'll probably go out drinking afterward, maybe dancing, and come back too sloshed to do anything."

"Great," she said dejectedly. "That means I've wasted a whole day and accomplished absolutely nothing."

"Get used to it," Mariah said.

"Where are you going?" Angie asked.

"I'm hungry. The caterer's truck came by not long ago."

All dressed up with no place to go . . . except the crew's mess. Angie threw on a coat and crossed the snowy driveway to the trailers. As her nice shoes stayed clean and dry, she understood why plastic was the snow of choice for this situation.

Although the trailers were still in place, many of the cars were gone, and only a couple of people walked around. Donna Heinz from wardrobe sat alone smoking a cigarette, an empty plate in front of her.

"Where is everyone?" Angie asked.

"Most of them have finished setting up and won't be needed again until it's time to shoot. They took off this afternoon. Beautiful dress, by the way. But a little elegant for trailer dining, I'd say."

"I wasn't heading this way when I put it on. Speaking of trailers, doesn't the cast usually stay in them? They've been given rooms in the house."

"This will be a short shoot. A few times in the past, they've stayed in the house for short shoots. In many ways, they preferred it. The house is sure as hell big enough for them, and comfortable. The catered food will be sent there, I suppose. Can't have them walk all this way, can we?"

"I see."

"For a few of the crew, like me and my assistants, our work begins now that the talent is arriving. I just hope they haven't gained too much weight over these past ten years or I'm going to have to do a lot more alterations than I'd expected."

Angie thought about Farrell's waistline. "Have you seen Bart Farrell yet?"

"No. Just a glimpse of Manning. Why?"

"Nothing." Let the woman enjoy her evening. She'd find out soon enough. "It was fun for me to see them together. In real life, they seem like Cliff and Natalie—kind of in love, yet troubled."

"You noticed that already, did you?" Donna said, taking a puff. "I'd have thought that'd be over by now."

"You mean there was something between them?"

"They tried to keep it hidden. Didn't work. She had her hands full, though. He was quite the ladies' man in those days."

"Was she jealous?"

Donna gave a raspy laugh. "Sometimes, when Natalie bashed Cliff with a book or vase, she did it hard enough we were sure she was getting even for something."

"Farrell didn't mess around with other women on the set, did he?"

"Is a lemon yellow?"

"Gwen Hagen?"

"She was more interested in Kyle O'Rourke, if you ask me, but that didn't stop Farrell from trying."

"What about Brittany, or was she too young for him?"

"Nobody was too young for Farrell. And Brittany was twenty-three when she died. She wasn't all that innocent."

"I still can't get over Brittany dying on this set," Angie said, spearing some asparagus. "How did you cope?"

"It wasn't easy, but you've heard the old adage *the show must go on*. That's what we told each other. We all felt her loss, though. She was . . . a presence."

"And Farrell had an affair with her."

"Suspected, not proven."

Angie nodded, trying to get a handle on all these people and their relationships. She was having a hard time. "Rhonda was in love with Bart, but he played around with others in the cast, including Gwen and Brittany, right?"

Donna eyed her curiously, then nodded.

"Gwen was having an affair with Kyle, who might also have been having an affair with Brittany."

"And don't forget Emery Tarleton," Donna said. "He isn't the first director to fall in love with his stars." She snuffed out her cigarette and stood. "Can't smoke in my trailer," she announced, as if purposefully changing the subject. "The smell will get on the clothes, and Rhonda will have a conniption. Goodnight, Angie."

With that, she went into her trailer and shut the door.

Chapter 11

Angie wondered if she was alone in the house. Aside from the plinking xylophone sounds of "We Wish You a Merry Christmas," all was quiet and still. She wondered if Sterling and Silver had gone out for dinner. And she still hadn't seen Junior.

As she headed up the stairs, curiosity about the second floor struck. It had two wings. She'd seen Sterling turn left at the top of the stairs. If that was where the family's bedrooms were, the guests' rooms were most likely to the right.

That was the direction she turned toward.

She knocked on the first door. After waiting a moment, she eased the door open to find a large bedroom. A beautiful floral display stood on a desk, and beside it were pictures of Kyle O'Rourke and his family. She neared the flowers and sniffed the air. Nothing. As usual.

Angie had never quite made up her mind about Adrian Roxbury. He was such a *nice* person, yet he had let himself be swindled out of half the brewery. Angie wanted to give him a good kick just to wise him up. Naïveté in the face of corruption was no virtue in her book.

She also didn't like the fact that he still carried a torch for his former girlfriend, even after she married Cliff. After all, he'd married the dark, sexy Leona. Angie wanted to tell him to get over it already! To have married Leona, feeling as he did about another woman, was wrong.

Angie hurried out of the room. What was wrong with *her*? They were just fictional characters, for Pete's sake, and she was carrying on as if what they did mattered!

Across the hall was another door. After another knock-and-wait, Angie entered. It, too, was large and airy and adorned with candles—at least they had a scent—silk flowers, a full-length dressing mirror, and pictures of Gwen Hagen made up to look like Leona.

Angie had always despised Leona. Everyone did. The woman was cold and calculating. She would have been a good match for Cliff.

As Angie turned to leave, she noticed a doll atop the pillows by the headboard. How sweet, she thought, crossing the room to see it better.

She gasped, put her hands to her mouth, and ran into the hall.

She reached the stairs just as Silver stepped out of a room in the family wing. "What's wrong? You look like you've seen a ghost," he said.

"No. A doll." She took quick breaths. "In Leona's—I mean, Gwen Hagen's—room. It has long, curly black hair, just like Leona, but it has a knife sticking out of it, and blood all over its stomach."

"Blood? Are you sure it wasn't catsup? It's got to be a joke," he said.

"If it was, it's not funny," Angie said. "Who would have done such a thing?"

"I have no idea," Silver replied. "If it's as bad as you say, we'd better remove it before Gwen gets here. If she leaves, the show will be canceled faster than a ninety-ninth-rated pilot."

It was catsup, as Silver had guessed. They removed the doll as well as the pillow sham. The incident added to Angie's unease. Something about the house and the people in it bothered her, though she couldn't pinpoint anything exact.

Nonetheless, she was ready to go home. Tomorrow, she'd have to get Tarleton's final decision on the menu—she remembered the kinds of traditional meals they'd served on *Eagle Crest* and had a good idea of what the one presented the night Julia died had consisted of—then she'd order any food supplies she needed, test a few recipes, and go back to San Francisco and Paavo until it was time to cook the actual Christmas feast.

Being here was far less a thrill than she'd imagined.

Silver took the doll, saying he'd dispose of it, while Angie carried the stained pillow sham to the laundry room. They reconnoitered in the family room.

Silver had a black leather jacket over his arm. "Want to join me in St. Helena for dinner? They have some nice restaurants, and you're certainly dressed for it."

"I've already eaten, but I'll join you for dessert. I'm feeling a little stir-crazy in this house, especially since I haven't done anything I'd intended since I arrived."

"Get used to it," Silver said.

"So I've been told."

They rode in Silver's brand new silver Aston Martin convertible. All his cars were appropriately silver. It was starting to shower. Angie pitied the poor crew, or what was left of it, who would have to freshen the outdoor props and scenery.

Silver chose a small French café on Main Street. He ordered veal medallions, and for Angie, a small Crab Louis just to have something to play with while he ate.

"I've been talking to people about Brittany," Angie said after a while.

"Brittany? Why?" he asked.

She explained how she'd been given Brittany's room, and the more she heard about the girl's death, the more uneasy she felt about it.

"She fell, that's all," Silver said.

The waiter brought a bottle of Beringer Brothers sauvignon blanc. Silver tasted it and nodded.

"You don't think her death had anything to do with the doll in Gwen's room?"

He looked at her as if she'd be talking about New World Order conspiracies next. "You're joking, right?"

"Well . . ." Now she hesitated to say what she was thinking. "Somebody left it. I'd like to know who. Bart or Rhonda might have, or Tarleton, plus the crew go in and out all day long."

"Don't forget Mariah, Tarleton's assistant—and more—from what I've heard," he said with a wink.

She wondered if he was laughing at her. "What do you mean?"

"I mean I saw her coming out of his bedroom in the middle of the night, and the way they act when they think they're alone." He added more salt to his veal.

Putting this news together with Donna's gossip, Angie was beginning to feel she was living in the midst of the soap opera.

"What about Bart or Rhonda?" she asked after sipping some wine. Silver had chosen an excellent wine for this meal. She wondered how he felt about having his name associated with wine that tasted like it should come out of a screw-top jug. "There's probably no love lost between them and Gwen since she's become a star and they're has-beens."

"Ouch! Never utter that anywhere near those two if you want to live!" He shuddered.

"It's true," she insisted.

He put down his fork, finally ready to pay serious attention to her concerns. "All right, I agree. On the other hand, I expect Tarleton, Mariah, or my dad has been with them from the minute they walked in the door."

"Do all the actors stay in the same part of the house?"

He explained, as Angie had seen, that the second floor was separated into two wings. At the end of the hall in the left wing was Sterling's room, then Silver's, and a couple of guest rooms.

Tarleton used one of them. The opposite wing had four more guest rooms, now used by the four lead actors. The third floor, where Angie was staying, was once an attic. Some years back, a crew converted it into four additional bedrooms for stars like Brittany Keegan as the Eagle Crest cast grew.

"You haven't mentioned Junior," Angie said.

"The maid's quarters off the kitchen is like an apartment. Junior took it over since our housekeeper lives in town with her husband. Junior doesn't care for these people and tries to stay as far from them as possible."

"I've wondered why I haven't seen him."

"You'll see him if he wants you to. Only then."

Angie didn't know if she liked that. "So, if Rhonda, Bart, and Mariah didn't leave the doll, did one of the crew?"

"It was a bad joke, that's all. Nothing to worry about."

"Tarleton wouldn't want to upset his star," Angie continued. "So I'd rule him out."

"And I haven't seen Gwen Hagen for ten years, you've never met her, and my dad wants the actors ecstatic to be here, not scared," Silver said, "which leaves exactly no one."

"Not so. There's the cook, Rudolf Goetring. He's a weird fellow and I haven't seen any evidence he can cook," Angie said. "Frankly, I'm not sure why Tarleton hired him."

Silver shook his head. "I'll agree that his presence is strange, but I don't know if he's *that* weird."

There was one more person that Angie hadn't suggested, and that Silver hadn't defended: his own brother, the elusive Junior Waterfield.

* * *

Late that night, Angie was standing at her window looking down at the courtyard. She couldn't sleep. The room was cold and depressing, she didn't know what to do, and she missed Paavo.

She was looking at the moon through the tall almond tree that was to the left of her window, when the corner of her eye noticed movement. She glanced down to the courtyard and saw a tiny man.

No, it couldn't have been a man. A child? Was that it? He darted across the courtyard, no bigger than one of Santa's elves.

She blinked a couple of times. Was she seeing things, or were Christmas and soap operas making her crazy?

Visions of the bloody doll . . . the gasoline behind the bar . . . the crew talking about sabotage of the props and equipment came back to her.

Maybe she wasn't the one who was crazy.

Chapter 12

"Angie, you have a visitor," Mariah said with a scowl. "Am I in a scene from *Groundhog Day*, or something? Is that what this is? Over and over the same thing?"

Angie sat at the breakfast table, which was covered with a variety of bagels and schmears. She wondered if Goetring was from New York. It wasn't a common Bay Area breakfast.

"Who is it?" she asked between sips of coffee.

"How should I know?" Mariah shrieked. "I'm having to take everything apart trying to find that damned drummer boy!" She stormed from the room.

Angie drained her cup and headed for the foyer. No one was there. Pulling open the door, she found the glaring black eyes of a stout older woman with black hair pulled straight back into a stylish bun, pursed lips, and an angry disposition. In other words, her mother.

"What kind of place is this, that the help leaves a guest standing outside the door?" Serefina bellowed.

"I'm sorry, Mamma," Angie said, "but Mariah isn't—"

"*Ah, come bella!*" Serefina marched into the house, uninterested in explanations. "Look at the little tree twirling around, and the music!" She handed Angie her navy blue Dior wool coat and matching handbag.

"Where's papà?" Angie said, sticking her head out the door.

"He didn't want to come. If I lived in the wine country, I'd have a home just like this," Serefina exclaimed. Her silk dress of soft navy print was slimming, almost. "I don't know why me and Salvatore don't live here. It looks just like Italia."

"Without all the people, cars, or pollution—except on weekends," Angie added.

Serefina waved her round arms, taking in everything around her. "It's been a long time since I've seen it."

"You've been here before?"

"Of course. Now, I wanted to see how you're doing here, and say hello to your father's good friend, Sterling." Serefina left the living room to poke her head into the dining room, and she continued down the hall to the family room.

Angie hung the coat in the closet. Her mother's explanations didn't wash. What was she *really* doing here? "Are you tired, Mamma? It was a long drive for you. You must have left the peninsula at the crack of dawn."

"Before dawn," Serefina corrected. "The more I thought about coming here and meeting Cliff and Adrian, the more I couldn't sleep." She sighed, smiling like a lovelorn teenager, and plopped

down on the leather sofa in front of the rock fireplace. "*Faccia brava*, that Adrian, so sweet and
handsome. My heart used to beat so fast when
he'd show up on TV it would make my head light.
But that wife of his, *Madonna mia!* How that Leona
could go to bed with his brother, I don't know.
What is this world coming to? If I see her, I'll slap
her face!"

"Mamma, relax," Angie said, sitting on the sofa
arm. "It's just a story."

"Sometimes I wonder. I lived with them for
years!" She placed her hands against her breasts.
"I raised my children to the troubles at Eagle
Crest. Maybe the characters aren't real to you, but
to me, they are like friends."

"They're an interesting group, that's for sure,"
Angie said.

"So, where is Adrian?" Serefina asked, swiveling around as if the star was lurking in the corners
of the room.

"He's not here yet. Cliff and Natalie arrived
yesterday, but they haven't come down to breakfast, I don't think. At least, I haven't seen them."

"I can wait. Where is Sterling?"

Wait? A sinking feeling hit Angie's stomach.
"I'm not sure. I look for him."

"First, which way is the bathroom? I want to
look my best before I see my old friend."

"Sure." Angie showed her mother to the downstairs bathroom, then ran up to Sterling's bedroom.

She raised her hand to knock on his door when
the peculiar way he'd stared at her face hit her full
force.

She'd almost forgotten about that. What *was* wrong with her face, anyway? Steeling herself, she knocked.

His hair was awry, making the plugs more visible than usual, and he was knotting the sash of his smoking jacket. In the background, the blue glow of a television lit the room. She wondered how it felt to hesitate to move about freely in one's own home. "I'm sorry to bother you," she said, "but my mother has come to visit. Are you free?"

His face took on a rosy glow. "Serefina is here? Now?" He glanced down at the floppy slippers on his feet. "Give me a minute. I'll be right down."

"Wait . . . one moment . . ."

He turned back.

"Yesterday, behind the bar I found gasoline in a wine bottle, and a bunch of rags . . ."

"Yes?"

"It's dangerous. I thought . . ."

"The crew does the strangest things. Don't worry about it, Angie."

"But—"

"Tell your mother I'll be right there. Don't let her run off, now!" He shut the door.

Angie couldn't imagine Serefina walking briskly, let alone running anywhere. And what was with the sudden animation in Sterling? She had no idea he was such good friends with her mother.

Angie had just finishing mixing a pitcher of Bloody Marys, Serefina's favorite morning drink, when Sterling entered the family room.

"Serefina!" He rushed to her.

"*Caro!*" She held out her arms. They kissed first

one cheek, then the other. She stepped back, as did Sterling, still clasping each other. Then both smiled, as if approving of what they saw.

Angie was sure, based on their broad grins, that it wasn't anything like what she saw: a too-chubby woman with jet-black hair due to her hairdresser's help, and a cadaverously thin, overly tanned gray-haired man.

"You are *bellissima*, Serefina. The years have been kind to you," he said.

"You were always such a charmer, Sterling. You were well named for your silver tongue." Serefina gave him a coy smile. "Although your *accento italiano* hasn't improved one little bit."

Angie handed them drinks in tall glasses with ice and a celery stick, forcing Sterling to let go of her mother. "I thought having your daughter here would be a pleasure," he said, his gaze never leaving Serefina. "It's even more of one now. Can you stay a while?"

"Stay?" Serefina asked, her eyes wide as if it was the most surprising suggestion she'd ever heard. Angie went on red alert. She knew that look.

"I'm sure you'd like to meet the cast, wouldn't you?" he coaxed. "Only two of them are here yet. We have plenty of room."

"Oh . . . well . . ." Serefina looked from Sterling to Angie, and back. "As a matter of fact, I just happened to pack a little overnight case. I was thinking I might be too tired to drive all the way home and could spend the night in St. Helena. But this is even better."

Angie's eyebrows rose so high they skirted her hairline.

"Wonderful!" Sterling cast a fleeting glance at Angie. "If you could find Silver, ask him to take your mother's bags up to the yellow guest room. It's a tiny one, Serefina, in the family wing. I'm afraid it's all we have left."

"I'm sure it will be lovely, *caro*."

Serefina took the car keys out of her purse and handed them to Angie. "Here. The car is locked." She batted her eyes at Sterling. "It's become my habit because of living so close to the city. *Madonna mia*, you can't trust anybody there, compared to an area like this."

"You should move here, Serefina." He held her hand in both of his. "You'd love it. Do you still have your Rolls Royce?"

"Dear God," she turned to Angie, looking like someone who'd just licked cream from a bowl. "This man even remembers the car I drive."

Before Angie could respond, Sterling said, "Shall I show you to your room? Maybe you can put on some comfortable shoes and we can go out to Silverado for brunch and a round of golf. Are you hungry?"

"I'm starving. I didn't want to stop and eat, I was so anxious to get here."

Sterling looked at Angie. "Do you mind? Your mother came all this way to see you, and I'm talking about taking her away."

Angie gazed at Serefina to see if her mother would give her "the eye," which meant that she was to object to whatever was being suggested. But Serefina simply smiled. Angie bit her lip. "No, I don't mind. I see my mother all the time. I'm sure she'd love to go to Silverado. It's a beautiful country club."

"And I'm one of their Gold members." He winked at Serefina. "Extra-special privileges."

"I can hardly wait," she said, and they sauntered toward the stairs.

When they were out of view, Angie tumbled onto a chair. What was her mother doing flirting like that? Where was her father?

And where was Silver to help her with the luggage?

She decided it'd be easier to carry an overnight bag upstairs herself than to hunt for Silver, who was quite possibly still asleep.

Her mother was no better at packing than she was because the bag was Pullman size. She rolled it to the foyer. Silver could take it from there.

By the time she returned to her Virgin Mary—sans alcohol—it tasted awful since the ice had melted. She nearly dropped it when her mother entered wearing a green polo shirt, white culottes, and white socks and sneakers, and carrying the satchel that held her golf shoes.

"We're going now," Serefina announced.

"You're really going golfing?" Angie asked.

"*Si*. It's been a long time." She sucked in her stomach.

"You always said the only thing you liked about golf was driving the cart," Angie cried, walking her mother to the door.

Sterling backed his classic MG out of the garage. Serefina gingerly crossed the slippery snow. "So maybe we'll do something else," she called. "I don't care. It will be fun. *Ciao!*"

This, Angie decided, was perhaps the most surreal experience she'd had in her entire life.

"Has Sterling found himself a new girlfriend?" Rhonda Manning tottered on stiletto heels toward the bar. Judging from her slurred words and wobbly demeanor, it wasn't her first visit. "She seemed a little old and chubby. Not his usual type at all."

"That was my mother," Angie said indignantly.

"Your mother? How cute. He usually goes after the crew's daughters. Now he's going after their mothers, too. What's this world coming to?" She stepped behind the bar and didn't have to search at all to find a glass, bourbon, and ice.

Angie neared. "I didn't realize Sterling was such a Lothario."

"I didn't say he succeeded with them, did I?" She laughed.

"Was Brittany Keegan one of his conquests?" Angie asked.

Rhonda's back straightened, her eyes hard. "What makes you bring her up?"

"I discovered I was given her bedroom—and that she died in this very house. It makes me curious."

"Don't you know it isn't smart to ask questions like that?"

Angie moved closer. "What can it hurt? The girl's dead. Her death was an accident."

"Maybe because it was such a sad thing. None of us want to bring it up again. Especially not around nosy little nothings who should stay in the kitchen, where they belong!"

Rhonda grabbed her glass in one hand, hesitated a moment, then took the bottle in the other and left the room.

Moments later, Emery Tarleton stuck his head in. "Have you seen Rhonda?" he asked.

"She went upstairs," Angie said, still smarting from the encounter. "Can I talk to you about the Christmas dinner?"

"No time, now." He dashed to the bar and grabbed a beer.

He had no time to talk, Angie thought, but he couldn't help but *hear*. Pretending to study the rustic Christmas ornaments on the tree, she broke into the love theme from *Titanic*, "Once more, you open the door . . ."

She'd never seen a man leave a room so fast.

Maybe he simply didn't care for movie music.

She was about to go into the kitchen to test the oven and do more planning when she saw Tarleton, Mariah, Bart, and Rhonda troop out the door without so much as a by-your-leave. Rhonda was steadier than Angie imagined she'd be, but the woman was an actress. How disappointing to find she was also a hard-drinking, vicious shrew.

They were soon followed out the door by Silver.

The crew was gone.

Angie hadn't seen Donna Heinz yet this morning. And even Goetring had abandoned the kitchen.

It was Saturday, and everyone seemed to be out enjoying themselves while she was here with a

Christmas tree that played "We Wish You a Merry Christmas" until she wanted to convert to Buddhism.

There was definitely something wrong with this picture.

Chapter 13

As Paavo left the city of Vallejo, he tried to reach Angie on her cell phone one more time. The call wouldn't go through. It was Saturday. How much work could she be doing on a Saturday?

He knew Angie, and even if she was working, she'd find a way to spare a little time for him. She had for Rebecca, and nothing could have surprised him more. If she was busy, he'd pitch in and help her.

He'd had a meeting with the Vallejo police captain to discuss trouble the town was having with a Mexican gang called Quetzalcoatl, named for an Aztec god represented by a feathered serpent. Despite the religious name, the gang was made up of ruthless drug runners who were violent about protecting their territory. If they were in the process of expanding to San Francisco, it'd mean war—which could be exactly what was going on. The men who had been killed had all been confirmed as gang members.

Vallejo was halfway to St. Helena. The meeting

went well, and since no emergencies had come in, he headed for the wine country. He hadn't told Angie his plan. If things hadn't worked out, he would have disappointed her. That'd be worse than not seeing her at all.

He could hardly wait to see her face brighten with surprise.

The city felt empty without her. And his apartment. And his life.

Although he often worked long hours, he'd stop by her place, even if just for a moment, even if there wasn't time for a real date.

It didn't matter what they were doing so long as they were doing it together. How he'd spent his time before Angie had entered his life was a mystery. He must have been bored silly and never even knew it.

One thing about Angie, she was never dull. She made life worth living. *His* life, at least.

A puff of black smoke shot from the rear of the ten-year-old Ford Fairlane he was driving. The car wasn't used to going freeway speeds. In the city, he rarely hit thirty.

He'd bought the Ford for a song from Yosh when his ramshackle Austin Healey completely gave up the ghost. When the engine fell out, the car was so old and rusted he had no way to fix it short of spending a small fortune. Angie had strongly hinted at giving him a brand new Corvette for a wedding present. Once they were married, even if she gave it to him, it would still be half hers, so he wouldn't feel as strange about accepting something so expensive.

Most of the time, her money didn't mean anything to him. Only when he felt she was being overly generous or overly frivolous was there a problem. Somehow, he had to learn to deal with it and not to allow finances to become an issue between them.

The car began to shimmy.

Progress was slow.

In more ways than one.

Angie pulled onto Paavo's street. As much as she told herself he might not be home, not seeing his Ford parked in front of his house was a bitter disappointment.

The possibility that his "new" car had broken down somewhere struck her. To her mind, it was every bit as dangerous as his job. Maybe more.

She rang the bell. No answer. They'd traded house keys, so she let herself in. Maybe he was asleep. Or hurt. Despite his constant assurances, she worried about him. And why not? Shortly after they'd first met, his longtime partner, Inspector Matt Kowalski, had been killed in the line of duty, and Paavo had nearly lost his own life. She'd saved him—to both his and her astonishment. They'd spent an extraordinary amount of time dodging bullets ever since.

The house was quiet. Paavo's cat, Hercules, asleep on the sofa, opened one eye when she entered. The bed was made, the kitchen clean, the refrigerator nearly empty. What was she going to do with that man to get him to eat properly when she wasn't there to cook for him?

So . . . where was he? She tried his cell phone. "Not in service" was the response. Odd, she thought, and left a message for him to call her cell phone.

She drove to the Hall of Justice. Homicide was empty.

Desperate, she phoned Yosh. Paavo had nothing special planned today that he knew of. Neither did he understand why Paavo's cell phone wasn't working.

A quick stop at her apartment allowed her to check the mail, make sure Stan hadn't looted her refrigerator and pantry, grab a couple more nice dresses to wear around Rhonda Manning, and finally, phone her sister, Frannie.

She no sooner finished explaining about being at Eagle Crest when Frannie shrieked. "Why are you encouraging Mamma to run around with another man?"

Angie bit her tongue and tried to calm Frannie down the best she could, which essentially involved her making scoffing noises during those infrequent moments when Frannie paused to draw a breath.

Finally, she got to the goal of the call: Junior Waterfield.

"He was such a disappointment," Frannie wailed. Angie could see her rolling her eyes. Frannie was a first-class eye-roller. "I hate to even think about him."

"Think about him," Angie ordered.

A long, irritated, martyred sigh blew through the receiver. Angie waited, impatient and annoyed, saying nothing. It was the best way to handle her sister.

Frannie's marriage was rocky, to say the least, and Frannie bore much of the fault. She tended to overly dramatize her problems and loved to play the victim. She was also good at pushing people away, believing she was better than anyone else, and subject to severe bouts of jealousy, all of which Angie had to take into consideration as she listened to Frannie's version of the brief romance.

"On our first date," she began, "he told me he loved me, and started making all kinds of plans for us. Can you imagine? I was looking for a boyfriend, a serious relationship, but he freaked me out. He called all the time, asking what I was doing, where I was going, who I was going with. We went out three weekends in a row, and I broke it off. I couldn't take it. For a while, that made him worse."

"What do you mean worse?" Angie asked.

"I had the feeling I was being watched. Sometimes when I answered the phone, no one was there. Finally, I warned him that if he didn't leave me alone, I'd tell Papa and he'd sic 'the boys' on him."

"You didn't!"

"Damned right I did. I told him I hated him and that my father's friends would turn him into mincemeat."

"Mincemeat . . . glad you reminded me." Angie made a mental note to include the traditional Christmas pie.

"What?"

"Anything else about Junior or Sterling?"

"Sterling always liked Mamma. His wife was

one of the coldest women I've ever met. Instead of Crystal, she should have been called 'Ice.' I think Junior's problems were because he was looking for someone to love him. All I knew was, it wasn't me."

Angie didn't want to ask, but she couldn't help herself. "Any idea how Mamma feels about Sterling?"

"I think she likes him, too."

Oh, dear!

Angie soon got off the phone and tried to reach Paavo once more. Unsuccessful, she finally shut off her phone in frustration, since the stupid thing didn't work at Eagle Crest anyway, dropped it into her purse, and traveled back to the Napa Valley.

Paavo inched along behind winery touring drivers who knew little about driving and probably less about wine. Now traveling at about twenty, the Ford was purring like a baby.

Not until he turned off the main highway onto the winding road to Eagle Crest did the congestion ease.

To his surprise, there was no activity around the estate. Empty trailers and a couple of cars filled a parking area. Angie's Mercedes wasn't among them.

He knocked on the door. When no one answered, he tried the doorknob. The door opened.

Was this what Eagle Crest looked like on television? After the reaction from others in Homicide, he must be the only person alive who had never watched the series.

He wandered through the downstairs rooms and didn't see a soul. The kitchen was the first place he'd looked. No Angie. Finally he went out into the courtyard.

A figure stood on the hillside. When he saw Paavo, he started to hurry away.

"Hey!" Paavo called. "Stop. Can you help me?"

The fellow turned. Tall and rugged, he had long black hair that was thick and wild, and a bushy black beard. He appeared to be in his early thirties, his nose and cheekbones sharply angled, his forehead high. He wore a rugged gray plaid flannel shirt and jeans and faced Paavo with a hostile glare. "What do you want?"

"Do you live here?" Paavo asked.

His bearded chin jutted out. He took a moment before answering, "Yes."

Paavo stepped outside the courtyard gate. "My name's Paavo Smith. I'm looking for a woman who was hired to help out with the TV special."

The man nodded.

"Are you one of the Waterfields?" Paavo eyed him closely.

"I'm called Junior." The name fell from his tongue with derision. He appeared nervous.

"You must know Angie Amalfi," Paavo said.

"I know her." Junior's eyes narrowed. "Why?"

"I'm her fiancé. Did she tell you?"

Junior shook his head.

That didn't sound like Angie. "Do you know where she is? Or where anyone is? The house appears empty. I was expecting a lot of people here."

"I don't know. It's Saturday. Maybe they don't work weekends."

Paavo looked at him skeptically. He wasn't sure what was going on, but whatever it was, he didn't like it. "I thought an entire cast and crew were in this house."

"Look, we get a lot of people trying to come in here, saying they're friends of this one and that one. We never tell where people are."

"Maybe this will help." Paavo held out his badge. "If you come down here, you can see the I.D. better."

"I don't need to." He shied even further up the hill.

People who took a step back at the sight of a cop's badge aroused Paavo's curiosity.

Junior cleared his throat. "The crew's gone for now, and the town's putting on some kind of shindig for the cast. I think everyone went into town with the director. Nobody's working. Everyone's having a good time. Angie's probably with them. The party will be over tonight. She'll be back then. Or, you can go to St. Helena and try to find her. It's not that big."

"Where's Silver?" Paavo asked. Angie had called him from a restaurant last night where she was dining with Silver. He wasn't a jealous man. He trusted Angie more than he'd ever trusted anyone in his life—but he wanted to take a look at this Silver character.

"I haven't seen him, either," Junior said. "He doesn't stick around the house much."

"Could he be at the town's festivities?"

"I doubt it. He's not a barbecue-and-speeches kind of guy."

"You aren't, either, I take it." Something about

Junior bothered Paavo the longer he talked to him.

"Right. I'm not, either. I want to go now," Junior said. His voice sounded strained.

"One question," Paavo said. "This place is called Eagle Crest on TV. Are there eagles out here?"

Junior looked over the hillside. "There used to be. No more, though. East of the valley, there's a wildlife preserve near the north shore of Lake Berryessa. Eagles, falcons, hawks. That's the place to see them."

"Thanks," Paavo said.

Junior nodded and headed back up the hill.

Paavo watched him a moment longer, thoughtful. As he went through the house, he looked for someone to question, but as Junior had said, everyone was out.

He left Angie a note on the foyer table.

In St. Helena, he found the park where the barbecue would be held later that afternoon. A woman who appeared to be in charge of the setup told him the mayor and city councilmen had invited the actors to an elaborate lunch at the Silverado Country Club. Afterward, they'd come to the park to meet the public and be given the keys to the town. They had a very complete day planned.

Angie was most likely with them. Leave it to Angie to rub elbows with actors and town politicians.

Time to head back to the city. He'd probably spent more time away than he should have anyway. If all he'd learned in Vallejo was true, the

Quetzalcoátl gang was involved, and they wouldn't be stopping with three murders.

St. Helena appeared to be a pleasant town. Angie was in good hands and was enjoying herself.

He was glad. Or, at least, that was what he told himself.

Chapter 14

Angie drove back from San Francisco depressed. Where could Paavo be? It wasn't like him to travel so far that his cell phone didn't work. She wasn't used to that happening. Before cell phones, how did people find each other?

In St. Helena, a banner proclaiming "Eagle Crest Day" was prominently displayed. A crowd had gathered at the town square.

Angie pulled into a grocery store lot, the only parking available. From there it was a short walk to the park. On a dais, wearing studious expressions, were Bart and Rhonda, and also Kyle O'Rourke and Gwen Hagen. They must have arrived after she'd left Eagle Crest.

The town's mayor read a proclamation and presented a plaque to Emery Tarleton. Photos were taken of the celebrities with the beaming mayor.

The speech ended to a short ripple of applause before the crowd mobbed the actors for autographs.

Several tables topped with food edged the park.

American picnic classics, barbecued beef and pork ribs, fried chicken, potato and macaroni salads, cold bean salads, and gelatin molds straight out of *Family Circle*, plus apple pie and ice cream desserts, were spread out.

A hunger pang reminded Angie that she hadn't eaten yet that day, having hoped to share a meal with Paavo. She made up a heaping plate, plus a glass of Mondavi chianti—she wasn't in the Napa Valley for nothing—then wandered back toward the actors.

Bart Farrell was holding court like a war-weary king.

Rhonda Manning was standing with a group of people, batting her round blue eyes, saying nothing more than "Yes," "No," or "I'm not sure." The force of her personality was stultifying.

Up close, Kyle O'Rourke was smaller than he seemed when playing Adrian Roxbury, although his body was well toned and muscular. A group of thirty-something women flocked around him. He must have been the teenybopper favorite on the show. Even when Angie was a teenager Adrian was too sweet and naïve for her taste.

Gwen Hagen had a surprisingly hard look to her face and demeanor. Her hair was boy-short and straight, which gave her a far different image from the long, sultry locks Leona Roxbury wore.

Kyle and Gwen's crowds were larger than Bart and Rhonda's.

Angie veered away from them, looking for a bench to sit on and enjoy her lunch.

"Psst!"

Had she just heard something? She ignored it.

"*Pssssssssst!*"

She turned to see a man with a camera dangling from his neck standing on the far side of a tree. He was of medium height, slightly overweight, with a loose, wrinkled sport coat over corduroy slacks. The battered brown fedora on his head made him look like the Internet reporter Matt Drudge. He waved her toward him.

"Yes?" she asked.

"Come back here, I don't want to be seen by the actors," he whispered. He had brown eyes and overly large teeth.

"That's your problem." She turned away again.

"It's important."

"I'm hungry." She sauntered toward a bench far from the actors.

Apparently, continuing to hide wasn't all that necessary, since he rushed after her. "I hope they don't look this way." He puffed along by her side. "They might recognize me."

She glanced at him. "Why should they?"

"Let's use that bench. I can sit with my back to them, and I'll tell you all about it."

Curious, she sat where directed. The bench had no back. He sat close beside her but faced the street, while she sat watching the activities in the park.

"I heard you're connected with the group out at Eagle Crest," he said, talking out of the side of his mouth like a B-movie tough guy.

"Where did you hear that?"

He grinned. "Actually, I guessed it from the

way you looked at Tarleton and the others. You don't appear the least bit interested in their autographs. And your clothes tell me you don't live in St. Helena. So I put it all together. I've got a nose for stuff like that."

She looked down at her heather and gray Jil Sanders wool pantsuit, a perfect San Francisco outfit. The crowd was mostly a hodge-podge of polyester, cotton, and denim. "Maybe I just don't like autographs," she suggested, not very convincingly. She began eating a rib, which was quite tasty. She preferred her barbecue sauce a little tangier and the ribs juicier, but for a town picnic she couldn't complain. The wine was delicious and welcome after her disappointing trip to the city. She suppressed a sigh. The food would taste better if Paavo were sitting next to her instead of this bizarre character.

"Do you mind?" He picked a rib off her plate and bit into it.

"Hey!"

"Are you from Los Angeles?" he asked, mouth full.

"San Francisco," she replied.

"Great. That means you don't know these people very well," he said, twirling the half-eaten rib as he spoke, "which is perfect."

"Perfect for what?"

He finished the rib and reached for another. She slapped his hand. "For giving me an open, honest opinion about them."

His audacity was laughable. "Why should I give you any opinion at all?"

"Because the public wants to know." He took a

sip of her wine. "It's my duty as a journalist and yours as a citizen to give them the information."

Her eyes narrowed. "You're a journalist? For which paper?" She moved her wineglass out of his reach.

"The *National Star*."

"A tabloid! Give me a break!" As she stood to walk away from him he snagged the last rib.

"You want your name in the news?" he asked. "What is your name, by the way?"

She stared at him as if he had two heads. "None of your business! The last thing I want is to have my name in any way associated with the *National Star*!"

"Don't you care about Brittany Keegan?" He concentrated on eating the rib as if he'd lost interest in her or her help.

She sat back down. "What do you mean?"

"Don't you want to know who killed her?"

Killed her? He was a madman, just as she'd first thought. "Her death was an accident."

"That's the official story," he said, studying the rib for any last iota of meat. "But I know better."

"What do you know?" she asked.

"That's the problem," he said, finishing her wine. "I haven't been able to put pieces together yet because I haven't had inside help. With such help—your help—I'm sure I will. I'll figure out who killed her. It'll be the scoop of the century!"

"I don't think so," she said.

"Aren't you in favor of justice? I thought you'd be on the side of the good guys in this."

"I'm always on the side of the good guys."

"Just like me."

"With the *National Star*?" She made a face. "How many visitors from outer space have you written about lately? Or interviews with the Abominable Snowman? Have you retired the Loch Ness monster yet?"

His face turned petulant. "Stop right there. I'm a journalist, and a damn good one. I've got ways to find out things. It's just that for this murder, I need some help. Anyway, you're really out of date as to current tabloid news. Loch Ness? Are you kidding?"

"I have a job to do, too," she said, "And I don't care at all about your tabloid news."

"You said you cared about justice."

"And I do." She proudly raised her chin and waggled her engagement ring in front of his nose. "My fiancé is a homicide inspector in San Francisco. It's his whole life."

"A homicide inspector! Hoo, man!" he shouted, rubbing his barbecue-stained hands together. "This is my lucky day, I mean, our lucky day! He'll be able to find out things about the investigation into Brittany Keegan's death that'd take me months and a fortune in bribes to turn up. This is wonderful!" He eyed the ring. "Nice rock."

She handed him the rest of her plate. He'd begun picking the fruit out of the Jell-O mold, and she lost her appetite. She was sure he'd scoop up potato salad with his fingers next. "This isn't his jurisdiction, for one thing. For the other, he doesn't help the press."

"Your fiancé would be disappointed in you." He used her fork on the potato salad, for which she was grateful. "Do you think he'd turn away a source? Someone who knows a lot about a case? Wants to be helpful? You know sources don't come wrapped up in sterile gowns, like in a hospital. We come in all shapes and sizes and job descriptions. I'm a source for your boyfriend and you're a source for me. In other words, you wash my back, and I'll wash yours."

She couldn't imagine anything much more dreadful than having this grungy fellow's hands, with their fingernails chewed to stubs and jagged cuticles, touching her, let alone washing her back. She didn't want to touch him in any way.

"I don't think so."

"Take my card." He handed her his business card.

"Digger Gordon?" she read. "Digger? Are you kidding me?"

He grinned. The smile made his face pleasanter to look at. "I've been called Digger since I was a kid and wanted to become a newsman. At age ten I used to write a newspaper about my neighborhood. It didn't make me popular, but it gave me a taste for reporting about people, a taste that's never left me, no matter what."

"Sounds like you and the *National Star* are meant for each other," she said.

"Someday"—his gaze was serious now— "you'll see my name on the *New York Times* front page."

"In the article where it talks about major scandals in the tabloid business," she added.

He stood to leave, clearly unhappy with her jabs at his work. "The card has my cell phone number on it. Call me when you're ready to talk.

You've *got* to be ready." Dark brown eyes held hers. The importance of this story seemed to go far beyond journalistic curiosity for him. "I need to do this. For the public, but most of all for Brittany Keegan."

"Not to mention for your reputation." Angie reminded herself that he was a reporter, a master at manipulating people with impressive words to get a story.

He shook his head and was about to speak when a cry rose from the crowd. Everyone stared open-mouthed at the road.

A woman who looked just like Brittany Keegan was standing on the back of a pick-up truck. She had long, straight blond hair and wore pink jeans and a cream-colored fringed shorty top decorated with silver embroidery—a typical Julia Parker outfit. The woman didn't look at the crowd but stared straight ahead. As the truck picked up speed, she raised both arms out to the side as if she were flying.

A few people ran to their cars to chase after her, Digger included. The truck would be long gone before they could get past the congestion they caused when all tried to pull out at the same time.

The faces of the cast were white and strained with shock. Rhonda leaned against a murderous-looking Bart. Gwen and Kyle shook their heads in disgust that anyone would have the bad taste to pull such a stunt. Tarleton was nowhere to be found.

Just then, Serefina and Sterling strolled across the park. "Angelina," her mother called. "Did I miss something?"

Chapter 15

Angie was conflicted. When she returned to Eagle Crest she'd phoned Paavo to learn he'd been in St. Helena at the same time as she'd been in San Francisco. They'd agreed it would be best not to try such "surprises" in the future.

Although sorry she'd missed him, at the same time she was moved that he'd come all the way to the Napa Valley to see her. How romantic! How touching!

How infuriating that she wasn't there!

The whole experience reminded her of O. Henry's "The Gift of the Magi," in which a woman cuts her hair to buy her husband a fob for his watch, and he sells his watch for a comb for her hair. The story was about love. Just like her and Paavo.

She learned he'd left her a note. Immediately she ran down to the foyer to retrieve it. Somehow, she'd overlooked it when she returned.

It wasn't there. She searched high and low. The stupid rotating tree's "We Wish You A Merry Christmas" sounded more and more mocking

135

with each passing moment. The note was gone.

Who would have taken it? Later, when she climbed into bed, dreams of Paavo and an electric blanket kept her warm in the frigid room until she fell asleep.

But the wailing of fire sirens woke her.

Disoriented, she put on a robe and ran downstairs. Tarleton, Mariah, Sterling, Silver, and Serefina huddled in the foyer, watching firemen check the situation in the living room.

"What happened?" she asked.

"Some man saw smoke coming from the sofa," Serefina said. "I heard him shouting about it." Serefina and Tarleton were the only ones who wore nightclothes.

"What man?"

"I don't know who he was," Sterling said. "Maybe one of the crew. He was dressed in brown, kind of scruffy, and wore a fedora. He ran out the door as I came downstairs. Whoever he was, thank God he was here. We were able to put out the fire before any damage was done."

"He wasn't one of the crew," Angie said. "He's a reporter. He's here looking into the death of Brittany Keegan."

Sunday morning Angie found herself at mass at St. Helena Catholic Church, a beautiful old building that was once a mission. She'd been so inundated with Christmas at Eagle Crest, she was expecting a service about the journey to Bethlehem. What month was it, anyway?

As they drove home from church, Serefina told her Sterling's story of the missing Little Drummer

Boy. Apparently, it had belonged to the Waterfield family for years. His wife, Crystal, had loved it and was quite upset when, years ago, it disappeared. Sterling was relieved when the set designer found it. He'd planned to reclaim it after the taping was over. Its sudden disappearance, once again, only added to the mystery.

They no sooner reentered the house when Sterling whisked Serefina away for breakfast and the wine train tour of the Valley.

Angie had wanted to ask him more about the missing music box, but when he gave her face another of his disconcerting stares, all she could think about was what could possibly be wrong with it. She was relieved, in fact, when he left.

In the breakfast room a choice of cold cereal, fresh fruit, pastry, and coffee had been set out. As Angie peeled an orange, Mariah entered.

"Have you seen Mr. Tarleton this morning?" Angie asked.

Mariah picked through the pastry. "He's planning a read-through of the script tonight."

"How exciting!" Finally she'd learn—

"It's for the actors only," Mariah added. "They'll use the living room, with the doors shut. He doesn't want the actors to feel self-conscious since they haven't had time to practice."

Angie shrugged. "That's okay. Where is he now?"

"I think he went for a walk. Kyle, too." Mariah bit into a glazed doughnut. "All he talks to me about is that damned drummer boy music box. How the hell should I know who took it? I don't even care."

"Will they be back soon?" Angie asked.

"Who knows? They took the path that leads into the hills just outside the courtyard gate. You could probably find them easily enough if you don't want to wait."

Angie didn't want to waste another day waiting for Tarleton. Muttering to herself, she quickly changed into jeans and hiking boots.

The path behind the house was well worn, probably a deer path that people had taken over.

For a long while the trees and shrubs weren't thick, and she was able to see the house. She hurried, hoping to catch up to Tarleton and O'Rourke.

The house disappeared and the path narrowed. She continued on, expecting that once she reached the top of the hill she'd be able to see how far ahead they might be. If she was very lucky, she'd run into them on their way back.

The path ran diagonally rather than straight up, and the top of the hill remained a good distance away. As she plunged deeper into the brush, she wondered why Tarleton was so anxious about the Little Drummer Boy when it belonged to the Waterfield family. And why had Silver taken the doll she'd found in Gwen's bedroom? What had he done with it? Was there a connection?

Not to mention last night's fire. The firemen said it was lucky someone—Digger, she suspected—had come by in time to smother the flames with pillows before it erupted into a full-fledged fire. They didn't know what had caused it, and suggested sending out arson investigators.

Sterling demurred, preferring to blame it on a cigarette. The firemen looked skeptical.

None of this made sense.

Weary, she was about to give up when she heard a noise.

She stopped. Silence. What could the noise have been? Was it human . . . or was it more like a roar or growl?

The city girl remembered that mountain lions were fairly common in this area. She glanced up, her head swiveling. They liked to climb trees and pounce on their prey according to Animal Planet. She didn't see any, but then, they were good at hiding. She began to back away. Could there be bears as well?

What was she supposed to do? She'd heard something about people not running away from mountain lions—that such behavior caused them to chase their prey. On the other hand, all she had to use as a weapon was a fingernail file in her back pocket.

Suddenly, she knew the true meaning of *"Lions and tigers and bears, oh my!"*

It meant *run.*

Rational thought left her. She careened straight down the mountain side as fast as her legs could take her, terrified that she'd come face to face with a mountain lion, wishing she were back home in her penthouse on Russian Hill, wishing for Paavo, wondering how long he'd mourn for her after they found her half-eaten body . . .

A figure reared up in front of her.

Unable to stop, she let out a scream and ran right into it.

Two more "Birds of Prey" murders, as the press had dubbed them, occurred Saturday night. Half of Homicide, including Paavo, Calderon and Benson, the chief of police, and the mayor's chief of staff met to talk about the murders and the panic the news media was trying to drum up about them.

It was clear to everyone working the cases that the cause was a turf war between gangs engaged in drug trafficking. The police had not yet released any hard evidence, however, and without it they could open themselves up to charges of besmirching the good names of fine people who came to these shores seeking a better life if they referred to them as drug dealers. So the situation became a tug-of-war between the police department and the press over facts and figures and truth—not an unusual state of affairs in San Francisco.

No one felt especially bad about drug dealers deciding to off each other. Their concern was about drugs flooding the area and innocent people getting killed in the crossfire as this war threatened to grow ever larger. An all-out effort to stop it was in the works.

Paavo threw himself into the investigation. The irony of it was that most intense manhunts like this one would have served to divert some of his thoughts and worry away from Angie and the strange people surrounding her in the Napa Valley. With this case, though, he was constantly coming up against the words "birds of prey" and "eagle," which only served as reminders that he wanted her home.

His concentration was completely shattered when Homicide's secretary, Elizabeth, brought him the copy he'd requested of Brittany Keegan's death certificate.

Multiple traumas to head and neck, the result of a fall, had caused Keegan's death. The California database held no files on the case. The determination of accidental death had apparently been so definitive to the medical examiner and detectives at the scene that despite the high profile of the victim, no investigation was launched.

How could they have been so certain? He was tempted to phone the St. Helena police department, but his call would be met with suspicion and irritation. He would be seen as the big city "expert" ready to second-guess a small town police force. Which was exactly what he was doing.

Napa County probably had sent people from the City of Napa's police department or sheriff's office to make sure the SHPD's findings weren't completely off the wall. He hoped.

He shoved Keegan's death certificate aside. No time for snooping around an eleven-year-old case existed with the city on the brink of a firestorm.

Rebecca Mayfield had been right. He had no business investigating everyone and everything Angie interacted with.

Chapter 16

Angie's scream was loud enough to scare away any bear, tiger, or lion within a ten-mile radius. Her momentum carried her into the object in her way. Luckily, the ground was even in this spot, and she managed not to mow them both down.

A shaggy-haired, broad-shouldered mountain man grabbed her arms, stopping her from falling over from the impact.

"Angie! Are you all right?" He winced as he tried to regain his hearing.

She blinked a couple of times. Under the hair, behind the beard, she recognized Junior Waterfield. "I don't know." She looked over her shoulder to see if she was being chased.

He let go of her. "I'd heard you were here working at Eagle Crest. Do you remember me?"

She tried to catch her breath and stop trembling. "Of course, Junior." Aside from having hair like a wooly mammoth, he hadn't changed all that much from the days when she was seventeen. She couldn't help but compare him to the handsome Silver. There was no comparison.

They bore some resemblance, but his features were too sharp, his eyes too small, and his brow too heavy.

"What are you doing climbing around up here?" he asked.

She fidgeted. "Maybe we should hurry back to the house. I heard a mountain lion."

He grinned. "You don't have to worry about them here. This area is filled with trails for hikers and horseback riders. No one's ever had a problem. Anyway, if there was one, you wouldn't have heard it. One reason they're dangerous is that they're quiet until they pounce."

"I heard a roar!"

He raised his eyebrows. That was one thing she hadn't liked about him when he came around the house to see Frannie. He always acted as if he were laughing at her—the cute kid sister. She didn't appreciate it.

Paavo out and out laughed with her many times, but never *at* her. It made all the difference.

"There are a lot of feral cats in the hills. Maybe you got too close to one. Sure you didn't hear a meow?"

"All right, if you say so." She glanced nervously over her shoulder. "Is this part of Waterfield land?"

"It is. Now, why don't you sit down and take a big breath? The last thing you want to do is go back down there with all those people and be talking about strange noises and mountain lions. They'll never let you live it down."

They found a grassy area and sat side by side, the sun warm on their faces.

"What are you doing up here anyway?" He curled an arm around his bent knees.

She told him about her search for Tarleton.

"I haven't seen him. Maybe he changed his mind. This hill is steeper than it looks."

"So I've noticed."

He studied her a long while. "I remember our family's plans for me and your sister. Did they send you to take her place?"

Shocked, she stared at him. "Don't be ridiculous."

"I am ridiculous, Angie," he said, scratching at his beard. "Everyone says so. And, I was just teasing you about us."

"It wasn't funny."

"None of my jokes are. Why haven't you run off?" he asked. "Most women run away from me."

"I have no reason to run, do I?" She met his gaze squarely.

"Aren't you afraid?"

"Should I be?"

"I'm the madman who spends most of his time alone in these hills instead of in a beautiful house, filled with beautiful people. My own father tried to turn me into one of them, but it didn't work, did it? I'm still the way I was. Still Junior, no matter what my face looks like."

His words puzzled her. She wondered if he was right and she should run to the house. "Are you talking about your beard? What do you mean?"

"Not the beard. Surely you know."

She shook her head.

He picked a clover and plucked off the leaves. "I was the homely son. That's how my mother used to introduce me. She'd say, 'Junior is our oldest. When Silver came along, we got it right.' Then she'd laugh." Swamp green eyes pierced her. "Frannie never told you that?"

Angie couldn't imagine such a thing. The strange way his father studied her face caused her insides to churn. How could a young boy handle it? "No. Of course not."

"No?" Now it was his turn to look surprised. He plucked another clover. "Do you know what I got for my high school graduation? Not a car, or a computer, or even an expensive wristwatch. I was given a plastic surgery job."

Angie said nothing. She suspected Frannie hadn't known. It wasn't the kind of thing Frannie would have kept to herself.

Junior tossed the clover stem aside. "Good old Dad made my nose thinner, my chin squarer, even removed some bags under my eyes. Once the bandages were off, you know what the first words I heard were?"

She shook her head.

"My mom telling my father that I was still 'no Silver.'" His fingers tightened around a bunch of clover and he pulled them from the ground. "She said she thought he was a better plastic surgeon than that."

Angie was sickened and horrified. How could a mother be that way? "I'm so sorry, Junior."

He grimaced, his voice harsh. "Why should you be sorry? I'm surrounded here by beautiful people, and a father whose entire life involves the creation of beauty. What more could any sane person possibly want?" He stood, dusted off his hands and held one out to her. "I'll walk you back to the house. I'd hate for a killer kitty cat to get you."

She hesitated a moment. His words and sarcasm troubled her, but then she took his hand. He pulled her to her feet.

"Did you always stay away from the actors?" she asked as they walked.

"Not like now. Earlier, I used to talk to some of them."

Angie's step slowed. "Like Brittany?"

His jaw tightened. "Like Brittany."

"They gave me her old room," Angie said.

"I know," he all but whispered.

"Do you think her death was an accident, Junior?"

His jaw worked. "It's best if you don't ask such questions, Angie. Don't ask anything about her."

Despite his warning, she couldn't stop herself. "Did you love her?"

He snorted derisively. "Did I love anyone? No, never. Not even my mother, who up and died on me. There's a saying about having a face only a mother could love. I never even had that."

"I'll admit your brother is exceptional, but you aren't bad looking in the least," Angie said. "I don't understand why she talked to you that way. She must have been a very unhappy woman."

He stopped as a family of mountain quail ambled across the path ahead of them. "Who knows? All I knew was that I wasn't good enough. I wasn't Silver, who she was so proud of. I wasn't good enough for Brittany either. I learned well from both of them."

The quails' heads bobbed. They darted from side to side, making slow progress as Angie watched. "Tell me about Brittany. You were both around the same age when she died."

He folded his arms protectively. "She was a slut. What more can I say?"

Angie studied him. "She slept with everyone?"

"That's right," he said bitterly.

"Bart?"

He hesitated, then spat out the answer. "Yes."

Somehow, she didn't believe him. "Kyle?"

He answered quickly. "Yes!"

Irritation filled her. "Tarleton? Silver? Your father? You?"

Hate gleamed from his eyes. "What business is it of yours?" His mouth twisted. "Do you want to take over for her? Maybe you'd like to sleep with me? Or, at least tell me you love me. No woman ever has, Angie. You can be the first." He loomed closer, scaring her. Instinct cried out that it was his hurt talking, that she wasn't in danger. She held firm.

"I'm sorry, Junior," she murmured. He told the truth as he perceived it, not a truth worth pursuing. "I'm sorry your family has made you so bitter, that they've caused you to waste your life this way. There are women who would gladly have gotten to know you, maybe to have fallen in love with you. I'm sorry you never learned that."

"Get out of here, Angie. Go back to your city, your fiancé, and forget about this family," he said.

"I hope to do exactly that as soon as I can."

"And take your mother with you. She's treading on dangerous waters." He laughed at his little play on words.

A chill went down Angie's spine as she hurried toward the house by herself.

"Paavo, I don't know why, but no one will talk to me about Brittany Keegan," Angie said into the bedroom extension phone. "Isn't that odd? They'll admit she died here. They all know it. But that's as far as it goes."

"If they don't want to talk about it," Paavo cautioned, "it's best not to. Who knows what memories you might be stirring up?" He told her about the lack of police records in the case. The findings were open and shut.

"There's more to it. I can feel it when they look at me."

"Keep out of it, Angie."

"I'm curious. Nothing more."

"I know it, and you know it, but it seems everyone else wants to keep whatever happened there a secret. Remember what happened when Pandora opened the box? Or to put it in terms more fitting to where you are, sometimes in Santa's sack you find a lump of coal and switches."

Chapter 17

The living room was in complete chaos. The damaged sofa had been removed from the room. The mantel and walls had been stripped bare, and Angie watched Mariah remove the beautiful Victorian die-cut Wedgwood porcelain, and Kugel glass ornaments from the tree. "What are you doing?"

"Em decided on a change," Mariah said tersely. "The new sofa will be here, special delivery, in a couple of hours."

"You've removed everything. Why?" Boxes of gold-colored glass ornaments were stacked in the center of the room. Something niggled in the back of Angie's memory. "Would you like help?"

"These are special decorations." Mariah backed Angie into the foyer. "I don't need anyone's help." She shut the doors in Angie's face.

As Angie headed toward the kitchen, she saw Bart and Rhonda at the bar. She developed a sudden thirst.

"I'll have Perrier with a twist of lime." Rhonda's speech was slightly slurred, her eyes glassy, like someone strung out on painkillers, Valium, or possibly something stronger.

Bart nodded. He was behind the bar, making himself a Manhattan.

"Hello," Angie said. "How are you two today?"

"I'm going to my room," Rhonda said. "My head is beginning to throb. Tell Em I'm too sick to do anything today."

"Here's your Perrier." Bart handed her a glass. He came around to the front of the bar with his drink.

Angie replaced him. "I'm sure I saw some Tylenol back here. I'll find it for you."

Rhonda sipped her water and eyed Bart's Manhattan hungrily.

"Did you hear I was given Brittany Keegan's room?" Angie asked Bart.

He glanced at Rhonda and put down his drink. "No, I can't say anyone thought to tell me that," Bart replied. "Should they have?"

"I guess not. Were you here the night she died?"

"Everyone was here," Rhonda answered abruptly. "We filmed the Christmas dinner scene. Haven't you found the Tylenol yet?"

Angie went back to rummaging.

"I remember that." Bart laughed to himself. "There was a big fight. Julia Parker—that was Brittany—had just told Natalie that she was going to become the next Mrs. Cliff Roxbury, and that I—I should say, Cliff—had grown tired of Natalie with all her whining about ice skating, and how she really should have stayed with Adrian, who was a much nicer guy than me. Natalie slapped

Julia in the script. Remember, Rhonda?" He chuckled. "You nearly knocked her into the next state. I didn't know anyone so skinny could pack such a wallop."

"Sounds like you two didn't like each other," Angie said.

"You idiot!" Rhonda addressed her words to Bart. "It was an act. We're actors, remember?"

"After a scene like that, you must have felt strange when she died," Angie said.

"I knew I shouldn't have come back here!" Rhonda cried. "I want to go home. I'm through with this."

"Wait, darling," Bart said. "You can't run out now. You need this job. Just try to relax."

"How can I relax around here?" Rhonda was near tears. "It's all coming back again. Just like years ago, when Brittany died. I can't take it!"

"What happened years ago?" Angie asked. She handed the bottle of Tylenol to Rhonda.

Rhonda began tearing at the childproof cap.

"Do you know, Mr. Farrell?" Angie asked.

"Not really. I thought everything was fine, a little tense, but then, it's always tense when you get this many actors around. Then, she died."

"You know there was more to it than that." Rhonda spat the words, her hands shaking with frustration at being unable to open the bottle. "You were sleeping with her."

"I never!"

"Everyone knew it," she screamed. "Don't try to deny it!"

"Rhonda!"

"Get out! Get out of my sight!"

"There's no talking to you." Bart stalked out of the room toward the kitchen.

The cap flew off and pills clattered onto the bar. Rhonda cast a furious glare at Angie and then also stormed away.

"Whew. That didn't go well," Angie muttered as she headed for the kitchen.

Bart Farrell's backside pointed at her, his head in the Sub-Zero refrigerator. At the sound of her footsteps, he tried to straighten and bumped his head on a shelf. He had a carton of eggnog in his hand.

"Are you all right, Mr. Farrell?" Angie asked.

Wincing, he rubbed his head. "I should have let you do this. Rhonda is getting after me for being too fat. She's not eating, I'm not eating. You saw the result. I heard about the raw food diet—that it gives extra energy, staves off disease, even extends youth."

"I don't know that I agree," Angie said, "but I can cook, I mean, slice or mash something for you to eat, if it'll help." The scene with Rhonda had unnerved her. Bart taking it so calmly was a surprise.

"Look at nature," he mused, arms wide, as Angie pulled cauliflower, peas, and zucchini from the refrigerator. "Animals stay healthy until old age. You never hear of deer or giraffes or elephants dying of heart disease, cancer, or strokes, do you? No! Raw food can not only prevent life-threatening disease, it can even cure it."

"You aren't sick, are you, Mr. Farrell?" Angie asked, concerned.

"Not yet, and I intend to stay healthy." He eyed the eggnog, looking ready to drink out of the carton. Angie took it away, poured him a glass, and put the rest back in the refrigerator.

"Thanks," he said. "Anyway, you saw how beautiful Rhonda is. Years ago she was a vegan. I thought it was extreme, but then I heard about raw food. I'll try it. She'll be impressed, I'm sure. Maybe you can whip enough food for both of us. Some people also recommend five daily enemas and radium therapy, but I don't want to go overboard." He drank down the eggnog.

"Heaven forbid," Angie said, trying to sound earnest. "I can mash the peas and add some spices and you can use it as a dip."

"That's good. The spices can't be cooked or dried. Only raw. And no honey. Rhonda used to say it was the product of bee enslavement."

"You seem to care for her quite a bit," Angie said.

"Rhonda?" He truly sounded surprised.

"You're more than a little in love with her."

His words were flustered and stumbling. "How could I not be? She's . . . everything. Perfect. For years . . . I just . . . I just . . ."

Angie smiled. "Have you seen her since *Eagle Crest* ended?"

"Now and then, at events. She made it clear she wasn't interested. My reputation preceded me. As with Brittany. I had no interest in that child. Not when a woman like Rhonda was near."

Angie plated the food in a way she hoped was attractive, and Farrell left with it smiling like a man who believed he might have found the way to Rhonda Manning's heart.

She shivered. The mere thought of eating so much raw food, without the heat that makes food taste good and improves digestibility, made her stomach ache.

Seconds after Farrell walked out of the kitchen, Mariah entered. Disgusted and on the verge of a nervous collapse, she told Angie someone was yet again at the door.

Angie wondered which friend or relative had dropped in this time to meet the actors. When she went to the door, there stood Digger Gordon. He wore his fedora and a rumpled brown sport coat over grease-stained khaki Dockers.

"Oh, no," she said, and tried to shut the door in his face.

"Hey! You're breaking my foot!" He'd wedged his foot between the door and the doorjamb. "You don't want me to sue, do you?"

"Your foot's the least of your worries. If you don't leave me and the people here alone, you'll have plenty more broken bones to worry about. Get out of here."

"I thought I was a hero!" he cried. "Didn't I save the place from becoming a cinder, and maybe you with it?"

"Yes . . . until I told them you were a reporter."

"We've got to talk, Angie." His words came rapid fire. "I'll tell you about the Brittany Keegan look-alike."

That gave her pause. "Do I care?" she asked.

"Sure you do. Or, at least you're curious about it. Aren't you?"

She thought about it a moment. Actually, less than a moment. He was right. "Come in."

"We need somewhere private to talk." Slack-jawed, he took in Eagle Crest's living and dining rooms. He darted down the hall to the family room. "Just like on TV," he said, marveling. He grabbed a plastic chocolate-covered cherry from a display and plopped it in his mouth.

Angie expected him to spit it out. He didn't.

"You ate that?"

"They aren't as good as they used to be," he admitted.

"Let's go up to my room. Since you're so fascinated by Brittany Keegan, you'll find it interesting." She started up the stairs.

He smiled, following. "You do trust me."

"Not one whit. However, this morning I phoned the *National Star* and talked to the news editor. He described you to a T, and even acknowledged you were in northern California. Great article about searching for Howard Hughes's heir, by the way. Real topical. When did he die? Twenty years ago?"

"That was clever on your part," Digger said, ignoring her slam. "We're going to make a great team. I can feel it in my bones."

"That's better than the cold chill I'm feeling." She opened the door. "This was Brittany's room. That's the window she fell from."

The aluminum framed window was about five feet wide. Digger opened it by pushing the left half over to the right, sliding door style. He stuck his head out. "Amazing. How did you end up getting this room?"

"Dumb luck."

"It's freezing in here," he said, shutting the window.

"It always is. Creepy, too." Angie rubbed her arms.

"Maybe the room's haunted," he suggested.

"Shut up!" She didn't really believe in such things. Much.

He studied the view from the window again. "You know, it isn't all that far down."

"Who knows how she landed, though?" Angie didn't want to look. Lately she'd had a strange feeling in this room, almost a premonition, of herself falling. She forced away the image and studied Digger, who was staring down at the pavement, lost in thought.

"Tell me all about it," Angie said, breaking the spell.

He turned his back to the glass, hands in pockets. "The pickup truck disappeared by the time I reached the road. I think it pulled into a garage not too far out of town. Maybe in town. It can't have disappeared on the open country that quickly."

"Why not?" She sat on the bed.

"There were too many cars and trucks going after it. Some of those yahoos have their trucks so souped up they could probably race in the Indy 500. My car didn't stand a chance."

"In other words, you have nothing to tell me,"

Angie said, disgusted with herself for letting him in. Why had she listened to him?

"Well, it does mean that it wasn't just some fan playing around. It means someone planned a way to spook people and then disappear. Maybe rented a garage, or storage facility, or something."

"Or, it was someone who lived in town, they had fun and went home! I don't get it, Digger. Why are you so sure Brittany's death wasn't accidental?"

He leaned back against the bureau, his eyes bleak, as if he was not so much the hardnosed reporter, but a man who cared about justice for a victim. "A gut feeling from the time I read the story. And I talked to her mother."

"Her mother?" Angie was stunned.

He'd learned that Brittany's mother had believed her daughter was happy with her life and career, and in love. Deeply, seriously in love. The mother's sense was that somehow the love had led to disaster, either from jealousy, or love not returned; she had no idea. Digger trusted her feeling.

"Who was she in love with?" Angie asked, intrigued. She thought of the houseful of potential prospects.

Digger shrugged. "Any of them. Talk is, though, she and Tarleton were close. He did all he could to beef up her part and make her scenes dramatic. Who knows? The mother convinced me something happened here, and I want to know what it was."

"What about Brittany's father? Did you talk to him?"

"She was raised by a single parent. Sounds like she never knew her father."

"Poor girl," Angie said. As much as her own father drove her crazy sometimes—like wanting her to drop Paavo for Silver—she couldn't imagine life without him.

Digger strolled toward the door. "Keep an eye on things here and let me know if anything else strange happens. Someone dressed up as Julia and drove by that picnic for a reason. I want to know why." He opened the door. "Don't bother to see me out."

With that, he left. She thought of following, but then, she'd just have to talk to him some more. She didn't want to do that.

She walked toward the window and looked out at the hillside. Junior stood on it facing her way as if he'd been watching her room the entire time. Startled, she drew back inside, her heart giving a little leap of fright.

The bedroom felt even colder.

Chapter 18

"Are you the owner of the house?" a woman called out as Angie hit the bottom step. She stood in the living room, a plain woman with straight brown hair, a turned-up nose, pointed chin, and glasses, and wearing a boxy gray tweed suit.

"Me? No, not hardly," Angie replied. "Are you looking for Mr. Waterfield?"

"No. I need the director."

"Don't we all?" Angie agreed. "He's out somewhere."

The woman nervously twisted the strap on her massive shoulder bag. "I'm here for tonight's read-through. I wrote the script. My name is Camille Spentworth."

"How nice to meet you." Angie introduced herself. "Let's go into the family room. I'm sure someone will show up soon."

Once they were seated on each end of the leather sofa, Angie said, "Now that I'm here seeing all the work that goes into a production, I'll be paying more attention to the behind-the-scenes

159

stuff than ever." She smiled, trying to set Camille at ease. "Without you scriptwriters, for example, where would all the directors, producers, and actors be?"

"That's how I feel about it." Camille's voice was whiny and woeful. "No one else does, though. They all seem to think it's easy to turn out sparkling lines of dialogue each week."

"I guess you weren't at the barbecue yesterday," Angie said. "They put it on to honor the show."

"I didn't know about it." Her mouth turned down. "That's what I mean about everyone forgetting the poor writer."

"You didn't miss a thing except when someone dressed up as Julia Parker and rode by in a truck."

"How strange," Camille remarked, eyes wide. "Doesn't anyone remember that Julia's dead?"

"Are you saying she won't be reappearing in your script?"

"Of course not." Camille looked at Angie as if she'd lost her mind.

"What is the story—"

Angie stopped talking when Mariah dashed into the living room. "Miss Spentworth! So glad you're here. I've run off copies of the script they'll be using. It isn't yours, exactly, but Mr. Tarleton wants to see how things play with a few ideas he's kicking around."

"What do you mean it's not mine?" Camille's voice crept higher with each word. "I accept revisions, but don't you think he should read my script first?"

"Don't worry," Mariah soothed. "It's not the whole script—just the last segment."

"The ending?" Camille squealed. She seemed to be having trouble breathing. "He's changed my ending?"

"Is he using Julia in the script?" Angie asked.

Mariah looked surprised. "Julia's dead." She glanced at Camille one last time as she left the room. "Eight o'clock."

Camille sat staring at the wall, looking miserable and saying nothing.

Angie decided it was a good time to test the kitchen appliances.

The California Park Service helped Paavo locate the wildlife reserve Junior Waterfield had told him about. The area was desolate, with a number of raptors and other wildlife native to the area. Varieties of falcon, hawk, and eagle feathers could readily be found there.

The feather on the victim he'd investigated was that of an osprey, a type of hawk.

The Park Service used mostly contract labor to handle the less pleasant duties, like taking care of outhouses, cleaning brush, and removing dead carcasses.

Paavo got the name of the service, and from them a list of names, Social Security numbers, and addresses of people employed. Two addresses given were in Vallejo and one was in Napa. Most of the names were Hispanic. It wouldn't surprise him if a number were illegals from south of the border.

He turned the list over to Calderon.

He hadn't heard from Angie today. The fire in the living room worried him, but she did say lots of people there smoked. It could have been accidental. Angie did have a way of exaggerating, and though Paavo didn't like to admit it, he had a slight tendency toward paranoia where she was concerned. Still, he'd be happier when she finished this little foray into filmdom.

He also wondered if he'd be hearing from her friend Connie soon. The missing person case she'd sent his way—Fred Demitasse—was so far on the back burner it was frostbitten. There was a lot about that case that made no sense, where the information didn't hold together.

He looked at the thick Birds of Prey homicides binder on his desk. First things first.

Rudolf Goetring sat at the kitchen counter watching *South Park* reruns, smoking, and eating a grilled cheese sandwich.

"I'm here to make a cheese soufflé," Angie announced, squaring her shoulders. She didn't give him a chance to argue. "It's the best way I know to check if the oven is too hot, too cold, how even it is, and everything else I need to know to make sure it'll do a good job for me."

He stared at her as if she were speaking in tongues.

"I don't want to argue with you," she said. "I just want to make my soufflé in peace and quiet."

"Fine." He shut off the TV and stubbed out his cigarette. "It's all yours."

Her jaw dropped. "You don't care?"

"Perhaps this isn't as important to me as you think." He gave a slight bow, grabbed his cane, and stiffly walked from the room.

His about-face made no sense, unless it was that Tarleton had explained who the head chef was around here. About time, too!

While the soufflé baked, Angie decided to check out the wine cellar. It was the one area she hadn't gotten to yet.

A door led down from the kitchen. The refrigerated room was filled with bottles of Waterfield wine. Only Waterfield, unfortunately. A small, old-fashioned grape press atop an open barrel and several oak barrels on their sides told her this was where small quantities of wine were not only stored, but also made and processed the loving, hands-on way done years ago before so many wineries turned into stainless steel mass-production factories. When she was a little girl, her father and his friend Giuseppe had used similar equipment to make wine over in Sonoma.

Engrossed in the old wine-making paraphernalia, she almost forgot her soufflé. Fortunately, it turned out perfectly. The appliances and equipment performed wonderfully. She was just about to dish some out for herself when Digger stuck his head in the door.

"I thought I smelled something delicious." He entered and immediately began searching through cupboards and drawers for a plate and fork.

"Are you related to a fellow in San Francisco named Stanfield Bonnette?" she asked wryly.

"Never heard of him. Why?"

"Nothing. I thought you'd gone long ago."

Angie scooped soufflé into both dishes.

"I was studying the place." He put a big spoonful in his mouth. "I heard Bart and Rhonda say they had to be ready at eight tonight. They were eating some green goo. It was sickening."

"It'll be the first reading of the script."

"You going to sit in?"

"No one is allowed to watch. They're shutting themselves in the living room."

"Is that so?" He got up and checked out the butler's pantry between the kitchen and formal dining room. "It would be interesting to hear it."

Angie didn't want to admit he was right, however . . .

She remembered back to the day she'd first arrived, when the crew was saying something about sabotage. Given all that had happened since, and having learned the script wasn't Camille Spentworth's, she wanted to hear it herself.

He handed her a folded piece of paper. "Angie" was on it in Paavo's handwriting.

"It's yours," he said. "I wouldn't have taken it if I'd known it belonged to you. You never did tell me your name . . . Angie."

Chapter 19

 At eight o'clock, Tarleton met Rhonda and Bart in the foyer. Angie had waited in the darkened kitchen and now crept into the butler's pantry. The dining room lights were off, the doors to the foyer open. She crept closer.

The double doors leading into the living room were closed, as expected, but the actors stood in the foyer.

"Is this necessary, Tarleton?" Bart asked, taking a seat on the stairs. "Today was supposed to be for getting fitted. Didn't that shrew Donna Heinz put me through enough grief for one day?"

"No sense wasting time," Tarleton said.

"I don't like it." Rhonda murmured absently, twisting a strand of hair around her finger.

"What are we waiting for?" Bart said. "Let's go in and get this show on the road."

"We need Gwen and Kyle." Tarleton glared at him.

"Oh, them." Bart sneered.

Sterling and Serefina tried to join the group.

When Tarleton asked them to leave, Sterling marched from the house in a huff, taking Serefina with him. Angie wondered where they were going this time. As much as she told herself not to worry, she felt like a parent with a wayward teenager. She was sure she'd be watching the clock until her mother returned.

Screenwriter Camille Spentworth showed up next. Right behind her, the last two stars walked in, laughing, their faces ruddy.

"Ready?" Tarleton asked.

The others stared at him as if bored. He opened the double doors to the living room with a flourish.

Angie crept into the dark dining room, the need to see the reading overcoming caution. She gasped, and then nearly screamed as someone tapped her on the shoulder.

Digger!

Instead of tossing him from the house, she pointed toward the living room.

The elegant, lush decorations were gone and had been replaced with a white-and-gold horror. Gold ornaments, bows, and tinsel filled the tree, long gold filigree cloth was draped over the top and sides of the mantel, gold streamers hung from drapery rods, and gold garlands crisscrossed the ceiling. Stacks of gold presents filled the floor under the tree.

Angie had seen the room decorated that way before. Her mind raced . . .

"These decorations look familiar," Gwen said, letting Kyle remove her mink jacket. "Haven't I seen them before?"

"They were used in the past," Tarleton replied.

When? Angie nearly shouted.

"So that's why they look so outdated," Bart said. "I think the other was prettier. You didn't change it all because of the missing Little Drummer Boy, did you?"

"What missing boy?" Kyle asked.

"It's what the audience wants. Trust me in this," Tarleton said.

I remember now! Angie thought, a sudden wariness running though her. What were Tarleton and Mariah up to?

"They go back to the show when Cliff and Leona were lovers." Gwen frowned at Tarleton. "Surely we aren't going to drag that old storyline out again."

"We're not." Tarleton replied.

"Thank God," Gwen murmured. She patted Kyle's face as if to show he was her preferred love interest. At least for now.

"Something else went on that season," Rhonda said slowly. "It was the year Brittany died."

Finally! Angie exhaled. Why had Tarleton wanted the room decorated that way? His decision to have her cook the same Christmas dinner as served on Julia Parker's last show was eerily similar. Why was he so interested in that time?

A bad feeling crept along her spine.

Digger inched closer. He gave her a questioning look, and she nodded.

"I think you're wrong about that, sweet thing," Bart said, with a loud, out-of-place laugh. "No one would have the bad taste to bring that up again."

"Here we go." Tarleton handed them copies of the script. "This is short. It's the ending segment of the show. I haven't read the beginning yet, but I'm sure Miss Spentworth did a fine job with it."

Camille smiled sourly. She stood in the doorway, leaning against the frame. As long as she was there, Angie thought, they might leave the doors open.

"How the hell do you know how something ends if you don't know how it starts?" Bart asked.

"This is a special ending," Tarleton explained. "It's a take-off on *A Christmas Carol*, but in reverse. We'll start out with the Ghost of Christmas Future."

"Goddamn, Em, you can't show it in reverse," Bart cried. "The audience is going to think we're ass backward."

"We are," Kyle offered. The actors sat down and began flipping through the pages. Probably counting their lines, Angie thought.

"We'll read the parts together," Tarleton said, "and go through it all, piece by piece."

"I like to read it to myself first," Bart said.

"You don't need to. It's easy enough," Tarleton offered. "It begins with Cliff sitting at the dining room table, a Christmas feast in front of him. Natalie is behind him. There's no place setting for her."

Angie's ears perked up at the words "Christmas feast."

Rhonda began to read. *"I am the Ghost of Christmas Future, and I'm here to show you your future, Cliff Roxbury."*

Bart scowled in confusion. *"What do you mean, you're a ghost? You're my wife!"* He looked at Tarleton and laughed. "Hey, that's exactly what I was thinking."

"No, not for many years," Rhonda/Natalie continued. *"I grew tired of your philandering ways, Cliff. I finally left you. Everyone left you."*

"Well"—he laughed—*"that didn't work out so well for you, did it? You're dead, Natalie, but I'm still alive."*

"You are alive, but you aren't living. You're alone, Cliff. Everyone's gone. You're nothing but a lonely, ugly old man. The people who know you are all waiting for you to die."

"No. My son loves me. Jon Royce doesn't want me to die."

"Your son hates you for driving away his mother. He's no longer in Eagle Crest."

"Jon Royce is gone?" Bart/Cliff sounded truly shocked and sad. *"What about Adrian and Leona? They're here. They wouldn't go."*

"They realized that to save their marriage, they had to leave Eagle Crest. And they did. It was worth it to Adrian to give up the wealth he had. The future he shares with Leona—their love—is much more valuable."

"Love? Those two? No way. This is ridiculous. I'm not alone. You're lying."

"Look into your future, Cliff, look at yourself in another five years."

"Stop there," Tarleton said. "At this point, we'll have make-up give Bart long white hair and gaunt gray skin. He'll be in bed alone. He'll ring the bell for the butler to come to help, but no one will. He'll call out, but no one will hear. Then he'll die."

"I'll die?" Bart asked with sudden enthusiasm.

Tarleton nodded.

"Wow!" Bart said. "I've never had a role where I got to die before. It'll be sad, won't it? I mean, I'd like to make the audience cry for once. Usually they just boo and hiss at my roles."

Gwen snorted, "After what Cliff's done, nobody's going to shed tears for you, and you know it."

Bart spun toward the director. "Damn it, Tarleton, if I'm going to die, it's going to be sad. Do you hear? Or I'm not going to do it. Look, it's the end of an era—the death of Cliff Roxbury. We've got to play it big time. I think it should be last, not first! We need to end with it. My death scene. Just like . . . *Hamlet*. *'Tomorrow and tomorrow and—'* "

"That's *Macbeth*!" Tarleton shouted, quivering with rage. He tried to calm himself. "We've got to continue. You're right about it being the end of an era, but keep in mind, it isn't the end of the story. We're doing Christmas Future *first*, and that's final."

Rhonda rolled her eyes and walked away, and Bart scratched his head, perplexed. Angie had to admit, she was with Bart. Why mess up a classic?

"Now," Tarleton said, "we're going to go into the Ghost of Christmas Present."

"Hey, I must be missing some pages," Bart bellowed. "I don't see any lines for me in this section."

"There aren't any." Tarleton's teeth were clenched. "It starts with Adrian looking into the dining room and seeing Cliff at the head of the table, a Christmas feast before him, and Natalie sitting at the opposite end, looking drunk and completely out of it."

Angie wondered if this would be the same meal as the one she'd need to prepare for the earlier scene. If it was up to her, she'd show a different meal, although that'd be a lot more work.

"Do we need to go into the dining room?" Bart asked, circling toward it. Angie and Digger, who had crept closer, tiptoed backward toward the butler's pantry.

"No need. We'll just read the parts for now," Tarleton said. "An empty place setting is at the table. It's Adrian's. Cliff and Natalie are waiting for him. He stops at the door and doesn't enter."

Tarleton himself picked up the script and read, *"I am the Ghost of Christmas Present."*

The actors all looked at each other. Tarleton nodded at Kyle, who began to read Adrian Roxbury's role.

"Where's Leona?" Kyle/Adrian read. *"I don't want Christmas dinner without Leona."*

"You have no choice, Adrian," Gwen read in Leona's little girl voice. *"You're all alone now."*

"Alone? You're my wife."

"But you didn't trust me enough to make me a partner as well as a wife. You learned too well from Cliff. I couldn't take all the lies, the suspicion, and the deceit, and so I left you. I'd made mistakes, but in time I came to love you, Adrian. Not Cliff, or Arthur, or John, or Graham, or . . . well, enough of that. You didn't love me back!" She began to cry.

Ham, Angie thought.

"I do love you, Leona! I've put Natalie out of my head. Along with Julia, Charlotte, Kathy, Beatrice—"

"Beatrice? That tub!"

"Forget Beatrice. I don't want to be here without you."

"You should have thought of that a long time ago. Good-bye, Adrian." Gwen/Leona cried harder.

"Don't go! What shall I do?" Kyle/Adrian wailed. *"How can I win her back? What shall I do?"*

"Hey," shouted Bart. "That doesn't make any sense. We know from the previous scene that Adrian does go away with Leona, so her statement about leaving him alone isn't true."

"No—it would have been true," Tarleton explained, "except that Adrian changed his fate. We can all change our fate. The viewer will remember the last scene, and know that Leona took Adrian back and the two are happy together."

"Ow! My head is hurting now," Bart whined. "No audience will understand it! Where's the scriptwriter?"

"And now, the Ghost of Christmas Past," Tarleton announced, ignoring the protest. "We've got a new member of the cast, plus an old one who returned especially for this scene. It takes place at the Christmas dining table—"

Angie had to cover her mouth to suppress a groan. *Three* big meals? He couldn't want three separate meals, could he?

"—Cliff, Natalie, Adrian, and Leona are seated . . ."

"Where's Jon Royce?" Rhonda asked. "Wouldn't our son be with us at Christmas?"

"He's . . . in the army," Tarleton said. "Quiet

everyone. Let's begin." He looked toward the doorway and waved his arm.

Rudolf Goetring, wearing a Santa Claus mask and red cap over his white chef's smock, stepped slowly into the room. The expressionless mask, with its fake, jolly smile, slowly focused on one actor then the other, brown eyes peering out at them. They shrank back. *"I am the ghost of Christmas Past."* He read, the words with a low reverberation in his voice. *"I am here, Cliff Roxbury, to help you remember why your present and your future are so lonely, and so wretched. Be silent, and you shall learn!"*

The room was silent as the actors looked at each other, waiting for someone to begin reading. No one did.

A young woman entered, a sheer white veil draped over her from head to toe. Her hair was straight and blond, she wore tight pink jeans, a fringed shorty top and high-heeled strappy white sandals. She was the ghost of Julia Parker, looking much as she had when she rode by in the truck.

Chapter 20

Rhonda half stood, then dropped back down in her chair. Bart clutched her hand.

The chef read, *"Julia Parker, the time has come for you to speak. Your death is a cancer eating away the hearts of everyone in this family. You will have justice; you will have revenge, and only then will eternal rest be yours."*

"I was told Julia wasn't part of this story," Camille said. Tarleton shushed her.

"Be thankful you didn't write that," Gwen nattered. "It's so hokey, my teeth ache."

"Hokey? It's claptrap," Kyle roared. "We already ended that storyline! Julia was killed when she walked out on her boyfriend to go to a cheap bar and let herself be picked up. A transient killed her. Everyone was speculating that it was Cliff, then up popped the real culprit and Cliff spent the next few episodes getting even with everyone who'd called him a murderer."

"This is horrible," Rhonda moaned, hands on her cheeks. She was pale beneath her make-up, and her eyes were dilated. "It looks like you're capitalizing once more on the death of that poor young girl. Wasn't one season enough?"

Tarleton strode back and forth, glaring at the four actors. The chef and Julia's ghost hovered near the doorway. "What did we learn during that season?" Tarleton asked. "Nothing."

"We learned that life has no value," Kyle tossed his script aside. "And its only use is to extend the storyline. It made me sick."

"Hey," Bart said, flipping through the script. "I don't have any lines in this segment, either."

Rhonda spun toward him. "Can't you tell this is a little beyond your lousy lines, you idiot!"

The Julia figure raised her arms and threw back her head. *"Murderer! You will pay for your sins. You will pay . . . for killing me!"* Then she ran down the hall toward the family room.

"Who was she talking to?" Bart demanded. He jumped up. "Me?"

Rhonda was on her feet, too. "I'm leaving. This is a travesty."

"Sit down!" Tarleton ordered. "We aren't through. We haven't talked about the most important thing. Who killed Brittany?"

"Brittany?" Bart looked from Tarleton to Rhonda, confused. After a second's hesitation, he and Rhonda sat. "Don't you mean Julia?"

"What are you saying?" Rhonda sounded strangled.

"Hold it," Kyle said, arms out, palms down as if trying to calm everyone. "We don't need this. Not again."

"If anyone killed Brittany," Bart shouted at Tarleton, "it would have been you! God knows, your directing nearly killed her career!"

"Somebody killed her," Goetring announced behind the laughing Santa mask. The others stopped bickering at once. He continued. "Two women were heard arguing right before she died."

"Two women?" Bart's brow furrowed. "I never heard that. How would you know? Who are you?"

"Who cares?" Kyle fumed. "Brittany's door was locked from the *inside* with an old-fashioned sliding bolt. If anyone was in the bedroom with her, they couldn't have gotten out. Brittany was alone and fell."

"Maybe someone broke through the door lock," the chef suggested.

"If so, that person would have had a very sore shoulder," Kyle countered.

"Is that so?" The Santa mask pivoted, the eyes focusing on the actors one by one. "How's your bursitis, Rhonda? Still have those shoulder pains?"

She stared at him a long moment, then grabbed Bart's hand. "I don't know what he's saying. What he's talking about. Take me away from this!"

"You know!" the chef shouted. His holly jolly mask seemed to broaden its smile. Bart's eyes were wide. He seemed unable to move.

Rhonda looked faint. "Who are you?" she screamed.

"The ghost of Christmas past, present and future," he said, and headed toward the dining room.

Seeing him approach, Angie and Digger scrambled through the kitchen and breakfast room to the courtyard, nearly tripping over each other.

"Did that make sense to you?" Angie asked. They hurled themselves at a nearby table and chairs. Angie sat back, legs casually crossed, and Digger lit a cigarette with an equally peaceful demeanor. Inside, she was quaking, expecting someone to dash out and accuse her of spying.

Digger pondered Angie's question. "Unfortunately, it made a lot of sense," he said.

"Let's meander into the family room," Angie suggested. "If anyone sees us, they'll think we were outside the whole time. I don't want to miss any more than we have to."

"Good idea."

They casually strolled back into the house through the patio doors. The family room was empty. They continued down the hall to the foyer to find the living and dining rooms now empty as well.

That was when Angie realized what had been bothering her the entire evening. Why everything seemed slightly out of kilter.

Someone had unplugged the foyer Christmas tree. It no longer twirled and was now absolutely silent.

Angie and Digger walked around the house to the front drive. "What happened in there?" Angie asked. "Did I dream it?"

"And where did this latest Julia disappear to?" Digger asked. If it was a dream, he'd had the same one. Their search had led them outside the house.

Angie rubbed her arms from the chill. It wasn't from the outside temperature. "Good question— and who was she?"

"You don't know?" Digger asked. "Wasn't she part of the cast? No wonder they looked so shocked."

"I wish I knew what was going on with Tarleton," Angie said. "Everyone knew Rudolf Goetring was his chef. It's clear now that Tarleton brought him here to put a scare into everyone. To read those lines about the Julia–Brittany death or murder."

"True, but even he looked shocked when the chef talked about Rhonda's sore shoulder."

The front drive was also empty. Everyone must have immediately gone up to their rooms. Angie looked at the house, bright and cheerful with Christmas lights, wreaths, and ornaments, and wondered what secrets had been buried there.

"I don't get it," she murmured. "They said Brittany's door was locked with a slide bolt from the inside. The door is the only way into and out of that bedroom, and yet it looks as if none of them thought Brittany's death was an accident."

"You noticed that, too, did you?" Digger said. "My nose told me there was a story here. Damn, I'm good! I'll be back tomorrow."

"Where are you going?"

"I'm a journalist. Who knows?"

* * *

Angie called Paavo and filled him in on this latest weirdness.

"The chef all but accused Rhonda?" he asked.

"I don't think anyone actually murdered Brittany," she said. "But Rhonda—or someone—might have driven her to jump. I'd say the others suspect it as well."

"Angie," Paavo said, "come home."

Chapter 21

The next morning when Angie went down to breakfast, not even cold cereal awaited her. Or coffee.

No one was in the breakfast area or the patio. She went into the kitchen. It, too, was empty. Mariah stood alone, looking helpless.

"Where's Goetring?" Angie asked.

"I don't know. I told him we'd cater lunch and dinner, but that he should put out a light breakfast spread for everyone in the house. He understood he was supposed to have coffee ready by seven A.M."

"No one else is here, either," Angie added, perplexed.

"I guess nobody's hungry," Mariah said. "They were all pretty upset about last night."

"Oh, really? What happened?" Angie made her expression as guileless and innocent as she could.

Mariah hesitated. "I'm not sure. I wasn't there either. In any event, if the cook doesn't show up, can you help with breakfast?"

"Of course." Angie was pleased with the opportunity to show off to one and all, and especially to Tarleton, how well she cooked.

Serefina walked into the kitchen. "Good morning, Mamma," Angie said.

Serefina eyed Angie, Mariah, and the pristine kitchen. "There was some trouble here last night, eh?" she asked. "No breakfast. No cook. Everyone's upset."

Mariah confirmed it.

Serefina nodded. "Let's make breakfast for them, Angelina. Nothing fancy. Maybe a little egg, a little toast. It'll cheer them up."

"We can do better than that." Angie began pulling ingredients from the pantry. "Want to help, too, Mariah?"

"Not me." She showed them her back. "I'm out of here."

Angie rummaged through the freezer while Serefina pulled out a few bowls, pots, and pans. Before long they began to work on a meal of Angie's poached eggs with crab and hollandaise sauce, and Serefina's frittata of pancetta, avocado, and chilies. With it, they planned biscuits, strawberries, coffee, tea, and a variety of juices.

As they cooked, Tarleton entered the kitchen. "Food. Good. Everyone's hungry." He turned to leave again.

Angie hurled herself in front of the exit. "Do you still want the traditional Christmas dinner from the last show Brittany played in?"

"Of course." He gave her a who-are-you-to-question-me glare. "The crew's returning, and we'll start shooting day after tomorrow. Two days after that, we need the dinner."

"Just one?" she asked, thinking about the three separate dinner scenes she'd witnessed.

"Yes, of course. What do you mean?"

Since she wasn't supposed to have heard anything from last night's rehearsal, she couldn't question him further. "Fine. In that case, I remember the show—"

"You do?"

"I remember the roast goose, but the trimmings are all vague."

"Whatever," he said, stepping to the side to get past her.

She stepped to the side as well. "I was thinking the roast goose should be maple glazed. It makes a beautiful centerpiece."

"Good, now—"

"With it, I'll serve corn pudding with smoked oysters, yams in orange cups, mushroom and parsnip soup, heart of romaine and persimmon salad—"

He took a few steps backward. She moved toward him.

"—Spinach with tasso ham, braised pork backs with bourbon gravy, green onion biscuits, a relish tray, pear-onion-fontina strudel—"

He backed further. She followed.

"—Little sweet-potato pancakes with caviar, broccoli with fennel, apple-filled acorn squash rings, cranberry sauce—"

He bumped into the far wall.

"—A Waldorf salad, and pumpkin chiffon and pecan pies for dessert."

"Stop!"

"That's it," she said with a smile. "What do you think?"

"I don't care. You fill the table with good food and Waterfield wines. That's all."

Her face fell. After hours of worry and planning . . . "You don't care?" she repeated, stunned.

"*I don't care!* As long as it looks pretty, Miss Amalfi, I . . . don't . . . care."

Anger, embarrassment, and frustration warred. It was all she could do to keep her tone civil. "If you don't care, why did you want a gourmet chef to cook it? You could have used plastic food, just like everything else in this house!"

Out of patience, Tarleton bellowed, "That's exactly what I told Waterfield! He said you needed to get away from the city for a while."

Angie felt the floor rock beneath her feet.

"What about the chef with the broken leg?"

"Broken leg? What broken leg? I don't know what you're talking about?"

From being flush with embarrassment, Angie suddenly felt as if all the blood drained from her face. She spun toward her mother. "What's going on?"

Serefina's gaze was sad and understanding. "Enough, Angelina," her mother said gently. "You were given a job to do. You'll do it, and make the food special. You gave your word that you'd help. In fact, this morning, it looks like everyone needs help more than ever. Now, *signor direttore, scusi!* We are cooking here."

As soon as Tarleton fled, Angie slumped into a chair. "What is Papà up to?"

Serefina measured flour into a sifter. "He has his little ideas. It's nothing."

Angie placed her hands on the counter. "Does having a couple of bachelors in this house—rich bachelors—have anything to do with it? Is that why you're here, too?"

"Angelina, I love Paavo. He's a good man." Puffs of flour billowed into the air as Serefina sifted too vigorously. "Your papà, though, he only sees money, or lack of it. He knows you won't look at another man on your own, so he suggested I come stay here a few days to help you realize what a fine man and good husband Silver would be for you."

"*What?* You agreed to that?" Angie couldn't believe what she was hearing.

"Of course." Serefina added eggs and milk. "I could use a vacation, and this is a lovely place for one. Also, Sterling has always been a little sweet on me. You don't know what fun it is to have a man pay close attention to me, like a woman, instead of a wife." She sighed dreamily.

Angie gawked.

"Not that I would ever do anything about it, but it's good for the ego." Her black eyes sparkled. She put down the whisk and wiped her hands. "Besides, when the day comes that I need a facelift, he might give me a discount." She smoothed her hair, making sure not one strand was out of place.

Angie stared at her a long moment, then broke into laughter. *That* was the mother she knew and loved.

*   *   *

Ignoring blaring horns and dirty looks from fellow drivers, Angie swung into a parking space when she saw Digger Gordon walking along a sidewalk in downtown Napa. Although it was the largest town in the valley, if anyone went there looking for great wineries, they'd be sorely disappointed. A few upscale restaurants and "gateway to the wine country" establishments helped, but not much.

Since the grocery stores in St. Helena were miniscule, Angie took her shopping list of gourmet ingredients to Napa.

She rolled down the passenger window of her Mercedes and called to Digger, "What are you doing here?"

He approached, surprised to see her. "After what we witnessed last night, I need to check something out."

She wanted to find out a few things as well, but didn't know where to start. It seemed Digger did. "What is it?"

"You don't want to know." With a good-bye wave, he continued past her.

She locked her car and ran to catch up with him. "Why not? I know all kinds of things about murder investigations. Didn't I tell you my fiancé is a homicide inspector in San Francisco?"

"Several times. Sounds like you agree this is a good story," Digger said without slowing down. "Maybe such a good story you want to steal it."

Shocked, her step faltered a moment. "I don't want your damn story! I want to know what happened, that's all."

"Maybe you want to sell the story, or make a book out of it."

"Oh, for pity's sake! We've got a bunch of TV stars and others acting peculiarly. We both want to know why—you for your job; me because it's important."

"Maybe it's important to me as well." Digger turned into a small building with *Napa Press Tribune* stenciled on the window.

"The newspaper office?" Angie asked. "Are you going to tell the local press about this?"

"Nope." He waggled his eyebrows. "If you must come along, keep quiet and watch an expert in action."

Digger showed his press credentials, introduced her as his assistant, and was given access to the morgue—the newspaper's back copies.

"Surely you've already read the newspaper accounts," Angie said as they entered a room filled with newsprint and microfiche.

Digger perused the dates written on the file drawers. "I've read the AP reports and those from a couple of San Francisco reporters who came up here, but I never saw the first stories from the site—what was written before it became big news."

"In other words, the first and maybe second stories out of here," Angie said, "before the big reporters took over and the Napa guys were shunted back to the obit page."

He found the right year and began flipping through the microfiche. "I like the way you think, Angie. Like a journalist."

"Actually, I was a journalist once."

"Do I have a nose, or what?" He gloated as he

found one with the dates he wanted. "I wasn't so out-of-line when I thought you wanted to steal my story after all. I must have sensed the news-hound in you."

"Actually, I wrote about food and recipes."

"For the *San Francisco Chronicle* or the *Examiner*?"

"The *Bay Area Advertiser*."

He stopped searching long enough to look at her and frown. "*Advertiser*? It isn't one of those newspapers delivered free with lots of ads, is it?"

"It was. I'm afraid it doesn't exist anymore."

He pulled out a fiche. "And you looked down your nose at me writing for a national tabloid?"

"We must have standards, Digger," she said, then added with resignation, "even if we don't live up to them ourselves."

Digger chuckled. At a microfiche reader he searched for the date of Brittany's death—November 15. The record of the fifteenth showed nothing, which wasn't unexpected. But the six-teenth also reported nothing, and the seventeenth only ran an AP report out of Los Angeles with a local sidebar in which Sterling Waterfield spoke of what a lovely, talented young woman Brittany had been, blah, blah, blah—all the usual things said about any dead star.

The lack of first-hand news reporting made no sense. Digger was out of the morgue like a shot. Showing his press badge, he asked if the editor was available.

"Daniel Gordon," Nicholas Clark said, extending his hand as Angie and Digger entered his office. "Glad to meet you. I've admired your work."

Angie couldn't believe what she was hearing. This newspaper had to be really small potatoes if the editor admired a *National Star* reporter.

"Thanks," Digger said, looking somewhat embarrassed. He told Clark what he was looking for.

"That was before I got the job, but I was curious about it myself," the editor said. "No one will say why or how, but the story was spiked. I can only speculate on what happened . . . and I won't."

"What about the cops and the medical examiner?" Angie asked. "Reporters often question them."

"They had little to offer." Clark explained that, almost immediately, the death was ruled an accident. Sterling didn't want any kind of investigation done in his house. He refused to let the CSI check things out unless they could get a court order stating there was a suspicion of foul play, and he refused to allow the police to talk to anyone in his family, saying they were too distraught over the death to do so.

Sterling had been the one who'd broken into Brittany's room. Clark said his reporters speculated that more happened when he'd broken in than he wanted to say—or to let CSI discover. Everyone assumed the door was locked with a slide bolt because they found the bolt intact on the door and the doorframe portion of the lock ripped from the wood molding. Sterling never said if the lock had been previously damaged or if the wood was bad. It was never questioned, and without the kind of investigation a CSI could do, no one would ever know if that was the case.

"He's my mother's friend . . . and my father's." Angie shivered, disturbed by the news editor's implication.

"All I'm saying is there was no proof for reporters to get a handle on," Clark explained. "Word of Keegan's death went out via press releases. All questions were handled by the studio's publicity department. A few reporters came nosing around and learned there was more to the story, but basically it was an accidental death. Whether she fell from her horse on her estate in Malibu, which was sad and romantic, or fell out of a window in St. Helena, which was clumsy and disgusting, the bottom line wasn't worth all the time, money, and effort to track down exactly where she fell. After a little speculation in the LA papers—even an eventual retraction of the Malibu story, I believe—the whole thing disappeared from the newsman's radar."

"You know a lot about it," Digger said.

"I'm a newspaper man. I want to know and print the truth—no matter what my predecessors did."

Angie and Digger soon left. "It's a dead end," Angie said as they returned to her car.

Digger pondered a moment. "Not completely. Rudolf Goetring seems to know a lot about what happened that night. I want to hear more about the two women who were fighting, and about Goetring, himself. His name is unfamiliar. I thought I'd checked out everyone connected with this case. I'll see what I can scare up on him."

"He didn't show up this morning to make coffee or anything," Angie said. "He wasn't in his bedroom."

The news interested Digger. "Now I've *definitely* got to check him out."

Chapter 22

Paavo and Yosh were driving to the home of a hostile witness with some tough questions when Angie called to fill him in on the latest twist in Brittany Keegan's death.

"Digger Gordon?" Paavo repeated the *National Star* reporter's name, feeling a headache starting behind his eyeballs.

"His name is really Daniel," Angie said.

"Daniel Gordon sounds familiar. Let me check with Yosh."

"Does Yosh know the name?" Angie asked when he came back on the phone.

"Daniel Gordon used to be a crime reporter for the *Los Angeles Times*. He was investigating a big drug dealer when his wife died. No connection was ever proven between his investigation and his wife's death. It was ruled to have been an accident. She slipped and hit her head taking a bath. Gordon insisted his wife never took a bath in the morning, only showers.

"No one believed him. He spent all his time try-

191

ing to find out who killed her, and lost his job as a result. He's made it his crusade to hunt down cases in which mysterious accidental deaths occur, to turn up hard evidence that it wasn't an accident. He does it as much to show up the police and crime investigators as anything, but he's managed to find some murderers who otherwise might have gotten away."

"That can't be my Digger Gordon."

"You never know," Paavo said. "I've heard him referred to as the John Walsh of the tabloid set."

"How long ago did Gordon's wife's die?"

"Seven, eight years at least."

"That must be an awful burden, especially since it sounds like he thinks she was killed because of his activities. He's got to feel horribly guilty."

"Yes." Paavo's voice was tight, and Angie remembered a time when she was a madman's targeted simply because Paavo loved her. She wished she could take back her words, especially when he said, "It's hard to imagine how he could bear it."

When Angie returned from grocery shopping the cook still hadn't shown up.

"I don't suppose you've seen the Drummer Boy music box in the kitchen, have you?" Tarleton asked when he saw her walk into the house with bags of groceries. Not that he offered to help, not even when she made it clear there were still groceries in the trunk of her car.

"No, I haven't."

"Is that food for dinner tonight?" he asked hopefully.

"Dinner? Isn't it catered? This is all for the

Christmas special," she said. "I had to order the goose—two, in fact. One for a test run I'll make of the meal day after tomorrow. The second is for the actual dinner that will be taped."

He followed her back out to her car and stood and watched as she lifted the rest of the bags of food. "You have to test it?"

"After I cook it once, I'll know exactly what I need to do to have the meal ready for television. And you'll be able to tell me if you want anything changed."

"Good idea," he said.

Back in the kitchen, he watched forlornly as she put groceries away. "What's the problem?"

"We haven't seen the cook all day," he said. "The caterer came by for lunch, but after the breakfast you served, it tasted like hardtack. Kyle and Gwen said they hoped to see real food at dinner. If Goetring was here, I was going to ask him to help you cook for us. Without him, though . . . what do you say? Would you do it anyway?"

She gaped. "They said that?"

"We loved your cooking, Angie."

"Oh, my." This was exactly what she'd hoped for! To be praised by Kyle O'Rourke and Gwen Hagen! A lot of big restaurants became famous because of celebrity word of mouth. "I can manage to scare up something for tonight. And everyone will be invited to my test Christmas feast as well."

"Wonderful." As he turned to leave she realized another chance loomed before her. She was feeling lucky. Why not go for the gold?

She burst into song, a jaunty Christmas song. "Sleigh bells ring, are you listenin'—"

He scowled at her. "Why are you singing again?
And so loudly?"

Although his frown was disconcerting, she
smiled. "I heard you're going to be directing a
musical. Can you tell that I'm interested? I've
sung in musicals." *One . . . but who was counting?*

"Where did you hear that? I hate musicals."

She snapped her mouth shut. So much for luck.

Angie had no sooner finished putting things away
when she heard angry voices in the maid's quarters. Junior had taken over the rooms, according
to his brother. Standing near the locked connecting door in the kitchen, the words became clear.

"Why are you pretending to be Brittany?" She
recognized Junior's voice.

"I'm an actress." The speaker was Mariah.
Angie pressed her ear to the door. "It's a part. I
was playing Julia."

"No. You were Brittany. Your hair is like hers
when you don't cover it with that ugly wig. I suspect you don't need glasses either. Why are you
doing this?"

Angie pressed her ear tight against the door.
She knew Mariah wore a wig, but she was astonished to hear the woman's own hair was blond
and attractive.

"Are you spying on me?" Mariah demanded.
"Keep away from me."

"You're working with Tarleton," Junior
shouted. "Tormenting everyone about Brittany.
What do you know of her? She was beautiful. Not
like you."

"It's none of your business." Her voice was piercing. "Why are you here? Why didn't you stay on that mountain, where you belong?"

"Because Brittany *is* my business. No one else is like her." Angie heard a scuffle, and was ready to shout at them when it stopped. "Take this ugly wig and burn it."

"Damn you!" Mariah screamed.

Angie could easily imagine Mariah as the one who'd played Julia. Why the charade?

"You don't even understand what you're doing to the people here." Junior's tone had turned low and deadly. "I feel sorry for you."

"At least I'm not *crazy*," Mariah shrieked. "You think you know Brittany? I didn't, but I know one thing—she could never have loved someone like you. Never! Why don't you go back up to that mountain where you belong? No wonder your father is ashamed of you!"

"With pleasure!" A door slammed, and all was quiet.

Angie's hand was poised to knock in order to console Mariah when she changed her mind. Junior was odd, but he was right about one thing: why was Mariah in disguise? It would have made sense if she'd put on a disguise to look like Brittany. Why, when she looked like Brittany normally, did she need to hide that fact?

There was talk that Tarleton and Brittany had been lovers, and now Tarleton and Mariah were. Had he chosen Mariah because she resembled the woman he once loved? Is that why he wanted to keep Mariah's true features a secret? Or was it done solely so that when she appeared, she'd shock people into saying things they might not have otherwise?

A casserole of manicotti filled with chicken, veal, and ricotta and covered with a béchamel sauce sat on the counter ready for the oven. Garbanzo and thyme soup simmered. Cooked polenta waited to be grilled with radicchio. Washed and sliced arugula and pears for the salad stayed cool and crisp in the refrigerator.

To complete the menu, Angie planned some bruscetta appetizers, and for dessert, chocolate rum mousse and zabaglione that would make them all sit up and take notice.

Waterfield wine was her biggest worry. It was bitter, vinegary, and with as much body as a sheet of tissue paper; she hated the thought of serving it with her meal. But she couldn't exactly serve someone else's wines with Sterling at the table.

A private reserve was stored in the basement. Maybe only the Waterfield wine sold to grocery stores or given away to friends was awful. She'd heard that with some small wineries, especially those owned by people with money, the best went to wine shows and family, the worst to unsuspecting customers.

If even the wine in the cellar was bad, Waterfield should turn in his vintner's license. She'd open a bottle and find out.

A switch at the top of the stairs swathed the staircase and ground floor in a yellowish light. The temperature sank precipitously as Angie descended the stairs. She grabbed hold of the banister, being careful not to trip as the unbidden thought came that if she were to fall and get hurt or knocked out, she could lie there for hours.

Where had that thought come from? She shouldn't be so paranoid. It was just a wine cellar, after all. She'd been there before.

She had almost reached the bottom step when she stopped, unable to believe her eyes.

The grape press lay on the floor. Rising out of the wine barrel it had sat on were white pant legs and heavy black shoes.

Angie immediately recognized the chef's outfit. "Mr. Goetring?" she called, and her heart all but stopped. "Mr. Goetring?"

It was as if someone had tipped him over and wedged him headfirst into the barrel.

She hesitated to touch him, but the thought that he was alive, possibly unconscious, overcame her squeamishness. She hoped fervently that the wine barrel was empty.

She grabbed his legs and pulled.

The bottom halves of both legs, from what should have been the knees down, came off in her hands.

With a scream, she flung herself back against the stairs, dropping the legs. In horror, she stared at the legless body of Rudolf Goetring.

She screamed louder this time, and continued shrieking all the way up the stairs, into the kitchen, and through the rest of the house, hoping someone would hear her.

Chapter 23

Everyone heard her. Angie wasn't sure if she'd fainted or not, but eventually she became aware of lying flat on the family room sofa. Silver was patting her hand, Kyle and Gwen hovered in the doorway, Tarleton was on the phone, and Bart was trying to comfort Rhonda.

Rhonda would have none of it and was pushing him away from her. She sat at the bar, eying Angie with bristling animosity and fear.

Tarleton hung up the phone. "The police will be here in five minutes. Everyone just stay calm and try to relax."

Slowly, Angie sat up. "What happened? Was it Goetring? He ... he ... he had four feet!" She shuddered as the memory of the pair of legs and feet coming off from Goetring, her dropping them and then looking at what she first thought was a legless corpse ... except that the corpse had another set of legs, albeit short ones.

That was when she'd completely lost it.

"It was a body suit," Tarleton explained. "Actors wear them to make themselves taller, fatter, shorter—whatever. He put it on to look taller and heavier."

Angie's head spun. "Why did Goetring want to look tall and heavy? Who cares how big or tall a cook is?"

Tarleton glanced at the others. "I don't know."

"And Goetring wasn't tall to begin with," Angie added. "Just a little taller than me, and I'm only about five-four . . ."

Her gaze jumped from one to the other. "Okay, five-two."

"Don't think about it, Angie," Silver consoled. "It's nothing to worry about."

Ten minutes later the police burst into the house. Right behind them was Digger Gordon.

"Who are you?" Silver demanded of the scruffy journalist.

"I'm Angie's friend." Digger made his way to the couch. "She looks like she's seen a ghost. What's wrong, Angie?"

"Is he your fiancé?" Silver's gaze raked Digger's ever more rumpled clothes. Angie nearly fainted again.

Digger didn't wait for her to reply as he noticed Tarleton leading the police to the cellar. He wheeled around and hurried after them, flashing his press badge.

"The press is already here?" Bart remarked in bewilderment. "They must listen in on police radio bands, just like in the movies. Isn't that special?"

"Shut up, Bart." Rhonda clutched her forehead.

"Rhonda darling, this is too much stress for you. I'll help you to lie down."

"Go to hell!"

"Now, I know you don't mean that, darling. Come on, let's go to your room."

"I suggest you wait until after the police talk to you," Silver said. "You remember what it was like the last time."

Rhonda began sobbing. Bart wrapped his arms around her and gave Silver a withering look.

"You remember the last time?" Angie asked, making room for Silver to sit beside her.

"It isn't every day a woman gets killed in your house. Even a self-centered teenager remembers the details of something like that."

"I'm sorry. What a horrible thing for you."

"It was." He took out a pack of Benson and Hedges and removed one, tapping the end against the box as he spoke. "Not nearly as sad as, say, my mom's death, or as freaky as my bro . . . or other stuff."

"Your brother? What did he do?"

"Nothing. I didn't mean anything. Don't know why I said that. My mind was wandering, I guess."

She looked at him skeptically.

He put the cigarette in his mouth and walked with it, unlit, to the courtyard.

At the bar, Kyle poured himself a straight shot of bourbon. "Shit! We don't need this! I want out of here."

"Goetring, in particular, didn't need it," Angie cried, unable to stomach the egos of these people.

"Poor fellow probably had a heart attack or something. It's very sad," Kyle said, his nice-guy Adrian persona suddenly in overdrive to undo any damage his last statement might have done. "If so, he was a walking time bomb. It's a shame it went off here and now. That's all I'm saying."

"Sure, sweet thing," Gwen drawled. "We understand."

The police soon began questioning, one by one, Angie, the cast, Silver, Tarleton and Mariah.

Serefina and Sterling soon returned. The two were horrified to hear what had happened, and Serefina babied Angie mercilessly.

The St. Helena chief of police, Donald McIntosh, arrived. Because of the prominence of the crime scene and the witnesses, this would be a high profile case. It wasn't as if there was other pressing business in town.

Waterfield worked to convince him that Goetring's death had to have been an accident—a horrible accident.

Perhaps it had been brought about by a heart condition? Or stroke? Or he might simply have hit his head on a shelf and, staggering from the blow, knocked the grape press off the barrel and tumbled into it?

Once inside, he didn't have the arm strength to lift himself out or to tip the heavy barrel over or do anything else to save himself. Poor fellow!

"Mr. Waterfield," Chief McIntosh said to Sterling, "Why is winemaking equipment in your basement? You own an entire large-scale winery elsewhere on your property. This seems very strange."

"That's the original equipment when the winery was first built. The vat is aged oak, over a hundred twenty years old. We use it for display purposes now and then, that's all. That's why it had water in it, so it wouldn't dry out and shrink. Now, I don't know if we'll ever be able to use it again."

"Sure you will, *caro*," Serefina patted his knee. The two sat side by side on a loveseat. "It's not a problem. In the old country, my father used to make wine. Sometimes things happen. You empty the vat, wash it out well, let it dry and start again. All this adds character to the wine."

Angie cringed. She couldn't imagine what kind of character a dead man would lend to anything.

The police chief frowned. "We'll remove the body. I'll be back with more questions soon."

A door led directly outside from the basement, so the police were able to bring a gurney down and load the body for the trip to the morgue without going through the house.

"I take it everyone who is living at the house is here now?" Chief McIntosh asked the assembled group. Fortunately the bar was well stocked. The sudden death had them all gravitating toward it.

"There's one more person," Sterling said after an imperceptible pause. "My son Junior. He's probably on the mountain, camping out. We haven't seen him in days."

Angie remembered that he was in the house that afternoon. She glanced at Mariah to see if she'd mention it. The woman stayed mute.

"He's in walking distance?" the Chief asked.

"Yes."

"Find him."

"Also, Camille Spentworth is staying with us," Tarleton added. "She's the scriptwriter."

"Has she been here today?"

"I haven't seen her," Tarleton replied. No one else had either.

"I'm the press," Digger said, waving his press badge.

The chief frowned at Digger. "That was fast."

"Yes, it was," said Tarleton suspiciously.

McIntosh cast a sharp glare, waiting until he had everyone's attention. "I'm inclined to agree with Mr. Waterfield that this was a terrible accident. However, until we are certain that's the case, I want all of you, with the exception of the press, to stay close to St. Helena. It should take only a couple of days to complete our investigation. If we have questions I'd like you nearby. I understand your work isn't completed, so it shouldn't be a hardship to stay."

"Stay?" Serefina whispered to Angie.

Wide-eyed, Angie nodded. "I guess that means us, too, Mamma."

"Come home," Paavo repeated later that night, after Angie had recounted the entire incident.

"I can't," she said. "The police said all of us need to stay nearby for questioning, even Serefina. God, Paavo. I can't believe he's dead! We argued all week. Now I feel so bad."

"The police are pretty sure it was an accident, though," Paavo repeated, as much to reassure himself as anything.

"That's what they said." Angie blew her nose. She didn't think she would shed tears for Goetring, but as she'd talked about his death, she couldn't help it.

"One thing is strange. Goetring was clearly no chef," she said, her composure back in check. "I've been thinking about this a lot, and I suspect the real reason Tarleton wanted him here is because of what Goetring saw the night Brittany died."

"You said he was disguised as a chef so the others wouldn't recognize him," Paavo said. "A chef's outfit isn't much of a disguise."

Angie drew in her breath. She didn't know what was going on, all she knew was that this was too strange to be coincidence. "That's the other part of the story I need to talk you about."

"Yes?"

"You remember how you said Connie sent a friend over to you to find a missing dwarf?"

A puzzled silence, then, "Yes . . ."

"I think I found him."

Chapter 24

Angie couldn't sleep. Her mind raced endlessly with her grisly discovery and what it might mean. Her head ached. She remembered the Tylenol behind the bar. Two of those and warm milk, if not a shot of brandy, should do the trick.

A night-light and the continuously glowing fake fire in the fireplace illuminated the room and revealed a figure seated on an armchair.

Angie started, surprised.

Emery Tarleton glanced up. "Angie," his voice sounded choked. "What are you doing still up?"

"I couldn't sleep." She hesitated at the entrance. "How are you doing? You were very quiet tonight."

"Do you know you're the only one who noticed? I sometimes think I walk around here and nobody sees the person behind the façade of 'director.' I'm a man, I have blood, emotions, a heart. Why doesn't anyone see them?"

And a bit of a ham, she thought, expecting his words to morph into a full-fledged *Merchant of*

Venice speech. His words were slurred, as if he'd had too much to drink. He also sounded like a man filled with great sadness, a man who needed someone to talk to.

She approached the armchair and froze. On the lamp table was an automatic pistol.

"Why is a gun there?" she asked nervously. "Is it a prop?"

"No. It's quite real," he replied softly, lifting bloodshot eyes to meet hers.

"What's it doing beside you?" She moved closer, close enough to see a stream of tears on his cheeks.

"I was wondering if I'd have the nerve to pull the trigger." His words were a mere whisper.

"On whom?" Angie asked, horrified.

"On myself." With shaking hands, he lifted the glass, drained it, then refilled it from the Jack Daniels bottle at his feet.

"Yourself? Why? What's wrong?" Angie sat on the sofa near him. Even with the gun she wasn't afraid of his harming her, only himself.

"A man is dead. A friend." His voice broke. She was sure he was crying silently. "We went back a long way. He offered to help me find out about Brittany's death. He knew things. He warned it might be dangerous, I'll give him that. But I was stubborn; I had to know. And what's the result? My friend is dead and I'm still not sure who killed Brittany, if anyone." He sobbed, and drank more liquor.

"The chef knew you suspected that someone killed Brittany?"

"Yes," Tarleton said, fighting to regain self-control.

"How would he even imagine such a thing?"

Tarleton shrugged. "People underestimated him because of his size. As a result, he learned a lot about everyone. Obviously, he'd learned too much this time."

"You don't think his death was an accident?"

He cast a long, soulful gaze at her. "No. Now, leave me alone."

"You think someone killed him?" She had to admit, she thought the same thing, but coming face to face with someone else who shared the suspicion was unnerving. It meant someone in this house was a murderer. "Who did it?" she all but whispered.

He shook his head. "I have an idea, but it doesn't make much sense."

"Who?"

"I won't say. Not until I'm sure."

"Rhonda?"

His head jerked up. He stared at her a long moment before averting his eyes. "Of course not." He was completely dismissive.

To her mind, Goetring had all but accused Rhonda of Brittany's death, yet Tarleton didn't think she'd killed him. Tarleton knew Rhonda a lot better than she did. What was she missing? "Put the gun away," Angie pleaded.

He drank more whiskey. Much more. His words grew more slurred, his eyes fiery. "No one cares, Angie, no one. The only one who ever cared was Brittany."

"You loved her?" Angie asked.

"I worshipped her."

"And she loved you?"

He sighed. "It took her a while to accept me, but yes, I believe she came to love me."

"Other people love you as well," she said. "Perhaps not like Brittany, but still, look at all the people you've helped, the work you provided, the careers you've launched."

Tarleton shook his head, then poured more whiskey. Some sloshed onto the carpet. Neither cared. "I don't think so, Angie."

"Bart Farrell was nothing but a blowhard," she began. "He played in two-bit situation comedies—the dumb husband. His marriages fell apart, his career was over until you made him into Cliff Roxbury."

"And now he can't do anything else."

"What else is there as lucrative as this? It isn't as if he was some Shakespearian actor. He knows it. Without you and this show, he'd still be doing situation comedy. He didn't have the fine features needed for Hollywood; he had no ability for theater. He would have gone from bad TV shows to playing bad guys in movies—the one the cops shoot halfway through the film and no one remembers. He's indebted to you for everything he has."

Emery shook his head. "He never said anything like that to me."

"Did you ever give him the opportunity? What about Gwen and Kyle? They were unknowns. You fought to give them roles. Even Rhonda—if it weren't for you, she would have been written off the script in the early years when she was a basket case who drank too much. You're the stuff of Hollywood legends, written about in all the star magazines. Everyone knows it."

"What is this, Angie, my own personal version of *It's a Wonderful Life?*" He tried to laugh. The sound was pitiful, then bitter. "I don't see myself as Jimmy Stewart."

"I see you exactly like him. You've done many wonderful things, and you should realize it. Now, get away from that gun and think about the people you've helped. You had no idea your friend would die. The police say it was an accident. It might have been."

He sat quietly for a moment. "I wish I could believe that. I told myself for years Brittany's death was an accident. I lied to myself." He sobbed openly. "I don't want to live a lie again! I can't bear the guilt!"

She placed her palm against the barrel of the gun, afraid he might reach for it. "You'll find someone else to love the way you did Brittany. Don't do this to yourself. It's been eleven years. It's time to forget about her."

"I'll never forget her!"

"What about Mariah? She's seems devoted to you."

His brow furrowed, confused. "Mariah? What do you mean?"

"Maybe you can learn to love her the way you did Brittany." Angie suggested.

More tears fell. "Brittany wasn't a girlfriend! She was—"

He stopped, staring at Angie. She had rarely seen a man with eyes so desolate and empty. He bowed his head, and his shoulders heaved with silent sobs.

"What is it?" Angie asked, placing her hand on his knee. "What was she to you?"

He spoke in a whisper. "She was my daughter."

Angie drew back, scarcely believing what she'd heard. "I'm sorry. I never imagined."

"No one knew. We had to keep it a secret so that she could get ahead in movies. I was once a movie director, but they don't even give you three strikes in Hollywood. Two, and you're out. I had my two. It ended for me. I didn't want that castigation to descend on Brittany. So, I didn't tell. She started out on *Eagle Crest*. She would have gone far. Instead, she died.

"My soul died with Brittany. And my heart." He shut his eyes, and a long moment passed. "I didn't want anyone to know, to slander her memory with my reputation. Being the director of *Eagle Crest* might have been lucrative money-wise, but it was a career killer as far as ever getting a chance at the high-budget, serious films I'd wanted to direct. Instead of making films like Milos Forman, or Robert Altman, I'm doing the *Eagle Crest Christmas Reunion*."

"It must have been difficult for you to go on, to act like a director instead of a father . . ." Angie shuddered. She couldn't bear to imagine her father's devastation if anything so horrible had happened to one of his daughters.

"I never should have kept quiet," Tarleton raged, running his fingers through his thin strands of hair. "When Brittany died, I should have stopped the show, called the police. I didn't want to face the possibility that someone killed her, even though I knew in my heart she wouldn't have killed herself, and as an accident . . . it just didn't make sense, despite the locked room she was in. I've lived with that guilt for eleven years, and I can't do it any longer. If someone killed her, I have to know who did it!"

"I'll do all I can to help you." She placed her hand on his. Everything he was doing, the decorations, getting Mariah to dress up as Brittany, all of it made sense. She even understood why all his drinking wasn't enough to chase away his demons. "The Little Drummer Boy has some connection with Brittany, doesn't it?" she asked.

"Yes," he whispered. "It was hers. She didn't like it and gave it to the studio to use as a prop. Still, it was one of the few things that I recall belonging to her."

She thought it had belonged to the Waterfields, but this was not the time to argue with the man. "Can I trust you to keep away from that gun, now?" Her smile was sad and slight. "It won't help, and we've got to find out—the two of us—if someone here killed Brittany and the chef."

"You'll help?" he asked.

"Of course . . . if you put the gun away."

Red-rimmed eyes studied hers as if searching for an angle, a scheme, in typical Hollywood fashion. "Can I trust you to keep my secret? Please, Angie?"

Her gaze was direct, open. She nodded.

"Your word?" he demanded.

"You have my word."

His relief was visible. "Thank you. Now, you've done your good deed for the evening. I suggest you go back to bed, Christmas Angel. I . . . need to sit alone for a while."

"I'll see you in the morning?" Her words came out more as a question than she'd intended.

He smiled wanly before giving a definite nod.

"Good night," she replied and left the room. If she still had a headache, she no longer noticed.

Chapter 25

As soon as Paavo arrived at work the next morning, he contacted the St. Helena police department. His ensuing conversation with the officer in charge of the investigation, Tom Baker, yielded one interesting fact. The dead man's real name was Larry Rhone. He usually went by the stage name "Fred Demitasse."

Paavo had no choice but to break the news to Minnie Petite, and get a few questions answered.

Rhonda sat at the breakfast table, slowly stirring a cup of coffee. Her eyes had heavy bags, her face was pale, and her usually flawless hair looked tangled and matted.

"Who made the coffee?" Angie asked.

"I did. I'm not totally useless, you know," Rhonda said bitterly. The spoon hit the saucer with a *clunk*.

Angie was troubled by the actress's appearance and words. She poured herself a cup and sat across the table. "Where is everyone?"

"Your mother went for a walk with Sterling. I haven't seen any of the others. They're still asleep, I suppose. Or dead." She chuckled to herself. "Isn't that what happens in this house? Accidental deaths to one and all. The actress, the cook, even the mother of the house, for all we know."

"Crystal Waterfield was ill," Angie said, horrified at the innuendo.

"Was she? How do we know? Whose word can we take for it? Watch your mother, Angie. And yourself. There hasn't been a death in the 'friend-of-the-family' category . . . yet."

Angie stood. "That's sick! Get a grip on yourself. You have no business insinuating things about the Waterfields. The police said Goetring's death was an accident."

Rhonda raised cold, hard eyes, chilling Angie to the bone. "You don't believe them, do you?"

Angie stood out in the courtyard. She couldn't stay in the same room, the same house, with Rhonda Manning. The woman was vile.

This morning, she'd spoken to Paavo again, listening to his warnings to be careful. She'd given him the names of everyone in the house. He'd be at Eagle Crest within twenty-four hours.

A shiver went through her. In the light of day, surrounded by scenes of Christmas joy, the cold fact struck her even harder than it had last night talking to Tarleton. If Goetring's death—or Demitasse's, as Paavo called him—wasn't an accident, it meant someone in the house was a killer.

The first time, Brittany Keegan's death looked

like an accident. This time, the accident theory wasn't so cut-and-dried.

She touched the tall outdoor Christmas tree and felt its rubber bristles, the plastic snow that hung on the branches looking so beautiful from afar, but up close, so very phony.

The ghost of Brittany permeated this house, as Marley's had when he visited Scrooge. Only if someone could find a way to right the wrong that had been done here would sunlight and truth fill these rooms and everyone's hearts again.

"I need to talk to you." Paavo stood on the doorstep of Minnie Petite's house.

"Have you found Fred?" Her voice was harsh, her glare fierce.

"I'd like to come in." He spoke softly.

Concern flickered across her face, then vanished. "All right."

"Have either of your roommates come home yet?" he asked, once they were settled in the living room.

"Not yet." She watched him, her body stiff and wary.

There was no way he could lessen the heartache he was bringing. Sometimes it was more difficult to face those left behind, those whose lives would be shattered by his words. "I've got bad news."

She nodded.

"Mr. Demitasse has been found dead." She shut her eyes. Paavo quickly gave her the details.

"Eagle Crest?" she murmured. "As a cook? Why was he there? He was no cook. He was an actor!"

"I'm sorry. Is there anyone you'd like me to call? Someone to stay with you for a while?"

She pursed her lips. "Stay with me? Hell no. I've been alone most of my life. No sense changing that now. Damned old fool! Falling in a wine barrel. He's lucky he's dead, or I'd have killed him for such a dumb stunt. Christ, but I'm going to miss him." She fought back tears.

"One quick question, Ms. Petite," he said, "then I'll leave you. Connie told you my fiancée was at Eagle Crest, and then you came to me to find Fred. I take it, then, you knew or suspected he was there all along. Why didn't you just go there to find him yourself? Why this charade?"

She stared at the wall to maintain her composure and, he couldn't help but suspect, to decide how much to tell him. "I wanted to know about the others there. How they were connected to Fred. I couldn't just show up. They wouldn't have told me anything."

"I don't follow," Paavo said.

"The police would have found out things, then you'd come and tell me. I've watched *Law and Order*, *The Shield*, *NYPD Blue*. I know how these things work." Her eyes filled with tears. "I didn't think he'd go and get himself killed!"

Although he still didn't understand what the TV shows had mistakenly led her to expect of him, it was time to leave, time to let her set aside her hard demeanor and brave front, and mourn for Fred and his untimely passing. "I've written down the phone number of the officer in St. Helena who can help you. He'll provide the contact you'll need for the . . . arrangements."

Her gaze was lost. "I didn't expect this," she murmured, her head bowed. "Of all the things I did expect, his death was not one of them."

"I will let myself out now, Ms. Petite," he said gently. "We'll talk more another time. Call me if there's anything I can do."

She looked up at him, tears rolling down her cheeks. "Forget it, Inspector. I don't want any more to do with cops."

"Angie, how are you doing?" She turned around at the sound of Sterling's voice. He had on a green and gray houndstooth cap and matching jacket, looking more like an Englishman ready to go for a country drive than a California plastic surgeon. He crossed the courtyard to stand beside her. "I'm so sorry about Goetring. Finding him must have been terrible for you."

She nodded.

"This time at Eagle Crest hasn't turned out at all the way I'd hoped it would for you. I'd hope it would be a happy time."

She studied him, and the little bit she'd learned about his life here caused her to ask, "Was there ever a happy time since this house became Eagle Crest? With these troubled actors, with the crew taking over and changing almost everything, I have my doubts."

His face fell at her question, and with it, all his years descended on him. "You don't miss much, do you, Angie? For all your sunniness and good nature, there's a serious streak that runs through you, the same as in all the Amalfis."

He placed his elbows on the adobe wall and

small, watery brown eyes peered hard onto the hillside. She joined him, saying nothing. Waiting.

"When I was first contacted by the producers, I thought it was a dream come true," he said. His breathing quickened and he folded his hands tightly. "Crystal was so excited. We never gave a moment's thought to what it would mean to our privacy, our home, the very nature of our relationship with each other or with our boys."

"More than your privacy was lost?"

"Crystal 'went Hollywood,' so to speak. It was all she could think of. She couldn't act, didn't try to, but she spent all her time there, meeting actors, agents, producers. People 'in the know.' Everything she'd known before *Eagle Crest* bored her. Her home, her life, me. Even our boys."

"Tell me about your boys," Angie urged. The more she got to know them, the more puzzled she'd grown by their behavior.

"What can I say? Silver is set on wasting his life the same way his mother did, watching the TV-and-movie crowd, wishing he could be a part of it, but not lifting a finger to give it a try, as if the 'wishing' was much more fun than trying, or the possibility of failure, could ever be. And Junior . . . how I've failed Junior."

"You're worried about Junior and Brittany, aren't you?"

His head snapped toward her. "No!"

"You knew he was infatuated with her, and that he had . . . troubles . . . with women."

"I knew." His hands clenched. "But he wouldn't have hurt her. No! Never! I'm talking about other things. Fatherly things . . . times I should have been there for him and wasn't; things I've never taught him; words I've never said."

"Perhaps it's not too late," she said.

"Isn't it?" He turned toward her, studying her face as intently as he had the hillside, and then smiled.

"Why do you do that?" She touched her face nervously. "Is something wrong?"

"Do what?"

"Look at me that way. As if you see something in my features that troubles you. Perhaps something that shouldn't be there, or should be changed."

"It's nothing—"

"Don't say that! I can see it in your eyes. Tell me." She lifted her chin. "Please."

With that, he burst out laughing. "Angie, my dear girl! Why didn't you tell me? It's nothing like that."

She felt suddenly very foolish. "What, then?" her voice was small.

"Come with me."

She followed him up to his bedroom suite. In one corner of the room was a table with several framed photographs. He lifted one and handed it to her.

Sterling, Crystal, and her parents stood in front of a brightly lit Christmas tree, presents and decorations all around them. The four were young and smiled happily.

"Look at Serefina's face in that picture, Angie," he said, his voice suddenly husky. "I thought she was the most beautiful woman I'd ever met. I see perfection in my work all the time—false perfection brought about by plastic surgery, implants, procedures that sound more like something Mengele would do than a physician. Your mother's beauty is natural and honest. She's full of life and love and warmth. I fell in love with her back then. I knew I wouldn't stand a chance, and never spoke a word of how I felt. Being around her brightened my life, my soul, in ways you couldn't begin to imagine. Having her here means very much to me."

"I see," she said, replacing the photo, stunned and bothered by his revelation.

"When I first met you, Angie, all I saw was the hair, the expensive clothes, the panache and polish. Serefina is earthier, more . . . full-bodied, even when she was young. But then I studied your face, and it all came crashing back to me, forcing me to remember. You are her, all over again. Even after all these years, I still love her, and I still know there's not one damn thing I can do about it."

His words settled deep in her heart as she studied the picture of the young couples. Of his disappointment with his own life and marriage. Of his unrequited love for her mother. Looking at her mother through another's eyes was startling, as was thinking of the force of her mother's sunny, loving nature, her joy in life, and what it must have meant to someone with the sterile, cold existence of Sterling Waterfield. He was a thin, scarecrow of a man, fit, tanned, wealthy, with more than one beautiful home, hobnobber of the rich and famous, and yet he lived in a plastic, artificial world of his own creation.

"I had no idea," she said, suddenly very sorry for him.

His hand lightly brushed the picture. "Neither does she. You won't say anything, will you, Angie? I wouldn't want to make her uncomfortable."

Angie saw tears glisten, and felt her own eyes fill. "It's our secret."

Chapter 26

"Thank you, Miss Amalfi!" Digger cried as he bounded into the kitchen waving a microcassette tape. "You've given me the story of the century!" He grabbed a stale doughnut. "Bye!"

"Wait. What are you talking about?" she cried as she ran after him. She caught up with him on the front porch. "What's on that tape?"

"You are one in a million, lady!" Digger exclaimed. "Who ever would've thought he'd admit such a thing! Hallelujah!"

"Stop!" She kept after him to his car. "Who are you talking about? Tarleton? What do you have?" A horrible thought hit her. "Don't tell me you bugged the place?"

"Would I do that? Journalists don't do such things. My tape recorder was running and it happened to pick up some conversation." He opened the car door and got in.

Angie jumped into the passenger side. "If you try to use that information, I'll go to your bosses and say it's a fake. I'll say it was me on the tape

222

and a man who was imitating Tarleton. I'll say we were thinking of coming up with a play, or something to blackmail Tarleton with. I'll ruin your credibility forever!"

"Angie," he sounded bored. "I write for a tabloid. We aren't talking the *Wall Street Journal* here."

She pounded her fists against the dash. "You will not publish this story."

"The public has a right—"

"The public be damned! We're talking about a man's life, and the death of his daughter. It can't be splashed across some sleazy paper!"

His mouth was firm, his jaw jutting. "I'm going to run it."

Her eyes narrowed. She considered trying to wrestle him for the tape, then she thought of a better way to win him over. "What if we come up with an even bigger story? What if we figure out what *really* happened to Brittany Keegan?"

"That's what I've wanted to do all along, only I'm not getting anywhere. Tarleton was my main suspect, and now he's been eliminated."

"I've watched Paavo ferret out lots of murderers. I'm sure if we do what he does, we'll figure it out. Then, once you've got the story and are about to print it, I think you should ask Tarleton if he'll consent to you revealing that Brittany is his daughter. If we're the ones who solve her murder, I expect he'd be more than willing. It's not as if it could hurt anyone at that time. It'll make your story even hotter. You might end up on *Sixty Minutes*. Maybe even *Imus in the Morning*."

"I'd rather be on *Howard Stern.* I'll have to think about it."

She wasn't sure she'd convinced him. "You once worked for the *L.A. Times,* didn't you?"

His eyes met hers, first with a question, then his own answer. "You're a pretty good investigator yourself," he said after a while. "Ever think of going into crime reporting?"

"Only if it involves the Food Network." She was glad to see him smile at her little joke, and then added, "I also want to say . . . I'm sorry about your wife."

Surprise flickered for a moment, then he nodded. "Thanks. I just said you were a good investigator, didn't I?"

"Have you found who killed her?"

His lips pursed. "Not yet, but I will someday. I know it wasn't an accident. The problem is that the prime suspects all have rock-solid alibis. I mean, really solid. So, someone else did it." His gaze was stronger than she'd ever seen it. "I'll find him. In the meantime, if there are others out there still free who should be behind bars, I'll find them as well."

"Like whoever killed Brittany?" Angie suggested.

"Exactly. And the chef."

"Good. That means we're on the same page. Now, all I need is for you to promise me you will *not* use Tarleton's story."

"Look, Angie—"

She was beyond frustrated with him. "You'd better not lie to me. I swear, Digger Gordon, if you lie to me on this, I'll devote myself to making your life more miserable than you ever imagined it could be."

His lips twitched, as if wanting to smile. "Why do I believe you?"

She glared fiercely.

"Maybe you should change your name to Antonia Soprano," he suggested. She was in no mood for levity.

"Think about what I'm saying, Digger. Are you going for the gold—finding the killer, or will you wreck everything on a two-bit story now?"

He rubbed his chin. "You're right. Do I have your word you aren't going to tell any other reporters about this?"

She could hardly believe how many people she'd given her word to in the past twelve hours. "Of course!"

He gave her a pointed stare. "Okay. I think I can trust you with it."

She slapped her forehead.

When she went back indoors, the house was quiet. Ever since the cook's death, the cast and Tarleton had barely spoken. Everyone went about their business somberly, and when not working seemed to spend most of their time in their rooms.

The smell of cigarette smoke in the family room surprised her.

"Busted!" Silver said. "I thought I was alone." He was about to put out the cigarette when Angie opened the door to the courtyard.

"I'll join you outside if you'd like," she said.

"Fine." He stepped outside. "Are you feeling it too? A bit jittery? The others seem that way."

"Can't blame them, can you?" she said. His father's concerns about Silver's future came to mind.

"No, I guess not."

"What about you?" she asked. "Your mother died in this house, too, didn't she?"

"Why do you ask? Because she was such a bitch? No one killed her, if that's what you're getting at."

She was taken aback by his vehemence. "I'm sorry."

"Don't be." He put out one cigarette and immediately lit another. "She wasn't the easiest person to get along with," he continued. "My parents stayed together for many reasons, but love wasn't one of them. My father found more warmth in one day with your mother than he got in a year from mine. Naturally, he reacted to that. Anyone would."

"How did she die, Silver?" Angie asked, remembering Rhonda's warning.

"She'd had heart problems for years—lack of heart, some said. Finally, it killed her."

How should she word her next question? "Was there ever any question about her death?"

His head jerked up, stunned, and then he laughed aloud. "Goetring's death got to you, didn't it? Seeing killers and cover-ups all around, are you? Her death was a natural one—in a hospital, even. It's ironic, though, that she died a month before Christmas, just as Brittany did."

Angie thought of the cheery decorations throughout the house, of the tree and shrubbery lights that brightened this courtyard at night. "I imagine Christmases aren't easy for you." Her voice was filled with concern. "Is it difficult, seeing all these decorations around you?"

"Don't worry about it, Angie," he said with a scowl. "Christmas never was good, that I can remember. Maybe when I was really young it was, but that was before I understood anything about what was going on. Later, I saw it was a time when my mother complained about the gifts she got. Dad never could get it right, and me and Junior gave up trying, which made things even worse. It was a time when she got us gifts that showed how unsuccessful we were in her eyes. She gave Junior a new suit every year. He stopped bothering to have them tailored when he realized he never wore them. And every year, she gave me a wristwatch—as if to say it was time to make something of myself. Believe me, Angie, the only thing these decorations cause me to feel is thankful we don't celebrate Christmas anymore."

He tried to add levity as he spoke, but Angie heard the sadness behind his words. For her, Christmas had a strong religious meaning, but she knew many people who weren't Christians celebrated the holiday as a time for families to get together and show their love of each other and life. The joy that was Christmas had many meanings that brought peace and hope. To find it so completely lacking in the Waterfields filled her with sorrow.

She often lived her life without giving much thought to the blessings she had. If she'd learned nothing else these few days surrounded by a fake Christmas, it was to be thankful for the happiness of her past and—she gazed at the engagement ring on her finger—for all that was to come in her future.

Chapter 27

At noon, Officer Baker of the St. Helena police department called to inform Paavo that Fred Demitasse's death had been ruled an accident caused by him falling into a vat filled with water and being unable to get out due to his costume. The ruling raised more questions than it answered in Paavo's mind, but he knew Baker hadn't called simply to chat, or explain, or to impress with the rapidity of the SHPD's work. Paavo waited for the real reason.

It soon came. The SHPD police chief wanted nothing to tarnish the good name of St. Helena or Eagle Crest—not the estate or the show. Chief McIntosh saw no reason for San Francisco Homicide to have any interest in the case whatsoever. He expected Paavo to keep everything he'd learned confidential.

Baker didn't say it, but Paavo heard the unspoken message. The SHPD would do anything necessary to stop him. Paavo thanked Baker. The officer had done what he could to let Paavo know which way the current flowed. The rest was up to him.

Paavo knew what he had to do.

At the same moment, Angie was speeding toward the St. Helena Hotel.

Off the lobby was a coffee shop. Seated at a table were her friend Connie Rogers and a tiny older woman. Very tiny. Fred Demitasse–tiny.

Angie and Connie embraced amid mutual squeals and cries of joy. After introductions, Angie gave condolences to Minnie.

"I wanted to meet the people Fred spent his last days with," Minnie said sweetly, dabbing the corner of her eye with a black handkerchief. In fact, she was dressed head to toe in black, a black pillbox hat on her blond hair, and a full-length black dress with jet buttons down the bodice. Angie wouldn't have been surprised to see her cover her face with a black veil. "It was kind of Connie to drive me."

"It was," Angie said. The fact that Connie had been another closet *Eagle Crest* devotee and could hardly wait to meet the actors had nothing to do with it—yeah, right.

Angie and Connie had discussed the situation at length on the phone after Minnie had asked Connie to drive her to St. Helena. Angie met them in town to lead the way through the back roads to the Waterfield estate.

"I hope Fred was happy here, and had an important role." Minnie turned an expectant gaze Angie's way.

Angie was taken aback. "I don't know what to say."

"What's that supposed to mean?" she snapped.

"Did you know he was disguised? He was pretending to be a chef named Rudolf Goetring."

"Goetring?" Minnie eyed Angie as if she were crazy. "That was the name of a character he played in a comedy about Nazis years back—back when people laughed at such things. Was he pretending to be Goetring when he was killed?"

"He was always pretending to be Goetring." Angie told her about his bleached white hair and body suit.

"Bleached hair? His hair was brown . . . before it turned gray."

"I don't know if anyone recognized him as Demitasse. There's some question in my mind— although not in the crime investigators—that someone in the house was responsible for Fred's death."

Minnie started, her gaze searching Angie's. "I was told it was an accident."

"That's the official version," Angie said with unhidden sarcasm.

Connie chewed her bottom lip. She'd heard all this from Angie already, but hadn't wanted to be the one to break it to Minnie.

"Paavo questions what happened as well," Angie said, "but the St. Helena police don't want to help him. The whole situation raises too many questions and too many coincidences. Are people who visit that house all clumsy? They fall out windows, into wine barrels. It doesn't make sense."

"Fred wasn't clumsy," Minnie countered, her jaw tight. "Of course, wearing those stilts . . ."

"An accident sounds reasonable to me," Connie

said hopefully. Clearly, she'd been involved in too many "unreasonable" deaths since meeting Angie.

"Living there has made me suspicious," Angie admitted. "Nothing is as it seems. That's the trouble with being around actors. They aren't who or what they seem, either." As she said this, she looked at Minnie, who'd been dabbing her eyes a moment ago. Her eyes, however, were clear and dry.

"You think one of them is a murderer?" Minnie asked, appalled.

"I think something happened to Fred that was much more than it . . . oh, no!" Angie cried. Digger Gordon entered the coffee shop.

"You know him?" Connie asked sitting a little straighter and with obvious interest. At least today Digger's slacks were clean and pressed. His corduroy jacket, however, was grungy. Angie wondered—once again—about her friend's bizarre taste in men.

"You ladies certainly brighten this corner of the room," Digger said as he approached their table. "Mind if I join you?" He smiled at Connie. Angie could practically see the wheels in his brain chug mightily as he studied the diminutive Minnie Petite.

Connie looked interested, Minnie wary, and Angie resigned. She made introductions and explained Minnie's relationship to the dead chef.

"Fred Demitasse . . ." Digger rubbed his chin. "I do remember that name. He was associated, somehow, with *Eagle Crest.*"

"I would have remembered if he was on the show," Angie said. "He wasn't."

"Are you here to write a story about my Fred?" Minnie asked, smiling daintily.

"I wasn't originally," Digger answered as the waitress came by to take his coffee-and-berry pie order. "I planned to write the true story of Brittany Keegan's death."

"I thought she died because of an accident in LA," Minnie said.

"That was the story given to the press." He gave Connie an I'm-connected-and-in-the-know smile. She smiled back.

Minnie's eyes widened. Digger's words made a definite impact on her. Angie waited for some explanation, but none was forthcoming.

"You think her death wasn't an accident either?" Connie asked Digger.

"That's what I was here investigating, and then this new death happened," he replied.

"Of course!" Minnie exclaimed.

"Of course?" Angie asked.

Minnie's head jerked toward her, her face pale. "I meant, *of course* a reporter would find it all quite curious." She glanced at her watch. "Hell! Look at the time. Come on, Connie, we got to get our asses in gear. Death certificates, papers to sign. A body can't just die anymore without the government's nose in every damn thing."

Everyone stood. Digger inched closer to Connie. "Are you staying at the hotel?" he asked.

"Yes," Connie answered, her manner friendly. "I expect to spend most of my time at Eagle Crest, though. I can't wait to see it."

"I'll be heading that way myself," he said. "In fact, I can help Minnie get through the red tape—

as a reporter I know what she'll be facing—and then I can show you the way to Eagle Crest."

"We'd appreciate the help," Connie said. "That means Angie doesn't have to wait."

Angie frowned. "Are you sure?"

Connie glanced at Digger. "Sure," she said.

Chapter 28

When Paavo returned to Homicide after getting a search warrant okayed on his part of the Birds of Prey murders, complete results of the search of the Eagle Crest group's arrest records were on his desk.

The first record belonged to Bart Farrell. Farrell had been arrested twice for assault and battery. Both times the charges had been dismissed. The first was in Brentwood fifteen years earlier, but the second was in St. Helena ten years earlier, which would have made it during the time the show was ending.

Paavo dug deeper into that assault. The complaint had been made by Emery Tarleton.

Rhonda Manning had received a DUI eleven years earlier, in Napa County. It was dated a week after Brittany's death.

Gwen Hagen showed two arrests and convictions for prostitution. The last was nineteen years earlier, shortly before she landed the role on *Eagle Crest*.

Fred Demitasse, aka Larry Rhone, Kyle

O'Rourke, Emery Tarleton, Mariah Warren, Camille Spentworth, and Brittany Keegan had no records. He'd learned long ago to always check on the victims as well. They weren't always as innocent as they seemed.

He then turned to the information about the Waterfields. Arrest records were blank for Sterling and Silver Waterfield. But a surprise awaited him.

Sterling Waterfield II, known as "Junior," had a restraining order served against him when he was twenty years old. He'd been ordered by a judge never to approach by less than three hundred feet, a woman named Julia Dean. He had been stalking her, and she'd pressed charges.

Paavo phoned Angie to tell her and for once, he was able to reach her in St. Helena.

To say she was shocked by the news was to put it mildly.

Camille Spentworth sat alone at a table in the St. Helena Hotel bar, a drink in front of her, her elbows on the table and her forehead pressed to her hands.

Angie left Connie and Minnie with promises to see them soon at Eagle Crest, and approached the screenwriter. "Remember me? Angie Amalfi."

Camille started. "I remember." She seemed even plainer and more tired than the day Angie met her. With no makeup and straight hair, her features were scarcely noticeable, giving her an overall appearance of beige—and just as lively.

"What are you doing here?" Angie asked.

"I had to get away from that house and all those Christmas decorations mixed with unhappy people . . ."

Angie wanted to hear an explanation, and she knew Camille was the type who would talk just to avoid the awkwardness of silence.

Camille sipped her drink. "It's been a long time since I celebrated Christmas," she said, "but my memories—I grew up on a farm in Iowa—are good ones. I suppose it made me a little nostalgic. Christmas isn't the same in L.A."

"I can imagine," Angie said. A cocktail waitress came over, and she ordered tonic with a lime twist, no gin. When Camille added nothing more, Angie asked, "How's the script coming?"

The writer rubbed her already red-splotched forehead. Forehead-rubbing was clearly something she did too much of. "I don't see how I'm supposed to integrate Tarleton's Christmas Carol story with mine. So far, he won't drop his."

"Director's prerogative," Angie said. "What's your script about?"

Camille swirled the maraschino cherry in her Old Fashion. "It was a typical *Eagle Crest* storyline," she said. "It was Christmas. Natalie wanted to prove she was still young and beautiful, so she planned to perform a solo version of the Nutcracker Suite on ice. While she was rehearsing, Cliff had time to fool around with Leona. Then, Leona's mother—and Cliff's first wife—managed to free herself from terrorist kidnappers, flee to the United States, and contact Leona. She showed up in St. Helena on Christmas Day, and all hell broke loose. She was the big surprise present Leona was planning for Cliff."

"Oh, my God!" Angie cried, so intrigued she

scarcely noticed that her drink arrived. All her love for *Eagle Crest*, the emotion that had brought her to this strange location in the first place, came back to her upon hearing the story line. "Finally, Natalie would have learned her marriage wasn't legal! After all she'd been through, too. That would have been so exciting! Then what happened?"

Camille smiled secretly. "I won't tell, in case Tarleton changes his mind. I'll only say *Eagle Crest* fans would not have been disappointed, and I also left the possibility very open for another special to tie up some of the new loose ends."

"If only!" Angie wailed, hands to her head.

"It would have been great." Camille sighed as if she didn't know whether to laugh or cry. "The least Tarleton could have done was tell me he only wanted to use the four main actors. Of course, nobody expected him to give his chef a speaking role, either."

"Did you hear the chef was actually Fred Demitasse?" Angie asked.

Camille looked genuinely shocked. "I had no idea. I didn't recognize him. I worked with him and Kyle O'Rourke a couple of times."

"So you didn't know he'd have a role either?"

"Not at all. Not that his role is a problem anymore." She drained her glass and motioned to the waitress for a refill. She ate the cherry. "I don't know what to do. I'm broke and I've already spent most of the money they paid me for the script, so I've got to go along with them."

"Aren't they working on your script at all?" Angie asked.

"They are. They want to go over it first without me there, which makes me nervous." She grabbed the drink before the waitress set it on the table and took a big gulp. Her eyes were beginning to glaze. "I'll have to get back by three p.m. and listen to all their ideas for changes. I don't know if I can stand it."

"I don't blame you," Angie said.

"I can't afford to pull out, but if they use my script and make a hash out of it like they're coming close to doing, my career could be ruined." She rubbed her forehead again. "Somehow, I've got to stop them."

"Rehearsals over?" Angie asked Kyle, as she stepped behind the bar for a lemon Calistoga water. She'd take it into the kitchen and get started cooking. Minnie and Connie should be showing up soon.

"I wanted a break." He sat on the sofa. No one else was in the room.

"I heard the rest of the crew gets in tonight," she said.

He nodded, uninterested.

"What do you think of the script?" she asked. "I hear Camille Spentworth isn't happy with it. Is the *Christmas Carol* segment still being used?"

"We haven't rehearsed it, if that's what you're asking. It's hard to tell how anything—TV or movie—will turn out since they're often shot in scenes, out of sequence. We just act and hope." He flashed her a nice-guy Adrian smile straight out of an *Eagle Crest* playbook as he picked up his beer and turned toward the doorway.

"You don't seem happy to be back here," Angie said hurriedly.

He stopped. "I don't?"

"Am I wrong?"

He strolled her way. "This show gave me my start. I owe everything to it—and Em for taking a chance with an unknown like me."

"He used a lot of unknowns, didn't he?" Angie asked. "You, Gwen, even Brittany Keegan hadn't done anything but bit roles, from what I understand."

"That's because we were paid shit when the show began," Kyle said bitterly, the façade gone. "No one dreamed it would take off the way it did."

She was frustrated. All his answers were trite, the same clichés he'd said time and again in interviews. "All of you must have grown close working together over so many years."

"We're like family," he answered, his gaze never leaving hers as he stepped to her side, leaning against the bar. "There's a lot of love between us."

"Fred Demitasse apparently worked on St. Helena in the past, but he wasn't in any of the shows. That surprises me."

Kyle looked annoyed by her mention of Demitasse's name. "Did he? I don't remember."

"Do you know why he was here?" Angie asked.

Kyle gave her a cold stare. "Em obviously wanted to surprise us by bringing up stuff about Brittany's death."

"Why?"

"How the hell should I know? Ask him."

"What do you think happened to Brittany?" she asked.

His eyes narrowed. "Are you talking about Rhonda, too?"

She studied him. Did he, like Fred Demitasse, think Rhonda had something to do with Brittany's death? "Rhonda?" she acted surprised. "No, not really."

"I'm sick of people accusing her. I'm sure she's innocent. Brittany died accidentally. Demitasse, too. Let them both rest in peace." He slammed his drink on the bar and left.

Angie stayed behind the bar after Kyle left. With this crowd, she knew someone else would show up before long. She wasn't disappointed.

"Well, well," Bart said, perusing Angie. "What have we here?"

"Call me Joe the Bartender." Angie smiled. "What'll you have?"

"Beer," Bart answered.

"Same." Rhonda said.

Angie found Heineken and glasses. "Have you both heard the chef was Fred Demitasse? Isn't it interesting no one recognized him? Surely, all of you knew Fred."

Bart and Rhonda stiffened like stone sculptures. "All I remember about Demitasse is he was a little fellow and grouchy," Bart said. "Frankly, I never paid attention to the chef. And, Fred had dark hair. Wasn't the chef blond?"

"And when Fred read from the script, he wore a mask," Rhonda added.

"It sure was strange behavior on Tarleton's

part, giving him a role and keeping him in disguise. Same as having Mariah disguised so she'd surprise you when she dressed as Brittany."

"That was Mariah?" Bart asked, his face flushed with surprise or anger.

"The thing that's the biggest puzzle to me," Angie said, handing a glass to Rhonda, "is why Tarleton set up this whole ruse. Why did he do it to you?"

"He set it up?" Bart asked.

"Now, a man is dead!" Rhonda cried, her hands clenched. "Why didn't Em leave everything alone? Why, Bart?"

He shook his head.

Rhonda glared at Angie, took her beer and fled the room. Bart followed like a whipped dog.

"Well, that certainly didn't go well," Angie muttered as she found a white and blue striped cloth and began to wipe down the bar top, humming "Our Love Is Here to Stay," as she did so.

Chapter 29

The leader of the Quetzalcoatl gang lived in the gray one-story flat-roofed shack that Paavo and Yosh watched. They were at the back of the house. Calderon and Benson would be approaching from the front. The SWAT team had it surrounded.

When Calderon found out one of the workers at the Lake Berryessa wild life reserve was a cousin of a leader of the Quetzalcoatl gang, that was the connection he needed to go in to make the arrest. The cousin could easily have supplied the gang with the feathers they'd been using on their victims.

The birds of prey feathers were most likely what was going to convict the murderers. Luckily, the gang hadn't used common ones from a pigeon, chicken, or goose.

Thoughts of a goose caused Paavo's thoughts to wander to the bizarre e-mails Demitasse had sent to the screen name "Etstar." It all fit together like the pieces of a jigsaw puzzle.

After Paavo got the list of people in the house

with Angie, the name Emery Tarleton had jumped out at him. On the Internet, he'd checked the IMDB director database for Tarleton. Sure enough, in the contact information was the e-mail address of "Etstar."

"Paavo, you paying attention?" Yosh asked suddenly.

"Sure," he said.

"Good."

Paavo tried to concentrate on the shut door, the windows, the roof, the grassy area behind them. Any move, any glimmer out of the ordinary could mean trouble. Once this was over, he'd be able to head north, finally, and see just what was going on at the Christmas reunion.

Christmas . . . looking around, he couldn't help but wonder if Christmas ever came to a neighborhood like this. If it didn't, that might be one reason why the area seemed so devoid of hope, of love, of a soul.

Demitasse's e-mails had to do with Christmas, and a goose. He could understand the one about Christmas coming more than once a year—a reference to the April reunion show.

"What gander plucked 'your' goose?" one had asked. Another made reference to the goose not being kosher.

He knew nothing about kosher food or kosher poultry. He'd ask Angie.

Earlier she'd left a message that Connie was bringing Minnie Petite to Eagle Crest. Petite bothered him. She knew lots more than she was saying—including about Angie and the soap opera. He needed to question her. How much longer?

He looked at his watch to see how long he'd been out here.

When he looked up again, the back door had opened.

A gunshot rang out.

Minnie Petite sulked, sitting at the center island in Eagle Crest's kitchen. She wanted to meet the director and cast, but Angie wasn't about to interrupt their rehearsal.

Using that as an excuse for not staying, Digger left almost immediately . . . after arranging to connect with Connie for drinks that night in St. Helena.

Connie was so gaga over being in the same house with Bart Farrell and Kyle O'Rourke that Angie had to watch her closely to make sure she didn't cut a finger as she sliced eggplant. Since the prior evening's Italian meal was such a hit, Angie decided a touch of Greece would be appreciated.

Serefina came in to greet Connie, then the two pitched in to help prepare moussaka, egg-lemon soup, stuffed grape leaves, cucumbers and tomatoes with feta dressing, shrimp and rice pilaf, and pastitsio. For dessert, rice pudding and baked walnut halva.

As they worked, Angie talked about her ideas for an engagement party until both Connie and her mother threatened to puncture their eardrums with shish kebab skewers. Could she help it if she had a lot to think about—date, time, place, colors, patterns, music, food, wine, guest list, gift registries, invitations, decorations, announcements, favors, her clothes, Paavo's clothes, the list went on and on. The details that had to be dealt with for a simple engagement party were so endless she had no idea how she'd cope with an entire wedding.

She'd hoped this time in St. Helena would allow her an uninterrupted opportunity to decide exactly what she wanted. Boy, had she ever been wrong.

"Will you knock it off, bird brain!" Minnie yelled across the room.

Startled, Angie looked up at her. "I'm sorry, I should have realized . . ."

"Hell, it's not like that. Me and Fred didn't have that kind of relationship. It's just that it's boring as hell to listen to you. Especially when there are more important things to think about—like why would anybody want to hurt Fred, let alone kill him."

"We don't know that anyone's killed him."

"Hogwash. There's no way he'd fall into a vat without help. We want to find out who. I think I know why."

"Why?" Angie asked.

"Let's just say I knew he was up to something. Fred was a player. Not much of an actor, that's all."

Angie thought about Minnie's words. Fred died because he was up to something and "knew things." If so, she'd have to be careful about what she learned! Tomorrow, Paavo would be here, and she'd feel a lot safer.

The question struck: why had Minnie involved

Paavo in the first place? Angie threw down her oven mitt and faced the little woman. "What's going on, Minnie? It wasn't coincidence that caused you to go to Paavo. What did you hope to find out?"

Minnie pressed her lips tight.

"You knew Fred was here, didn't you?" Angie sat beside her. "What did you expect Paavo to do? Did you know Fred was in danger? Is that why you didn't come here on your own?"

"I didn't know anything like that!" She pulled her black handkerchief out of her little black handbag and dabbed her eyes. "You're upsetting me."

"Why didn't you tell the police? What were you hiding?" Angie yelled, sick of the acting and deception around her.

"I wasn't hiding anything, for cryin' out loud!" Minnie yelled right back. "Fred was." She glared hard a long moment, then eased her shoulders and shook her head.

"Fred was . . . damned old fool! He'd found a way to get work. He wouldn't tell me how. I suspected it had something to do with the people at Eagle Crest, but I wasn't sure."

Minnie's eyes darted back and forth between Angie, Connie, and Serefina, who had stopped work to listen. "Connie knew I used to act. When I was in her shop, she told me about your job. Later, when she mentioned your cop boyfriend, it gave me an idea. She said he was more thorough than a lot of cops, tried real hard to be helpful. I thought I could weasel out of him a list of the other people at Eagle Crest, and maybe something about them—if one had a past he didn't want known for example. Instead, he found Fred. I guess Connie was right: he is thorough."

"What do you mean that Fred found a way to get work?" Angie asked.

"I mean, he got paid. All the time. And he wasn't in that many actual shows. I thought, if I could find out how he did it, I could get a cut, too. I'm not getting any younger. Old age can be pretty bleak without a good retirement income."

"Have you considered," Angie asked, "that whatever it was that Fred knew that kept him employed is the same thing that led to his death?"

"Blackmail," Serefina said, her eyes wide.

Angie nodded.

Minnie breathed deeply. "You're right. It's what I'd suspected for years. He wouldn't tell me! He wouldn't share! All I wanted to do was find out for myself. It's not so bad of me, is it?" For the first time that day, Minnie's tears appeared genuine.

"It's not good, Minnie," Connie said honestly.

Minnie cried harder.

"Do you want to find out who killed him?" Angie asked. "I've got an idea that might work."

Puzzled, Minnie nodded. "Poor old Fred. Too damn smart for his own good. What do you want me to do?"

The four women huddled closer, and Angie explained.

Digger couldn't hear Angie's plan, much as he pressed his ear to the door between the kitchen and breakfast area. It didn't matter. He knew no one in that house would confess to a crime unless there was no alternative.

Her plan was doomed before it began.

The blackmail angle was much more interesting. It made sense—if Minnie Petite was telling the truth.

Now, he did leave Eagle Crest, even though he'd said his good-byes earlier. It was amazing the information he picked up simply by saying good-bye and then taking his time leaving. That little phrase seemed to force people to talk openly . . . and if he happened to overhear, was that his problem?

In his hotel room, Digger opened his laptop and did an Internet search of Minnie Petite. It turned up a couple of films she'd been in decades earlier, but nothing more. He then called his office, asking for a Lexis-Nexis search of both Minnie Petite and Fred Demitasse. He wanted everything they could turn up. Next he called the Screen Actors Guild and requested a bibliography of Petite and Demitasse's films and television credits. He left the hotel's fax number and gave the *National Star*'s credit card for billing.

Something here didn't add up.

Ouzo flowed freely as the cast, Tarleton, Mariah, Camille, Sterling, and Silver scarfed down Greek food. Angie found it interesting that despite Bart Farrell's talk about a raw food diet and Rhonda's veganism, both ate her cooking, meat included, and appeared to enjoy it greatly.

Angie convinced Connie and Minnie to stay in

the kitchen while she and Serefina joined the diners. They ate by candlelight.

When everyone was quite full, Angie cried out. "I just heard Rudolph Goetring's voice!"

Connie had been listening in the butler's pantry for the cue. As soon as it came, she whacked the counter with two cookbooks—*thud, thud*. Then she did it again. *Thud, thud*.

All heads turned toward the pantry. Sterling stood. At that moment, Angie pointed toward the foyer. "Look!"

In the darkness, Minnie Petite stood in a white chef's gown and hat. As soon as Angie pointed at her, she ran down the hall.

"What?" Bart shouted. "I didn't see anything."

Rhonda was frozen to the spot.

"I saw it, too," Gwen shouted. "Is this a joke?"

"It's no joke," Silver said. He started toward the door.

"Stop," Serefina said. "It's just Angie. Cooking in that kitchen makes her nervous. She sees Goetring everywhere. Sometimes, when a Christmas tree light burns out, it glows a little brighter for just a moment. That's probably all you saw. Or perhaps the moon peeking from behind a cloud cover. It's the full moon tonight, you know. Don't let Angie scare you."

Silver sat again.

"It would be Goetring's ghost," Serefina explained, "only if someone killed him and he returned to accuse his murderer."

"Oh, ho, ho!" Sterling laughed. "A fine joke, Serefina. Look at them, they're all white as sheets now." He turned to Angie. "Why didn't you tell us you were troubled? You don't have to cook if you don't want to."

"I love cooking," Angie said. "Mamma's right. I'm sorry. It couldn't have been a ghost . . . could it?"

"Wait," Tarleton said. "We all heard the footsteps. What was that?"

"Maybe Junior getting his dinner," Angie said.

"I think anyone who scares us like that should just go home," Rhonda shrieked. "I didn't come here for this!"

Mariah sat like a statue. "I saw something," she whispered, "and it wasn't a light. It was Fred Demitasse."

As Angie looked from one to the other, she saw that they all had heard about Fred being Goetring.

"The hell it was!" Kyle threw his napkin on the table and strode down the hall, Angie and the others following in a cluster behind him.

He went through the family room, breakfast room, and into the kitchen.

"Who are you?" he roared.

Angie tried to push her way ahead of the others.

"Adrian! I mean, Mr. O'Rourke!" Connie squealed. "It's such an honor to meet you!"

"*Who are you?*"

"I . . . I'm Angie's friend. I got here a short while ago, and saw everyone was eating, so I came in here. I didn't want to disturb Angie's dinner." She had a half eaten plate of food in front of her. "I helped myself. I hope you don't mind." Her gaze turned moony and she stood, stepping near him.

"I simply must tell you how much I loved the scene when you told Natalie that you would love her forever, even though she ditched you and married Cliff. It still brings tears to my eyes whenever I think about it. I taped it and watched it over and over. Someday, I hope to find a man who loves me like that."

Kyle backpedaled out of the kitchen. "Don't let me disturb your dinner. I'm sure Angie will be happy to see you."

Connie clutched her hands together, lifting them to her breast. "The way you kissed her good-bye. Only your lips touched hers. It was the sexiest, most sensual kiss I've ever seen in my whole life! God, I don't see how she didn't throw her arms around you! Hold you tight and kiss you back until you were dizzy from it! It was so, like . . ." She sighed. "How could any woman resist you?"

"Excuse me." He dashed out of the kitchen, eyes wild, and fled. Gwen and the others went after him. The show was over.

Smiling from ear to ear, Angie entered the kitchen. "Where's Minnie?"

"Hiding under the sink. We cleared a space just in case something like this happened."

Minnie crawled out. Connie put her hand on Minnie's shoulder. "We were great, weren't we? Spooked them good!"

"Wonderful," Angie said. "You really got to Kyle, too. It was all I could do not to laugh."

Connie's smile vanished. "Laugh? Why? I was dead serious about him!"

Chapter 30

 That evening was not the time to spring Minnie and Connie on the cast or anyone else. Angie needed to sneak them out of the house first chance she got and let everyone stew about the "vision" they'd seen—or feared seeing.

All three were about to begin with the cleanup when there was a knock on the kitchen door.

Since they'd refilled the area under the sink with cleaning supplies, the only place Angie could think of to hide them was the wine cellar. She pointed to the door.

Minnie headed for it. Angie motioned for Connie to join her. If Minnie realized she was hiding where Fred had been killed, she might scream or otherwise freak out. Hopefully, Connie could keep her calm.

Angie called, "Come in."

Gwen Hagen entered and offered to help with the cleanup.

"I didn't think stars like you even realized that someone had to clean pots, pans, and dishes,"

Angie said, amazed. Gwen filled the dishwasher while Angie scrubbed pots and pans in the sink.

Gwen smiled. "You wouldn't believe the kinds of things I did before I had money. Washing dishes is nothing. My only regret is that I never had a big family to do them with. I gather, talking to your mother, that you have sisters and brothers-in-law, and nieces and nephews. All the things that money can't buy. You're lucky, you know."

"Does that mean I should be used to washing up after a big dinner?" Angie said with a laugh.

"Exactly. To me, it sounds like fun. Where's your friend, by the way? She wasn't the one out here scaring everyone . . . or was she?"

Angie swallowed. "She . . . she's in the court-yard. Enjoying the fresh air, I think. She couldn't scare a soul."

Gwen's face turned hard, almost cruel. "She's not a midget, is she? Was she wearing Fred's body suit with stilts?"

"No," Angie replied. "She wasn't the ghost I saw. Or thought I saw, if that's what you're asking."

Gwen continued with the cleanup, not speaking for a while.

Eventually, the two began to talk amicably again, Angie about her family and her fiancé, and Gwen about growing up dirt poor and never having a Christmas until she was old enough to make one for herself.

Angie commented on how surprised she was that so many traditional Christmas foods and plants and decorations were fake in the house. Fortunately, she hadn't gone too far when Gwen told her she decorated her home in much the same way. It was much easier on the waistline when the mince pies, iced sugar cookies, fruitcake, and sugar plums were made out of plastic or sculpted foam; easier on the carpet when trees didn't need to sit in stands filled with water and didn't drop needles all over the place. Her maid sprayed the house with pine aerosol so that it smelled Christmasy . . . or like a bathroom. Take your pick.

They were almost finished when Rhonda walked into the kitchen. "Oh! I didn't realize you were here." She swayed slightly as she took in what they were doing. "I should have helped."

"It's all right," Angie said.

"I just wanted some ice for my water. There's none left at the bar. I'm going up to bed."

"Already?" Gwen asked. "I was thinking of going into St. Helena tonight. To see something besides these four walls. Want to go?"

"No. I'm tired." She filled up a bowl with ice, and then grabbed a tall glass. "Goodnight."

Angie frowned. Something was very wrong with that woman. "Goodnight."

They soon finished the dishes and went out to the family room. Kyle, who'd been talking with Tarleton, jumped to his feet with a smile at Gwen. Angie thought it was more than a "friends" type smile.

The three chatted a while and then Kyle asked, "Are you ready? Emery's going with us."

"Great," Gwen said. "Angie, want to come along?"

It was tempting, but she had to do something

about Connie and Minnie. "I don't think so. All that cooking was exhausting."

"I can imagine," Gwen said. "Let's go, everyone."

As soon as they were out of sight, Angie dashed into the kitchen and opened the door to the wine cellar.

"You can come out now."

Silence.

Oh, God! "Connie? Minnie? The coast is clear."

More silence.

She didn't want to go all the way down the stairs to that cold, dank cellar again. She really, really didn't want to do that.

She crept down a few steps, but couldn't see much of the cellar. She went down a few more. "Connie? Don't play games. This isn't funny."

Taking a deep, courage-enhancing breath, she marched to the bottom without letting herself stop.

The cellar was empty.

A door led out to the side of the house. It had been unlocked.

Outside, she took a few steps toward the front of the house. Connie's car was still in the parking area.

She made an about-face to the courtyard.

"Over here!" Connie called. She and Minnie stood a few feet up the hillside, enough so Minnie could see over the adobe wall and into the courtyard and the house. Angie joined them. "How could you have sent us down to that cellar?" Connie cried. "Are you crazy?"

"I'm sorry," Angie cried. "Minnie, I hope it didn't upset you too much."

"Me? I didn't give a damn. Connie here looked ready to wet her pants. I said 'Boo' and she scaled the walls. Had to get her out of there."

"Anyway," Connie said, not hiding her irritation well, "from the hill, we could see into some bedrooms. The one with the lights on is Rhonda's."

Connie pointed to a window just below and to the left of Angie's. In front of it was an almond tree.

"I wonder what she's up to," Angie murmured. "It's hard to see with that tree in the way." An idea came to her. "Connie, let's you and me go down to the courtyard. Minnie, wait right here."

At the base of the almond tree Connie said, "You aren't thinking what I think you are, are you?"

"Of course I am." She put her hands on the trunk. "Give me a boost."

"You are crazy!" Connie declared.

"Rhonda is hiding something and I want to know what it is."

"You can't spy on her!"

"It's not spying. It's investigating. What if she's up to something terrible? What if she's a homicidal maniac? Or suicidal? What if she's about to kill herself and I'm the only one who can save her? I need to see what she's up to." Angie kicked off her sandals with four-inch heels and gestured impatiently for Connie to come closer.

"I give up." Connie laced her fingers together. She'd been through this before.

Angie used her hands as a step and Connie lifted as Angie jumped, reaching for the Y in the tree trunk. She landed on her stomach and crawled to a sitting position. "I didn't realize how high this was. These branches are *round*, and they're slippery!"

"You've got to go up a couple more limbs," Connie urged. "You can't see anything from there."

Carefully, Angie got to her feet, clutching the trunk. Slowly, she climbed a few boughs higher. The words to "Rock-a-Bye Baby" ran through her head. What a nasty little song!

Clutching a tree limb, she looked right into Rhonda's bedroom window.

Rhonda stepped into view and behind her, Bart Farrell. Angie gasped and nearly lost her balance.

Bart wrapped his arms around Rhonda. They kissed passionately. Angie's eyes nearly popped out of her head.

Rhonda criticized Bart constantly and publicly, but hers was not the face of a woman hating what was going on. Bart apparently knew what he was doing with all the "darling" this and "darling" that, and being so solicitous. He'd acted like a man in love—possibly one who'd been in love for a long time.

"Get up here!" Angie whispered down to Connie. "You've got to see this."

"How am I supposed to do that?" Connie whispered back.

"You won't believe it!"

"I won't?" That got Connie moving. She reached for the Y of the tree and tried to lift herself onto it. She couldn't. Maybe she should spend some time at a gym. Angie climbed back down and grabbed her hand, and while Connie's feet scrambled against the trunk, Angie pulled.

"Oh, my God!" Connie cried, finding herself clinging to a thick branch. "I can break my neck from here."

"You aren't that high," Angie said. "And I'll hold onto you."

Connie wasn't sure if that would help or hurt. Clutching Angie's hand, she climbed higher, looked into the window, and gasped. "Those two? I thought she hated him."

"Isn't it wild?"

"Like on TV, only better," Connie squealed.

At that moment, Rhonda began to unbutton her dress while Bart walked toward the bed. He pulled back the covers and kicked off his shoes. Angie and Connie's eyes grew round as saucers.

"Uh . . . Angie," Connie whispered.

An X-rated *Eagle Crest* was not part of Angie's viewing pleasure either. "I never did like those reality shows," she said. "Time to get off this tree."

Connie began down. "Stop stepping on my hand!" she said. "Let me go first. Once I'm on the ground, I'll guide you."

"Okay." Angie tried her best not to glance back at the window—just a peek or two. Things were definitely getting steamier by the minute.

Connie climbed down, and near the bottom, jumped.

Angie slowly moved her feet down one limb and then another. The tree bark was hard and prickly, the twigs and branches hurt the tender

soles of her feet. If she wore practical shoes like
Connie's one-inch pumps she could have left
them on and not had to endure this torment, but
now . . .

All of a sudden, Connie turned and ran.

Angie didn't move, listening and wondering if the
tree leaves would hide her from whatever had
scared Connie. She certainly didn't want anyone
to know she'd climbed a tree right outside
Rhonda's bedroom. Now what?

She stood there, about five feet up, clutching
the trunk. She'd never realized how far five feet
was. No way was she brave enough to jump. At
best, it'd hurt. She could easily twist an ankle or
worse.

"Angie?" Junior looked up at her. She could understand Connie running. He looked like a wild
man of Borneo, even if you didn't know he was
once charged with being a stalker.

She felt trapped.

Once, she read that sexual predators never
changed, never could be rehabilitated. Was stalking the same thing? She wished she'd asked
Paavo more about it.

"Why are you up there?" he asked.

Everything about Junior disturbed her, but she
didn't want to stay in the tree any longer. "Help
me down, please."

She lowered herself to a sitting position. Leaning forward, she placed her hands on his shoulders. He took hold of her waist. Slowly, he eased
her from the tree down to the ground. Their bodies touched, and he used his for leverage not to

drop her. She felt more of his body than she ever
wanted to.

"Why were you up there?" he asked when her
feet touched the ground, his arms still around her.

She didn't want to upset him. "I . . . used to
climb trees all the time when I was a kid," she
said, easing herself away from him. "The going
up was easier than coming back down."

"Like a cat." He smiled, touching her cheek. He
stepped closer.

"Let me go, Junior," she ordered.

He did as she asked, his expression wary. "I saw
your friends," he said. "It seems I'm not the only
one with secrets here."

"There are too many secrets in this house," she
said. "Why don't you come inside, join everyone.
There's no need for you to continue to hide."

He looked at the house, at the cheerful Christmas lights. "Yes, there is." He studied her. "Do
you know where the music box is?"

She was growing more nervous. "Music box?"

"The Drummer Boy. *'Come, they told me . . . '* " he
softly sang.

His voice made a cold chill ripple down her
spine. "I don't know where it is. Do you?"

"You should know, Angie. It's important," he
said.

His affinity with the poor child with no gift to
bring struck her. His loneliness, his lack of gift, of
any social grace or self-confidence, was sad to behold in one whose life should have been filled
with so very much. On the surface, it was, but inside, she'd rarely seen such a hollow shell of a
man. Her sister said he wanted someone to love

and to love him. Maybe that's what was behind the stalking charge—desperation rather than perversion. Still, it was wrong.

"I've learned more about your mother since I've been here, Junior," she said, wishing she could find a way to get through his solitary shell. Curious, he gazed down at her. "She was an unhappy woman. Unhappy, unfulfilled. Her bitterness wasn't about you." Angie ached to touch him, to comfort him, but something held her back, some sense that she needed to be careful not to cause more upheaval than she knew how to handle. If she said or did the wrong thing it could tip the scale in a dangerous way.

"You weren't the problem," she continued. "It was her. There wasn't anything you could do, no way for you to change, to make it up to her. You've got to understand that."

"I don't know what you mean," he said stubbornly.

She didn't know what else to say. The possibility that Brittany, unknowingly, had set off Junior worried and sickened her. He could have been a good man.

"I'm going inside now, Junior. I have to find my friends."

"Your friends?" He touched her cheek once more. "You're my friend, Angie. My only friend."

She hurried into the house.

Chapter 31

The Quetzalcoatl gang member who'd come out the back door firing got off one shot before he was wounded by the SWAT sniper on the opposing roof. The other SWAT members fired until the back door was pulverized. Then they stopped and waited.

In a matter of minutes, the other members surrendered.

Since Quetzalcoatl had been the gang moving into the city and upsetting the perverse balance of power that existed among the drug dealers there, with them out of the way, the city could go back to the status quo.

Ironically, that meant the police had helped the dealers return to selling, rather than hiding in order to save their own lives.

Paavo and the other cops knew it; as they made the arrests, they could see it in each others' eyes. All they could do was shake their heads over the situation and hope that arresting and jailing the members of one ruthless gang would create an overall drop in drug traffic. Still, many of them were probably going to have a long struggle with their consciences over this case. According to the law, they'd done the right thing.

As soon as he could, Paavo left the city. Worry about what was going on at Eagle Crest nagged at him. Often, Angie managed to stir a pot in ways that caused trouble to bubble up even when it wasn't there before—or was there, but hidden under the surface.

At night, Highway 29 through the valley was nearly empty, far different from the weekend parking lot he'd dealt with the last time. When he turned off it for Eagle Crest, the narrow road was pitch black. He put his headlights on high, but he could have been alone in the world for all that was visible around him.

He drove for five minutes before he saw a light in the distance. A shining light in the East. He chuckled to himself. Angie's talk about Christmas had impressed him more than he'd imagined.

He followed the light. As he got closer, he saw it wasn't one light but many, strung around the house, over the roof, porch, and windows to look like something out of a Hallmark advertisement.

He turned into the parking area. In this light, even the fake snow looked pretty.

"Angie, the door," Mariah said, her lips pursed, but she didn't look nearly as irritated as she had in the past.

Angie was in her room. After leaving Junior, she'd found Connie and Minnie on the front veranda. She saw them off, with plans to return the next day. Since then, she'd thought a lot about Junior, as well as holding a full-fledged debate with herself over whether her "ghostly" dinner party ruse had been helpful, harmful, or simply a foolish waste of time and energy. Unfortunately, she was leaning toward the latter.

Now who? she wondered. Had Connie returned for some reason? As she headed downstairs, she expected the foyer to be empty, that her guest would have been left outdoors as usual.

He wasn't.

Paavo stood in the foyer wearing a brown leather jacket, cream-colored sports shirt, jeans, and looking so handsome she could hardly stand it.

She threw her arms around him, showering him with hugs and kisses. "I'm so glad you made it. I wasn't expecting you this soon."

He kissed her back with equal enthusiasm. "I couldn't wait. At least this time, you aren't on your way to San Francisco."

"Thank goodness!" She hugged him again before stepping back, his hands in hers. "Now that I've dragged you up here, though, I can't help but wonder what you could possibly do. Maybe I'm just imagining things. Maybe I'm putting my nose where I shouldn't and—"

"Why don't you show me the scenes of the crimes?"

"That's easy." She led him through the main floor, then to the wine cellar, the family and guest wings of the second floor, and finally to her bedroom. It was a good spot, she decided, eyeing him, to end the tour.

* * *

"A kosher goose?" Angie looked incredulously at Paavo later when they got around to talking once again.

They were side-by-side on the narrow single bed. "There's a lot involved," she said. "In kosher cooking, you aren't supposed to eat anything that's been strangled, for example. For poultry, that means the bird can't be killed by wringing its neck. I can find out more for you, if you'd like."

Paavo shifted his arm under her shoulder. "So if the goose isn't kosher, a simple meaning would be that its neck was twisted, or broken. Interesting." Paavo then told Angie about the e-mails Fred had sent to Tarleton. "They tie in somehow, I'm sure. Keep an eye on Minnie. She's an actress. I don't know that you can trust her."

"Same as all the others in this house," Angie said, her arm across his bare chest.

Paavo was silent, thoughtful.

She shivered and pulled the covers higher. "This room is always so cold," she said. "Some say it's caused by Brittany's ghost."

"Very funny. Isn't there a thermostat around?"

"The house has central heating, but none comes in here."

"That doesn't make sense." He got out of bed and put on his jeans. Angie switched on the small lamp by the bed.

Behind the bureau he found a wall register. "Maybe this is your problem." He shoved the bureau to one side. It actually looked better since it was now centered.

Paavo held his hand in front of the grate. "There's no air. I wonder if some inside vents are closed."

"I looked, but they're open," Angie said.

He studied it. In the dim light, it did appear to be open. He knelt closer, then got up and grabbed Angie's rat-tailed comb and pushed the handle inside the grate. It didn't go in far at all.

"Something's blocking it."

"There is?" Angie wrapped herself in his cotton shirt and knelt down beside him.

"Do you have a screwdriver?" he asked. At her blank expression, he continued. "Knife? How about a fingernail file?"

"That I've got."

He used it to unscrew the cover from the wall. A piece of black cardboard had been pressed against the register cover so that, to the casual glance, it appeared one was looking into the open cavernous maw of a heating system.

He pried the cardboard off. "Someone wanted it cold in here."

"Or someone wanted to hide something," Angie said. She reached into the opening and pulled out some papers.

They were from an obstetrician–gynecologist in San Francisco. The patient's name was Brittany Keegan. As Angie and Paavo read through all the medical jargon and the billing records, one fact became clear. When she died, Brittany Keegan was pregnant.

Chapter 32

When Angie awoke the next morning, she discovered that much of the crew was on the job, and the craft service was back. She'd been relieved of breakfast duty, which was good since this was her big day: the day she was going to cook the test-run of her Christmas feast.

As they ate breakfast, Angie took the opportunity to introduce Paavo to the cast, plus Tarleton, Mariah, and Camille. Soon after, Sterling and Serefina showed up, and Silver joined them briefly.

Angie made it clear to one and all that Paavo was a homicide inspector. She'd hoped that would cause one of them to fall to their knees and confess.

No such luck.

No one even looked especially guilty.

"Now that you've met everyone," Angie said to Paavo when they were alone in the kitchen, "what do you think? Did you see the shifty eyes, the guilty demeanor of a killer?"

"They all look like they're hiding something," he replied.

"Sterling and Silver, too?" she asked. She couldn't believe either of them had anything to do with murder.

Paavo wasn't so quick to judge. "Sterling's a ladies' man. We know he and his wife didn't get along at all. You mentioned rumors of his interest in Brittany as well as Rhonda and Gwen."

"That doesn't make him a killer," Angie said.

"I'm not saying he is, only that you can't rule him out. Same with Silver. Hormones making a sixteen-year-old boy go a little nutty are not unknown. Or, an older one for that matter. What was Junior at the time, twenty-one or -two? He already had a record as a stalker."

"True," Angie agreed.

"Fred Demitasse knew more happened in this house than was ever made public," Paavo said. "When he heard about the *Eagle Crest* reunion, he wanted to be part of the show and sent those e-mails to Tarleton. 'Aren't you curious about the gander who plucked your goose?' and so on. That means he also knew who Brittany was having an affair with."

"Minnie said something to me and Connie once," Angie added thoughtfully, "that others didn't see 'little people' as people—they only saw them in relation to their size. Fred could have silently gone about, watching and listening, and no one paid attention."

"Let's think about this a bit more. And about Minnie Petite. Why is she here?"

Angie filled him in on her blackmail theory. "Fred was blackmailing someone to keep quiet about what he saw the night Brittany died. Maybe Rhonda?"

"If she was paying him blackmail money, why would he cast suspicion on her?"

"Good point . . . but Rhonda has to be the killer. Fred publicly confronted her with her tale of bursitis."

Paavo shook his head. "Rhonda looks like a strong wind could blow her away. Fred was short, but solid. I don't see how she could lift him."

"So it can't be her," Angie said. Everyone seemed guilty . . . and no one.

But it was time for Paavo to leave. He had plans and needed to get started with them.

"Don't be late for dinner!" she cried. "Seven o'clock."

"I'd like to review Brittany Keegan's autopsy report." Paavo showed his SFPD badge to the clerk at the Napa county coroner's office.

The young clerk had apparently never been given a request like that because she grew flustered and went back to talk to the coroner. In a moment, a stoop-shouldered man with gray-streaked black hair, sunken chin, and silver-framed glasses approached.

"Steven Ellsberg," he said, extending a long-fingered hand. "I'm the medical examiner for the county."

Paavo introduced himself and again showed his credentials.

Ellsberg studied them. Satisfied, he said, "I understand you're interested in learning about Brittany Keegan's death."

"I am."

He regarded Paavo a moment. "Please come into my office."

"This was a very sensitive case," Ellsberg explained, seated behind his desk. "We nearly didn't do an autopsy on her because the people involved were afraid any results might get leaked to the press. For over ten years, we've kept the findings quiet, and I don't expect that to change."

"Are you saying the autopsy threw the accidental death ruling into question?" Paavo asked.

"No, I'm saying autopsies can provide information about a person that isn't known to the general public. *Private* information."

"Which you want to make sure remains private," Paavo added.

"Exactly."

"Unless it would in some way have material bearing on the case I'm looking into, I would have no reason to make anything in the autopsy public."

Ellsberg folded his hands on the desk, his eyes flinty. "What is the case you're looking into?"

"Fred Demitasse's. You might know him as Rudolf Goetring or Larry Rhone." Paavo explained his own involvement in the case. "Two accidental deaths, two actors. It's possible, but it appears suspicious."

"Put that way, I'd tend to agree," Ellsberg admitted. He leaned back. "I worked on Mr. Demitasse this morning, in fact."

"You did an autopsy?" Paavo asked.

"No. None was requested, and it doesn't seem any is needed. They're rare in this county. Most deaths here are caused by auto accidents—tourists, mostly. Or old age. That'd be the residents. People here live a long time. It's the wine, if you ask me. On the other hand, of those who die young, it's often the wine there, too. I guess it all evens out."

Paavo didn't like there being no autopsy. He'd witnessed a number of them that resulted in a cause of death far different from what was first suspected.

The ME rambled on, clearly relishing the chance to talk about his work.

"It's a good community," Ellsberg continued. "Changing, but what isn't? We're far enough away from big cities that most of the crime you deal with hasn't reached us yet."

"Except for Eagle Crest," Paavo said.

Ellsberg's gaze met his. "True."

"Did you find anything surprising when you looked at Demitasse's corpse?" Paavo asked.

"He's in the morgue." Ellsberg's eyes twinkled. "Want to see?"

"You're looking thoughtful this morning," Serefina said as she entered the kitchen to see if Angie needed help.

"I am," Angie confessed. "What am I going to do about Paavo and Papà? Why won't Papà accept him? Making up a story to get me to come to Eagle Crest—"

"Your father only wants what's best for you,"

Serefina said. "His problem is he thinks he knows what that is, and it's not easy to convince him he doesn't."

"Even if I convince him," Angie said, "I want them to like each other. How can I make that happen? Paavo has an open mind, but it won't stay that way if Papà keeps putting him down."

"Sometimes, in families especially, there's nothing you can do," Serefina admitted. "*Madonna*, but my father was unhappy with my choice for a husband. Salvatore and I can laugh now, but at the time . . ." She shook her head.

"Nonno didn't like Papà?" Angie was shocked. She'd never heard that before, and she was quite sure she'd heard everything involving the family.

"I don't like to talk about it, and your father definitely doesn't. It was all because of our first Christmas together."

Now Angie was even more confused. "Christmas?"

"Your father had no money and many bills. As my present, he bought me a necklace from Weinstein's. You probably don't even remember that store, a little five-and-ten. When I wore the necklace, it turned my neck green. Nonno saw it and was furious! He said Salvatore had no prospects, no money, and even worse taste. He never did get over that suspicion completely."

Angie chuckled at the story, but knowing history repeated itself wasn't exactly a comfort. "Papà didn't treat Bianca or Caterina's husbands this way. And Maria married a jazz musician and Frannie's husband is a jerk. Why pick on Paavo?"

"Because you're your father's baby." Serefina tried to explain. "He didn't like seeing Bianca marry. The first child to leave home is hard, but Johnnie had a business—and he's Italian. Your father could accept it. Caterina had to one-up her sister by marrying a lawyer, also Italian. What's not to like?"

"Well . . ." Actually, Angie couldn't stand Caterina's husband, but this wasn't the time to bring it up.

"Your father was sure Maria would become a nun. When she got married, he was so shocked he forgot to complain. And Frannie, poor Frannie—I think he was more relieved than anything that she found anyone who'd marry her. She isn't the easiest person to get along with."

About as easy as a great white shark, Angie thought.

"But you . . . when you're married, Angelina, another phase of our jobs as parents will be over. Salvatore doesn't want to give it up, yet." She brushed Angie's hair back from her face. "For most of your life, he was the man you ran to when things went wrong or you needed advice. Even as the older girls left, little Angelina was always there for us. You still needed us.

"Now, you've found someone else to go to. The man you love and want to share your life with. Let me tell you, Angelina, this isn't about Paavo as much as it's about Salvatore. I think if Paavo was president of General Motors, your father would find something to complain about. Now, do you understand?"

"Thank you, Mamma," Angie said, as Serefina gave her a hug, and then added a little more pepper to the sweet potatoes.

A spring developed in Ellsberg's step as he led Paavo through the county office building. "It isn't often I get to talk to someone who isn't squeamish about these things. I suspect you've watched more autopsies in a month than most cops in this county see in their careers."

"I don't know if I'd go that far," Paavo said. Ellsberg's glee was a bit ghoulish.

"I would." Ellsberg chuckled.

In the morgue, he rolled open the drawer with Demitasse's sheet-covered body.

"There was a blow on the back of his head." Ellsberg turned the head and pointed to a spot with his pen. "You can see the early stages of a bruise, even a slight tearing of the skin here. But look, no swelling. That tells me the blow was either surprisingly light—which is inconsistent with the bruise and tears—or occurred very shortly before death."

"What was the actual cause of death?"

"Drowning. The barrel had been half-filled with water."

Paavo had seen drowning victims before. Usually a residue of dried white foam—mucus mixed with water—was found around their mouths. Demitasse had none. "What confirms drowning?"

"The way he was found. What else?"

"Is it possible that he was hit on the head, knocked unconscious, and then shoved into the barrel?"

"Certainly. The police theorize he was in the cellar looking for wine and removed the barrel cover. At some point he hit his head, causing the contusion. Dazed, he stumbled about, fell into the barrel, couldn't get back out and drowned. If he'd had the height of most adult males, and if he weren't wearing that strange body suit, he never would have gotten stuck the way he did. It was a strange confluence of events."

"The unlucky, clumsy contortionist theory of death," Paavo said, frowning.

Ellsberg covered the body and shut the drawer. "You've heard of that, have you?"

The two men walked toward the exit. "Every so often. Defense attorneys are especially fond of explaining ingenious ways people do themselves in. Police, in my experience, aren't usually so creative. We tend to take a much more straightforward approach."

"Medical examiners, too. We go along with Occam's Razor—that the simplest explanation is most often the true one," Ellsberg said, "except when a death takes place on the Waterfield estate and the police chief himself shows up for the investigation. That's reason enough for investigating offices to become very creative, indeed."

"I understand." Paavo had had more than a few of those cases, himself. He'd always managed not to buckle under, however.

Ellsberg stopped before entering his office. "You still want Brittany Keegan's autopsy?"

"More than ever."

"Wait here. I'll be back with it in five minutes."

Chapter 33

Connie burst into the kitchen flush from having Cliff Roxbury himself greet her at the door. She felt as if she were living in a television series, and she loved every minute of it.

The kitchen looked completely chaotic—food, bowls, and knives everywhere. Angie was up to her elbows in flour, bread stuffing, and chopped vegetables, fruit, onions, and garlic. Stuffing, pies, hors d'oeuvres, and vegetable dishes were spread around her as she prepared for the feast.

"What's going on around here today?" Connie asked. "It's a madhouse outside, and even worse in here."

"The cast and crew will start filming tomorrow. I don't know what else they're up to, but I can tell you that no one confessed. Our little farce with Minnie apparently didn't phase the killer in the least. Where is Minnie, by the way?"

"She didn't want to come this afternoon. I think she's a lot more upset about Fred's death than she let on, and added to it, all these Christmas decorations . . . she said she'll show up later if you need her."

"I'm not surprised," Angie admitted.

"What do we do now?" Connie asked.

Angie told her about finding Brittany's OB/GYN papers, and about Junior and their strange conversation.

"Why did he ask about a music box?" Connie asked.

"He said I should know who had it. I wonder . . . Sterling said it belonged to the Waterfield family, but Tarleton thought it was Brittany's. He said she didn't like it. Could one of the Waterfields have given it to her, and then she gave it away to be used as a prop? Would that be a motive for murder?"

Connie's eyes widened. "I certainly should hope not! I've given away a few gifts I didn't like myself."

Angie tried connecting some dots—those visible to her, at any rate. Junior was young, like Brittany, and thought he loved her. Everyone knew he'd watched and followed her.

Yet, she spurned him, gave away his present. Perhaps he broke into her room to confront her and ended up pushing her, causing her to fall. Breaking into her room wouldn't have been a problem for a strong man like Junior. Angie had looked at the doorframe in the bedroom—it was weak, inexpensive wood. The whole attic had been converted into bedrooms cheaply and quickly.

Junior being responsible for Brittany's death was quite possible, she thought.

Then, when he saw Brittany's music box, he took it—and Fred Demitasse saw him. He might have confronted Junior about taking the music box now, as well as over what he might have seen in the past. And so, Junior killed him.

Connie was confused. "I thought you said Fred accused Rhonda?"

"It seemed that way. Maybe that was a red herring—he'd throw everyone off the track, so they'd never suspect Junior. That way, as long as Junior paid the blackmail money, Fred was safe."

"I don't know, Angie." Connie shook her head.

"It all hinges on the Little Drummer Boy," Angie insisted. "If it's in Junior's room, we know he's the killer."

"How are we going to find out?" Connie wondered why she bothered to ask. She already knew the answer.

"Now, Connie, is that question really necessary?"

The two knocked on the door between Junior's apartment and the kitchen. No answer. Angie tried to find a way to spring the lock, but she couldn't fit a credit card between the door and the frame, and there was no keyhole to unlock with a bobby pin, like in the movies—not that she or Connie wore bobby pins or even owned any, or she'd know how to tumble a lock mechanism if she had one.

"We have to go outside," Angie said. "There's an outside entrance."

"Outside? But you said Junior's always up on

that hill. He might see us! I don't want some homicidal stalker finding me in his room. No way. Good-bye!"

"Don't worry. His room faces north. The hill is east. We'll be fine."

"I don't think so."

Angie lowered the cooktop flame to simmer, grabbed Connie's arm, and hustled her friend around the house. Near Junior's entrance, a window was opened about an inch, just enough to bring in a little fresh air. The house, though, was on a slope, and the window was fairly high.

"I'm still sore from boosting myself up into that tree last night," Angie said. "Your turn. I'll watch and if someone comes, I'll divert their attention."

"Why don't I divert while you go into his room?" Connie suggested. "What if he's in there?"

"He didn't answer the door," Angie pointed out.

"Gee, a homicidal maniac who isn't friendly? Doesn't want to greet people at his door? How amazing is that!"

"If he's inside," Angie said, "simply excuse yourself and jump back out again."

Connie looked ready to tear her hair. "Sure—if I'm not hog-tied and duct-taped."

"Look, once you're inside, open the door to the kitchen for me. If you don't, I'll get help and we'll burst in like the cavalry. You're wasting time. Now, go! No—wait!"

A member of the crew walked by, smiling and waving at the two women. They smiled back.

As soon as he was gone, Connie turned, slid the window open wide and scrambled up onto it. Her feet kept slipping against the outer wall, so Angie positioned her shoulder under Connie's butt and lifted.

Connie toppled in head-first.

"You okay?" Angie called, trying to look non-chalant—as if she was nonchalantly talking to herself—in case anyone else passed by.

"Uh . . . I think so," came a muffled reply.

As Connie pushed the window back to where it was, Angie ran through the house. Connie had just unlocked the kitchen door when she reached it.

The simplicity of what had once been the maid's quarters was a marked contrast to every-thing else in the house—a pine bed, bureau, and desk, a colorful comforter on the bed, and travel posters for decoration.

Angie pointed toward herself and the closet, then at Connie and the bureau. Connie nodded.

In no time, Angie found the Little Drummer Boy in the back of the closet under some old blankets.

"Got it!" she cried.

"It's lovely," Connie said. "Look at the work-manship, the delicacy of the paint, how lifelike the eyes are, the pensive but loving expression on his face. I have nothing this fine in my shop." Connie ran Everyone's Fancy, a small gift shop in the West Portal district of San Francisco. "How could Brit-tany not have loved it?"

At that moment, the sound of a key entering the outside lock was like a sonic boom. They stared at each other, then broke for the kitchen.

But as Angie swung the connecting door shut, she remembered that she'd left the closet door open.

Digger was sitting outside the St. Helena police station trying to come up with a reason to question the chief about Fred Demitasse's demise that wouldn't get him tossed out, when he saw someone familiar getting out of an old Ford.

He remembered—Angie's cop. She had his picture on the bureau in her bedroom. What was he doing here?

Digger waited. Over an hour passed before the cop came back out. Obviously, he got more than the runaround from the authorities.

Digger introduced himself. "I know cops don't like to share evidence with the press, but I know a lot about this case. I've been studying it for years and came up here for the reunion show. I thought the show might yield some new evidence. I never imagined things would get this out of hand."

Paavo headed steadfastly toward his car.

"Angie's in the middle of it," Digger said. "Don't you want her out of there? Don't you want to get whoever is behind these murders?"

Paavo stopped and eyed him harshly. "It's not your concern."

"Look," he was almost pleading. "Tell me what you know. I'll put it together with my information—which I'll give you—and together we might have something."

"Forget it," Paavo reached his car.

"What about Demitasse being involved in blackmail?" Digger asked. "Did Angie talk to you about that?" He gave a quick rundown of Fred-as-blackmailer.

Paavo stopped and listened. "It could be." Paavo studied Digger closely, and then decided to give him a new piece of information. He told Digger about an e-mail in which Fred said Brittany's death wasn't kosher, most likely meaning she died from a broken neck.

Digger frowned. "Everybody knows her neck was broken in the fall. That's what killed her. Why would he put it in an e-mail? It was hardly news. Why bother?"

Paavo stared at Digger, chagrined. He'd been so wrapped up in the Birds of Prey case, he hadn't thought about this case clearly enough to ask himself those very questions. "You're right," he admitted. "Everyone would know it . . . if that was the case. And Fred's own death . . ." He stopped.

"What are you thinking?" Digger asked.

"Can you get some movie-business information right away?"

Digger stepped back from the intensity of the cop's gaze. "I can sure try."

As Angie cooked, the spicy aromas of the food drove away uneasy thoughts of killers and music box thieves and filled her mind with memories of past Christmases, of the days when she was a child and the whole family would gather at her parents' home.

Her mother would cook a turkey or lamb or a ham, but the most loved part of the meal was a huge platter of homemade ravioli. Angie and her sisters helped Serefina make it Christmas morning. When she was very young, Angie resented the time spent away from her new toys. As she grew older though, she came to appreciate those hours in which the six women worked in the kitchen together.

She tested the parsnips in the soup. Finally, they were soft.

The first one to stop participating was Bianca. As her children grew older, and her husband's parents wanted their "share" of time, she began to develop her own Christmas morning rituals for her children to remember.

Caterina and Maria soon followed suit. Last year, Frannie gave birth to her first child. Although she was there to help Serefina, she spent most of her time caring for Seth, Jr., who was a colicky, fussy child.

Angie plugged in the hand blender—the appliance Chef Emeril called a "boat motor" on his TV show—put it in the soup pot and turned it on to cream the parsnips and mushrooms.

By next Christmas or the one after, the ravioli would be made only by Angie and her mother. Once she and Paavo were married, she wondered how long she'd continue to help, and what traditions the two of them would develop. Paavo's stepfather, Aulis Kokkonen, couldn't be left alone on the holidays.

Angie saw it as a cycle. The gathering around the Christmas table would grow larger each year until the time came when her parents grew too old and frail to handle the get-together any longer.

Then it would be time for her sisters to take over, perhaps Bianca as the oldest, or herself, as the gourmet cook.

Whoever did it, she knew that, for her, it would never have the magic of her childhood years when her aunts and uncles and friends of the family would all come together. Her father would take an old accordion out of the closet, one that once belonged to his father in the old country. He knew how to play exactly one Calabrian tune on it, a tarantella that his father had taught him when he was a boy. No one ever tired of hearing it. The older women would sing, and the young ones would dance to Salvatore's music.

Angie prayed that in the future, her own children—hers and Paavo's—in these much more serious times would come to know Christmas as a time of joy and laughter, and that she and Paavo could provide them with strong, happy memories just as her parents had given her.

The parsnips were creamier than she'd ever seen them; the mushrooms all but disintegrated. Enough daydreaming. She needed to concentrate. If the meal was a disaster, she didn't want the fault to be hers.

The coroner's office was closed when Paavo returned. It took him a while to track Ellsberg down and explain what he needed and why. As much as Ellsberg enjoyed Paavo's earlier visit, he didn't sound happy about returning to the office again that day.

"I don't need an autopsy," Paavo said into the

phone. "Just an X ray. A simple X ray will tell us if
we're on the right track."

"I guess it won't bother the mayor's office too
much if I do that," Ellsberg responded with a
weary sigh. "After all, the guy is on ice. We should
do something with him since we're spending all
this energy just keeping him here. I'll be there
soon."

Over forty-five minutes passed before Ellsberg
and his assistant arrived. Paavo watched them set
up Demitasse's body for the X ray. He got himself
a cup of coffee while the film was being developed. Seven o'clock had come and gone. He only
hoped Angie hadn't started dinner—or, if she
had, kept her murderer theory to herself.

A half hour later, Ellsberg found him. "Want to
come see the results with me?" he asked, waving
the large paper envelope that contained the film.

"Absolutely."

Ellsberg flipped the switch to backlight the X-
ray holder and placed the film over it. He studied
the lower head, neck, and upper back area of the
deceased a long while. Paavo studied it as well.
He thought he knew the result, but waited for the
professional opinion. "The tear is right here," he
said, indicating an area above the first vertebrae.

"Is it possible," Paavo asked, careful not to edge
too close to the medical man's territory, "that
Demitasse was dead before he was pushed into
the vat?"

Ellsberg stroked his chin. "Judging from the
trauma to the neck and vertebrae, I'd say beyond
a doubt—to put it in layman's terms—this man's

neck was snapped. And that was the cause of his death."

Not kosher, Paavo thought, then quickly gave his full attention back to Ellsberg.

"This definitely calls for an autopsy, at which time I could look at the bruising, the contusions, and try to figure out exactly what happened, and when. This, however, is a definite indicator of foul play."

Paavo thought about this a moment. Demitasse wrote to Tarleton that *his* goose, Brittany, was not kosher. That meant Demitasse knew her neck had been broken as well, but not in the fall. It was broken some other way. And Demitasse witnessed it.

"Thank you, doctor," he said. "One more thing. Can we take a look at Brittany's autopsy files again? I'd like you to look at any descriptions or photographs in them of her neck injuries."

Chapter 34

Seven o'clock arrived: dinnertime. The actors and Waterfields impatiently waited in the living room. Although Paavo still hadn't returned, Angie decided she couldn't delay any longer. It was time to put her ideas into play.

She left the dining room and began to shut lights through the house and outdoors. Last of all, she shut the lights in the foyer, leaving the guests in darkness anticipating her display.

After a moment's dramatic pause, she flung open the dining room doors, revealing a magical scene. A white-and-silver Christmas tree sparkled in front of the windows. The dining room table had been extended to nearly twelve feet. It was ablaze in candlelight. The flickering lights dancing off cut crystal wine and water goblets and white and gold Wedgwood dishes cast a red aura over the food—a maple-glazed goose surrounded by elegant gourmet side dishes, appetizers, soup, and salads.

"Beautiful!" "Mouth-watering!" "Better than

Spago's." The compliments went on and on, to Angie's delight.

"*Bellissima!* My daughter cooked all this," Serefina proudly announced as each person entered. Nametags directed them where to sit. Twelve were at the table, Sterling at the head, and Junior opposite. His presence was a surprise to everyone. Angie had talked to her mother about getting him to attend the dinner, and Serefina had spoken to Sterling. Whatever she'd said had worked.

When Paavo arrived, he would be the thirteenth guest. The symbolism wasn't lost on Angie.

Connie entered the room wearing a central casting maid's outfit of a black dress and frilly white apron. She served Mondavi Fumé Blanc as an aperitif. Fortunately, Waterfield didn't make a dry white, so Angie didn't have to worry about hurt feelings or outraged palates.

Minnie arrived, but stayed in the kitchen dressed in Fred Demitasse's chef's outfit. They had agreed she would wait quietly, and only appear if needed.

Individual bowls of mushroom-parsnip soup, plates of romaine-persimmon salad, and appetizers of small caviar-topped sweet-potato pancakes and pear-fontina strudel were at each place setting.

"Turkey!" Bart said as he settled in between Serefina and Camille. "My favorite!" He reached for his wine.

"It's goose," Angie corrected.

"Goose?" Bart's hand stilled, his face scrunched as if trying to remember something.

Others did remember, however. The room fell silent.

"It's traditional at Christmas," Tarleton intoned with a sly smile. "We were gathered this way over a Christmas goose eleven years ago."

"Damn it, Em!" Gwen shouted. "Why the hell are you doing this? All this old Brittany shit. What are you trying to prove?"

"Nothing, dear." Tarleton's smirk grew. "Nothing at all. Let's eat."

Angie waited for everyone to dig in. Waited for the words of praise that usually accompanied meals she'd worked hard on.

The diners glanced at each other, at the food, at Tarleton. They sipped wine. Serefina began to eat, then Camille. Slowly, the others picked up spoons and forks. They looked like death-row inmates facing their last meal.

Angie should have realized the shock of a Christmas dinner featuring a goose would deaden appetites. It was all part of Tarleton's scheme to flush out the killer, a scheme that she'd gone along with wholeheartedly. Still, as she watched everyone but Serefina pick at the food, she was ready to cry. Or murder someone herself.

Even Paavo apparently found it more important to talk to the coroner or whoever than to enjoy her cooking while it was hot and at its best. He'd been right when he suggested she go home immediately. These people didn't deserve the work she'd done. They didn't deserve the beauty around them.

They didn't deserve Christmas!

She began to carve the goose. The only way to save this meal from becoming a complete fiasco and waste of time was to get the killer to confess. To do that, she needed the wine to flow freely.

At Angie's signal, Connie entered the dining room with bottles of what appeared to be Waterfield Cabernet Sauvignon. Earlier, Angie had dumped out the contents and refilled the bottles with Freemark Abbey Cabernet—a fabulous wine.

She wondered how many of the diners had the same reaction as she did when looking at the label: the image of Fred Demitasse in the wine barrel.

Connie poured a little into Sterling's wineglass and watched his face light up with pleasure at the taste. "A particularly fine year," he said, reading the date on the bottle. "My, I'm surpr—er, yes! A very fine year!"

Serefina vehemently shook her head when Connie tried to pour her some. "Try it," Angie urged, catching her mother's eye. At Serefina's pleased reaction, the others also agreed to the wine.

Silver tasted it and lifted his eyebrows at Angie. He knew what she'd done.

Still, even though they drank lots of wine, no one spoke. They passed the platters and bowls of food but took only small portions, as if quietly determined to get through the meal as quickly as possible. This wasn't going the way Angie had expected.

After reviewing Brittany's files, Paavo asked to borrow a telephone. He needed one more bit of information, and he didn't trust his cell phone to hold the call while he waited for the information he needed.

He checked his watch. He needed to get back to Eagle Crest, but some places, like U.S. Government offices after hours, you knew even before dialing you'd be on hold a long, long time.

* * *

When Angie saw Rhonda remove the napkin from her lap as if ready to excuse herself, she knew she couldn't wait any longer. She stood and everyone's attention turned her way.

"There have been troubles in this house," she said. "Accidents. Deaths. It's time for them to stop."

"Here, here!" Sterling shouted.

The others scowled at him.

Angie continued. "When Brittany Keegan died, the police ruled her death an accident. We believe there is more to the story."

Now, the scowls turned on Angie.

"Her bedroom was locked," Sterling shouted. "I was there. I had to fight to get the door to open. The police were right in their conclusion."

He rose to his feet, grabbed the platter with the goose and waved the carving knife. "Who wants another slice? This is a wonderful meal, Angie. We really don't want to talk about ugly things now. Why don't you sit back down? We're enjoying your dinner very much." He smiled, but she didn't sit.

"You said the door to Brittany's room was locked." She directed her words at Sterling. "Are you certain it was due to the slide bolt? You aren't! You do know, however, that Junior was troubled, and that he was infatuated with Brittany—"

"That's none of your business!" Junior shouted.

No one else spoke; a suffocating silence gripped the room.

Sterling began carving the goose even though no one had asked for seconds. "Sit down, Angie," he said, his teeth clenched. His slices were torn and mangled.

"Is there a reason to bring this up again?" Bart demanded.

"Haven't we been over it enough?" Kyle shouted.

"This might be new and interesting to you, Angie dear," Gwen added, "but frankly, it bores me. You really should stick to cooking."

Angie ignored them, all her attention on Junior. "Years ago, Junior was charged with stalking a young woman. You worried about him, didn't you, Sterling? You worried that he broke into Brittany's room and that she fell trying to get away from him. You pretended to struggle to break into her room so everyone would think the slide bolt was holding the door shut."

Junior jumped to his feet as well. "That stalking charge was a lie! I just asked her out a few times!" He glared at Sterling. "Is this why you insisted I attend this dinner? So you could accuse me?"

"I never . . ." Sterling's eyes were watery. He continued to hack at the goose.

"I'm out of here!" Junior yelled.

"Wait!" Angie cried. She glanced toward the doorway. Still no Paavo. "I have proof. Your father and your brother can't hide your guilt any longer."

"Proof?" Junior's stunned gaze searched Angie's, then lingered on Sterling and Silver. "You believe her?" he asked. The other diners watched with rapt curiosity. "You think I hurt Brittany? Why would I? She was the most beautiful person I'd ever met. She . . . she had no interest in me, but I didn't kill her. Don't you think I'm used to women not caring if I live or die? Not wanting to date me, or even have a conversation." Sad eyes gazed at Angie. "I once said I thought you'd run away, too. When you didn't, I thought you were special. I should have known. This is even worse."

The others stared at Junior as if seeing him for the first time.

"There's been sabotage on this set," Angie said. "Wires crossed, props destroyed, fire, a bloody doll left on Gwen's bed—"

"What?" Gwen shrieked.

"—And the Little Drummer Boy stolen. Everyone knows you didn't want the show here again. The doll was to scare Gwen away, to cause her to walk out, which would have destroyed the show—"

"What bloody doll?" Gwen asked. "I never saw—"

"Silver took it away," Angie replied. "He did it to protect his brother."

"I don't know what you're talking about." Junior pounded the table. His fist hit his soup spoon, splattering creamed mushrooms and parsnips over the table. The others recoiled to avoid the airborne side dish. "I never did anything like that!" He glowered at his brother. "You felt you had to protect me? You? I thought you, at least, had confidence in me. I know Dad has none. He thinks I'm crazier than a loon."

"I never said that!" Sterling cried. He slammed down the carving knife. Glasses, dishes, and flatware shook and rattled. The goose was hash. Angie gaped at it.

"You didn't have to." Junior stared at his father with dismay. "You, me, and Silver all know the slide lock to Brittany's door was weak, the wood bad. It wouldn't have taken any effort to break it open. Your acting job at trying to show that you tore it from the wall was better than anything seen on *Eagle Crest*. I thought you did it to protect yourself . . . or Silver."

"Me?" Silver cried. "You *are* crazy."

Sterling held up his hands. "Both of you, stop. This is going too far. Angie, I don't know why you're bringing this up. Why are you making these accusations? It's time for you to apologize."

Under Angie's chair was a paper bag. From it, she lifted the Little Drummer Boy music box and placed it on the table. Junior started, then sank back into his chair. "This once belonged to Brittany," she said. "That's why it was so important to Emery to find it. It was a reminder to him of Brittany, as was everything that he did—from the decorations he used, to his rewrite of the script, to tonight's meal."

"Why?" Gwen swiveled toward Tarleton. "I never understood why Brittany meant so much to you when she was alive, and especially now that she's dead. It's been years, and we can all see Mariah is far more devoted to you than Brittany ever was."

"It's nothing," Tarleton said, his voice choked.

"Nothing?" Mariah cried. "Gwen is right. She's all you think about. She's dead, Em. I'm not . . . not that I seem to matter to you."

Tarleton's gaze traveled from Mariah to Angie and settled there. Finally, he shut his eyes a moment, and when he opened them again, he studied his fellow diners, one by one. "Brittany," he said quietly, "was my daughter."

The very room seemed to gasp. Those four words opened a floodgate within Tarleton. He explained why he'd kept the news secret, and what torment that secret had been to him. He had suspected Brittany's death was more than an accident. Fred Demitasse's e-mails to him affirmed it. He had to do something. "I wanted to know who killed my daughter," Tarleton said, teary eyed. "But as a result of my questions, my friend died as well. I believe he was murdered."

"This music box is the key," Angie said. "I believe the person who killed her is the one who couldn't bear to look at it, to have it remind him, day after day, of Brittany and the way he loved her. I believe Fred saw him take it, and that's why he, too, was killed. I found it in your room, Junior. This is my proof."

Digger stayed close by the hotel's fax machine waiting for the information he needed. It had cost the newspaper a pretty penny to order it, and to request it quickly as possible, but if it would result in the story he thought it would, it'd be worth every cent. The time crawled by; he needed to meet Paavo, to get back to Eagle Crest.

Finally, the desk clerk waved him over.

He grabbed the first page to spit out of the machine and began reading. It wasn't what he'd expected at all. He had to be patient, he told himself, not go too fast, and make sure he had all his facts in order before acting.

"Damn you!" Tarleton lunged for Junior, knocking over the platter of acorn squash rings. The rings rolled and raced across the tabletop, and the painstakingly added apple stuffing spurted out and left a trail a snail could envy.

"I didn't do anything to her!" Junior pushed Tarleton back. Tarleton's arm smashed onto Junior's plate, knocked over his wine and water glasses, and caused the bowl of spinach and tasso ham to crash to the floor. "I gave her the music box. My mother loved it. I thought Brittany would as well. Instead, she laughed at it and gave it to the set designer. When I got my chance, I took it back. That's all! I had no reason to kill her! I liked her!"

"You had a reason," Angie said, trying to be philosophic about her ruined spinach dish. "It's here, in my hand. Do you want me to go on, Junior?"

"Yes, damn you!"

The other diners exchanged anxious, puzzled glances at each other, but didn't interfere. Angie and Junior were center stage, with Tarleton held back and ineffectual by Junior's strong arm.

"This is a report from Dr. Philip Chambers in San Francisco. His specialty is obstetrics and gynecology. Brittany was pregnant. Whatever this news caused between the two of you, it was the impetus for murder."

"No!" Tarleton whispered, dropping his arms. His face was ashen.

Angie's heart ached for the man. "She hadn't told you?"

He shut his eyes, shaking his head.

"I never made love with her," Junior cried. "I never made love with *any* woman! I'm not the one who got her pregnant. It was Bart. He was always mooning after her."

"Me?" Bart leaped to his feet.

"You bastard! I knew it! I knew it all along!" Rhonda stood and picked up a glob of corn pudding and smoked oysters and hurled it across the table. It splattered on his forehead and oozed down onto his face.

"Stop!" Angie shouted.

"I didn't!" Bart cried, blinded by corn pudding. He used his fingers to scoop it away from his eyes. A piece of oyster remained above his left eyebrow.

"Don't you lie to me," Rhonda screamed. "I was a fool over you years ago, and you dumped me for that little snot. I thought I had you out of my system, but you came back, all charming and repentant, and I believed you. I stupidly *wanted* to believe you! Now I find out I was right back then. Damn you!" She hurled more corn pudding. This time he ducked, and it sailed over his head to decorate the Christmas tree behind him.

"All right!" Bart yelled. "I tried with her—I was stupid, okay? I never got anywhere. It wasn't me, Rhonda. It was him." He pointed at Kyle.

"I only met with her to talk about work," Kyle yelled. "To hell with you, you has-been!"

"Everyone!" Angie cried. "Please!"

"Has-been?" Bart turned ruby red. "Nobody talks about their roles at two in the morning. They *roll*, if you get what I mean, loverboy."

"I'm happily married," Kyle said. "The only thing that surprises me is that you could knock her up, old man."

"Stop right there!" Bart grabbed a goose leg and shook it like a weapon toward Kyle. "Stop, or you'll be as dead as this goddamn goose." He threw the leg back onto the meat platter. It bounced off the edge and landed in the relish tray, sending pepperoncini and kalamata olives bounding into the air as the tray skittered across the tablecloth, caroming into the plate with cranberry sauce. The cranberry shot off the plate and landed on Gwen's lap.

She screamed, grasped at the sauce and flung it right back at Bart. "You bastard!"

"Maybe you're the one," he yelled at her. "You wanted Kyle all to yourself. You didn't like Brittany horning in on him."

"I'll show you about horning in!" She picked up the platter of baby back ribs in bourbon gravy.

"No!" Angie shrieked.

Gwen swung the bowl back and then forward. The ribs and gravy flew out like someone tossing slop to hogs. It missed Bart and hit Silver. Drenched with sauce, he picked up a rib and threw it right back at Gwen.

Everyone got into the act. The tension broke as food flew, curses sounded, and accusations rang out. Soup, caviar, and sweet potatoes filled the air, as did the random plate or glass.

The room darkened as the candles went out one by one, some knocked over, others snuffed out by landing food, until only lights from the tree remained.

"Relax, Gwen," Kyle said, trying to hold her back. "Don't listen to them. If you were jealous of her, it's not important. All actresses are jealous."

"You think I'd be jealous of you?" She hit him with a green onion biscuit.

"Bart is right," Serefina shouted. "It was Leona! I never could stand her. On so many shows I wanted to smack her myself. Look, look what she's done to my daughter's dinner! I will slap her!"

"Mamma, stop!" Angie grabbed Serefina's arm, and Sterling took this as his chance to finally put his arms around her.

"Everyone!" Angie screamed. "This is getting us nowhere."

No one listened.

"Sit down!" She yelled again.

They didn't.

What next?

Enter Connie carrying a tray. On it were two huge chocolate soufflés and a pecan pie covered with whipped cream. Her jaw dropped as she watched the celebrity food fight. Gawking at the chaos instead of where she was going, she stepped on a ring of acorn squash. Her foot slid out from under her.

Connie and the tray started to fall forward. The tray teetered ominously. Angie saw the impending disaster and rushed to save the tray, when she was bumped by one of the food warriors and went into her own downward descent.

Angie, Connie, and tray collided. Sticky pie flew up and landed on the remains of the Christmas goose. Gooey soufflés fell to the floor with a thud then a whoosh as all the air went out of them making them flat as pancakes.

Connie sat on the floor, dazed, picking caviar

from her hair and wondering how it got there. Angie sat beside her, rubbing her head. That tray had been hard.

On the table was the Little Drummer Boy music box, now covered with the remnants of her dinner. Her beautiful dinner had been ruined.

The table was a mess.

The diners were a mess.

She was a mess.

Why had she thought accusing Junior in the middle of her wonderful dinner would be a good idea?

Rhonda broke for the door. Bart grabbed her. "I swear to you, I didn't kill Brittany!" he yelled.

"I didn't say you killed her. I said you had an *affair* with her. I know you didn't kill her!"

"How do you know that?" Tarleton asked.

Her head whipped back and forth from Tarleton to Bart.

The room became still, as if everyone sensed that a new, more important drama was about to unfold.

Angie and Connie stood.

Rhonda stared at them like a tiger caught in a cage, her gaze turning harder and more hate-filled by the minute. "I knew something like this would happen if I returned. I didn't want to. For the past five years I've been able to live without having to get dead drunk in order to forget about Eagle Crest and what happened here. Without thinking about Brittany and how she died . . . about Bart, and how I gave him my heart only to watch him trample on it." She drew in a deep breath. "I never wanted to be here again, never wanted to see any of you. I hate you all! I hate what you've made me. Most of all, Bart Farrell, I hate you!"

Tarleton grabbed her arm. "Damn it, Rhonda. How could you kill her?"

"Let go of me!" she screamed, yanking herself free. "I'm leaving. I quit."

She turned to leave the room, and froze.

Paavo was in the lead, Digger following, as the two pulled into the parking area at Eagle Crest. They had reconnoitered at the St. Helena police station. Putting together what both had found, the sergeant on duty was convinced. He had to talk to the chief, who'd already left for home and was probably enjoying a leisurely dinner, to get an arrest warrant signed.

Paavo and Digger knew who the killer was. Now, all they had to do was make sure everything stayed quiet and peaceful at Eagle Crest until the police arrived.

They didn't want to tip anyone off. Paavo hoped everyone would be enjoying the elaborate dinner Angie had worked so hard over, and that accusations of murder would be the last thing on their minds.

The sound of china breaking as they opened the front door was their first indication that something was seriously wrong.

A goose's leg in the foyer was the second.

Rhonda backed up at the sight of Paavo and Digger in the doorway. Everyone knew Paavo was a cop, and their eyes jumped from him to Rhonda.

Bart rose and took Rhonda's arm. "You don't

have to say anything. He has no jurisdiction here. Let's go upstairs."

"No," she pulled her arm free, her eyes on Paavo's. "I can't take it any longer. I've lived with it too many years—if it was living."

"Rhonda, don't!" Bart began.

She raised her hand to silence him.

She stared at him. "I didn't kill her. I wanted to kill this show. I arrived early in San Francisco and drove up here to destroy things, set a fire, freak out Gwen with the bloody doll, but no matter what I did, you wouldn't stop!" She took a deep breath. "No one killed Brittany. I know, because I was there."

Tarleton held himself rigid. "Go on," he whispered.

"I had a fight with her," she began, "but it wasn't about love. I . . . I felt I had already lost that fight. It was about jealousy—professional jealousy. She wanted me written out of the series, wanted Natalie killed off. She swore she had the power to do it. Judging how close she was to Em, I believed her. Her character would become Cliff's wife—the second-most powerful person on the show. That was what we fought about. She ran into the room and locked the door, and I threw myself against it. I was shocked when it flew open, and so was she. She stumbled backwards, away from me, and her foot caught on the throw rug. The window was open, and she fell."

Rhonda was shaking, her expression wild. "I didn't want to hurt her. I just wanted to stop her from going to Tarleton with those ideas. I was afraid. Afraid for my job, my career, my future.

When she fell, that ended all of them. I couldn't
bear the show after that. I honored my commit-
ment to the last year in a haze of alcohol, then
quit." She gazed down at Bart. "I never touched
her."

"I believe you," he whispered, taking her hand.

"You do?" She stared, her eyes filled with surprise.

"Of course. I know you. You could never hurt
anyone. These past years, alone and without
work, I've had time to think about you and all we
had together—and all I'd stupidly thrown away. I
love you, Rhonda. I always have."

Tears came to her eyes as she stared at him.
"Thank you," she whispered, then drew in her
breath and faced the others. "I was in pain that
night—my shoulder was burning—and in the
early-morning hours, I went down to the kitchen
for ice. Fred saw me. I told him I suffered from
bursitis. He didn't react, and I thought he believed
me. I never heard any more from him until last
week after the rehearsal. After he spoke, I immediately recognized who he really was.

"I followed him into the kitchen, and when we
were alone, I asked him what he meant. He said
we should go down to the wine cellar to talk pri-
vately. He wanted money to keep quiet. I told him
no, but he grabbed my arms and was pushing and
pulling, shaking me, demanding money. He was
small, but incredibly strong. I pulled my arms
free, and suddenly, he fell over, flat on his back.
There was a loud thunk as his head hit. His eyes
were shut. I ran. It can't be happening again, I
thought. It can't." Her gaze met each person, fi-

nally resting on Paavo. "That was the last time I saw him. I never touched him, and I didn't lift him into a wine barrel."

Rhonda swayed. Bart caught her and helped her into her chair. She gripped his hand like a lifeline.

Angie's gaze went to the Little Drummer Boy and her certainty of Junior's guilt fizzled. She didn't know what to think.

"Aren't you going to arrest her?" Gwen screamed. "You don't believe her do you? She's an actress! It's all lies!"

Paavo and Digger caught each other's eyes. And in his hesitancy, it was obvious that Rhonda was not the one he suspected. "Brittany survived the fall with a few broken bones. It isn't what killed her."

Suddenly, the Christmas tree lights went out, plunging them into complete darkness.

Chairs, food, the Christmas tree crashed. Bodies flew about, shoved hard against walls and to the floor. Panicked, everyone pushed and fought.

Paavo heard Angie's cry among the others, first clear, then muffled. He tried to reach her when Gwen fell against him.

Climbing over furniture, Silver reached the light switch. Slowly, everyone picked themselves up and looked at the chaos around them. One by one, they studied each other.

Two people were missing.

Chapter 35

In the darkness, shortly after the tree lights went out, Angie felt a strong arm circle her waist, capturing her arms in a viselike grip. A hand covered her mouth. She fought and struggled and tried to cry out, but her captor was too strong for her.

She was lifted off the ground, the wedgies falling from her feet. As easily as if she were a doll, she was carried out of the family room and up the stairs.

Even as Paavo hurried out the opened front door into the dark night, something told him that wasn't the way the killer would go. It was too obvious. While others ran forward, searching the front driveway, Paavo turned back inside.

In the foyer, he stopped in his tracks.

Minnie stood before him dressed up as a chef and holding a Santa Claus mask and hat. He didn't need to be told that had been Angie's idea.

"I was in the kitchen," Minnie said. "What happened?"

He had no time for explanations. He rushed out to the courtyard.

He tossed her into Brittany's bedroom. She hit the wall and landed on the floor, dazed. He slammed the door shut, then slid the bureau in front of it.

"Why are we here?" Angie asked. "Why don't you run? You'll be caught."

"What am I supposed to do? Try to drive to the border? Sure, that'll work." He gave a snort. "I've got a better way to escape. You'll help me."

"Why did you do it?" she asked. "Why kill Brittany and Demitasse?"

"The cop had it right about Demitasse. He blackmailed me for years. When I tried to make him stop, he went nuts. Contacted Tarleton about Brittany, and Tarleton hired him.

"I told Fred he'd won, that I'd give him his blood money, but first, we had to get Tarleton off our backs. The only way to stop him was to throw the blame on Rhonda. We came up with a plan to do that. Fred thought he was just supposed to scare Rhonda into a breakdown. To me, it was a way to get rid of them both."

"That doesn't explain Brittany," Angie said. "Why kill her?"

"Because she went and got herself pregnant! She expected me to leave my wife and marry her. When I said no, she threatened to go to the press. Do you know what that would have done to me? To my career? Every bit of popularity I had was built on my nice guy image. What would the public say if they heard Adrian Roxbury was no good? I'd be finished.

"I was in the courtyard and saw her fall. That was my chance. A twist of the neck, and it was over."

Tarleton came in the front door, frantic and then frightened as he gawked at Connie, now standing beside the trembling Minnie. "Where's the cop? And Angie?"

"I don't know, but Paavo went that way." She pointed at the courtyard.

Digger ran in right behind Tarleton, but screeched to a halt in front of the two women.

"They're taking too long." Kyle O'Rourke grabbed Angie by the arm and lifted her to her feet with one hand. With the other he slid open the window.

"What are you doing?" she screamed, trying to get away from the madman. Her engagement ring flashed as she tried to break away from him and desperation filled her. "Let me go, please!"

"This will get their attention."

He pushed her out the window.

Angie's scream rose from high above.

Paavo's blood froze. He was in the courtyard heading for the gate.

He looked up.

O'Rourke stood at Angie's window. She was more than halfway out. Her legs were inside, but her arms flailed. It looked like he was holding her by gripping the top she wore at the neckline and waist. If he let go, she'd tumble to the ground.

Her face was white with fear. As he watched,

she was able to reach back with one hand and grip
the window frame. She tried to pull herself back,
but O'Rourke's strength was too great.

"*Madonna mia.*"

Others had run outside. Among them, Paavo
heard Serefina's whispered prayer. He didn't turn
her way; he didn't take his eyes off Angie.

Someone flipped switches and one by one inside and outside lights came on, including the
Christmas lights strung over the house and courtyard. The courtyard sparkled, creating a fairyland
setting despite the life-and-death struggle going
on high above it.

"Give it up, O'Rourke," Paavo said. He moved
closer to the house, closer to Angie, three stories
above him. Fear and nearly uncontrollable anger
clutched his heart. "We can bargain, but not if you
hurt her."

Against the red and yellow twinkling lights,
Kyle O'Rourke's usually handsome face appeared
shadowed and contorted. He looked evil.

"You think I'm a fool?" O'Rourke shouted. "It's
all over for me. And it's all her fault. Nosy bitch
ruined everything." He pushed Angie farther out
the window, so far she lost her grip of the frame.
She screamed, as did everyone below.

"Stop!" Paavo shouted. "What do you want? A
lawyer? We'll get you what you need. You've got
lots of outs right now. You know it. Think about
some of the movies you've been in. It's not cut and
dry. It never is. We can talk as long as you don't
take this any further."

O'Rourke laughed as he watched Bart and

Tarleton come out of the house with a blanket. "You jerks think you'll catch her?" he ranted. "Didn't you understand what the cop said? I was in the Special Forces. I know how to kill with my bare hands. Do you really think I'd toss her without making sure she's dead first?"

Silver began to climb up the almond tree to the left of Angie's window. As he crawled out onto a long limb, it began to dip and lower. He went out farther, until he was lowered to a spot beneath Angie.

He sat on the bounding branch, holding himself in place with his legs.

"Let's negotiate, O'Rourke," Paavo said. "You want to get out alive, I want Angie. We can deal."

"I know what I want. A private plane, fully fueled, and a pilot—the one I flew here in. Gwen knows him. To get me from here, to the plane, I want a helicopter."

"Sure," Paavo said. "Anything you want. To arrange it, though, we'll need the help of the local police—"

"No cops!" O'Rourke yelled.

"Okay. We'll deal directly with the airport," Paavo said.

Sterling appeared at the door, with him the police. Brittany's autopsy photos, Kyle O'Rourke's Special Forces training, and Digger's paperwork that placed O'Rourke at nearly every job Fred Demitasse held over the past eleven years had apparently been enough to convince the police chief to issue a warrant for the actor's arrest . . . a few minutes too late.

Paavo gave an almost imperceptible shake of his head. He didn't want O'Rourke to see the police for fear of how he might react.

At the same time, Digger peered over the courtyard wall, then motioned to someone at the far side of the house.

"We'll get you a private plane," Paavo continued, his voice calming. "Gwen will help and we'll have one ready for you. How big a plane do you want?"

"A Gulfstream."

Just then, Digger's plan became clear. The crew's truck with a crane and cherry picker basket on the end came into sight. The crane was extended higher than the roof of the house.

"How big?" Paavo shouted, needing to keep Kyle's attention on the possibility of escape.

When the crane's tip was directly over Angie's window, the cherry picker began to lower. Connie was in it, while Minnie sat on the rim, her legs dangling in the air. Straps bound her chest and hips.

"Big enough to get me to Mexico—deep into Mexico," he said. "I'm keeping her with me until I know you aren't lying."

"I wouldn't lie about this," Paavo said, stalling. "We're going to need time. Pull her inside so we'll know you're serious about negotiating."

Angie was able to grab the window frame once again.

Paavo nodded to Digger.

Digger gave the signal to Minnie. She didn't move. He gave it again. Nothing. Then Connie pushed her.

Wearing the white chef's gown and hat, Minnie fell from the basket. Everyone below cried out.

Held by the straps, she dropped almost to Angie's window and looked like she was flying— a flying, angelic chef.

Kyle shrieked at the sight, his body straightening as he did so. "No!" he shouted.

A shot rang out, and Kyle fell back into the room. Paavo glanced quickly behind him. The shot came from high on the hillside, the area where Junior spent his days watching, alone and lonely. Paavo turned back, his heart in his throat, to Angie, aching to help her, and not sure how.

She had hold of the window frame and was struggling to pull herself back into the room. He knew the police would be breaking into the bedroom any moment. They'd help her.

"Hold on," he shouted.

"I can do it," she cried.

Digger began to lower the crane, while Connie reached over and helped Minnie get hold of the end of the basket so together they could lift her back in.

Angie's second hand gripped the ledge. She was about to hoist herself inside when Kyle stood filling the window.

"No!" she cried as he shoved her hard. She lost her grip and fell.

Everyone screamed.

Silver lunged, arms outstretched. As he took the full brunt of her weight, she nearly yanked him off the tree. The branch bent even lower with the two of them.

She dropped low enough that Paavo grabbed

her legs. She let go of Silver to wrap her arms around Paavo's neck, wanting to never let go again.

Without her weight, the tree limb sprang upward. Silver was jettisoned from the tree into the open arms and full, well-cushioned breasts of Gwen Hagen.

Gwen tumbled onto a thick bed of plastic snow, Silver sprawled on top of her.

She gazed up into his handsome face. "I think I've just found the leading man for my next action flick."

Paavo slowly and carefully lowered Angie to the ground. Other than strained and sore muscles—and being petrified with fright—she seemed unhurt.

Holding each other tight, the two of them peered up at the window she'd fallen from. Kyle was draped over the sill, head and arms dangling, bleeding and unconscious. The police were just then pulling him back into the room.

Chapter 36

Three days later, Angie stood on the veranda at Eagle Crest gazing out at the horizon. The phony snow had been picked up, revealing spring flowers and a lush, green lawn.

The *Eagle Crest* special had no chance of surviving Kyle's arrest for two murders. Immediately upon hearing the news, the producer pulled the plug on it. The crew packed up and went home. Tarleton and Mariah soon followed. With the guilt of the past eleven years lifted, Tarleton was like a new man.

Gwen had convinced the producers of her action movie to let Silver try out for the leading man role. He flew in her private plane to Hollywood.

Rhonda gave her story to the police, Bart at her side the entire time. She was finally free to accept his love, and give love in return. Flying commercial to save money, they departed for Southern California together.

Minnie Petite headed for New York to do the talk show circuit to take advantage of her fifteen minutes of fame as Demitasse's girlfriend. She was slated for an appearance on *Larry King Live*.

As soon as the police allowed, Serefina shouted "Arrivederci," kissed everyone on both cheeks, and fled home to Salvatore.

Sterling openly puzzled about what to do with his life. Eagle Crest would never again have the glory of its soap opera days. He considered selling it and moving permanently to Los Angeles. At least there he could keep an eye on Silver.

Paavo had stayed with Angie through the police questioning and to help security keep newshounds and paparazzi far from Eagle Crest. He ended up working side by side with Officer Baker and others in the SHPD to make sure their case was airtight. Finally, everything had quieted down and he and Angie could move on with their lives.

Now, he stepped up behind her and put his arms around her waist. "Are you glad Christmas is over?"

She leaned back against him, enjoying his strength, his love. "Just one more night," she replied mysteriously.

"Do you miss the film crew and cast?" he asked. "I know you hoped for a career—"

"Stop. Don't even talk about it. I never want to deal with people like that again. My father meant well . . ." She hesitated, not sure how much she had to explain. She turned and caught Paavo's eye. He understood. Smiling, she gazed back at the front drive, the budding vineyards, and in the distance, the rolling hills that separated the Napa and Sonoma valleys. "He meant well, but he was completely mistaken. Someday, he'll come to understand that."

"He worries about you," Paavo said, holding her close. "I don't blame him for that. But if he ever parades some young, rich, movie-star handsome guy in front of you again—"

"I'll ignore him completely," Angie said. "I have only one thing on my mind—"

"So do I." He turned her around, ready for a kiss.

"Our engagement party."

He gawked. "You're kidding, right?"

She looked shocked. "Of course not! It's going to be the best, biggest, most beautiful engagement party the city has ever known."

He felt woozy. "Didn't you say that about our wedding?"

"That, too." She glanced at her watch. "I'd better see to dinner. It's almost time."

She dashed off to the kitchen.

All in all, he'd rather elope.

Since Angie had one more goose to cook, she decided to prepare an elegant dinner. For her, Paavo, and Digger—who had remained these few days to cover the story and its aftermath, which even resulted in a byline in the *Los Angeles Times*—it was a going-away dinner. For Junior, Sterling, and Camille—who hadn't figured out what to do next with her life—she hoped it might be a new beginning.

The meal was considerably simpler than the last, rolled goose breast with juniper berry rub and a caraway and apple stuffing, spinach au gratin with potatoes, braised peas and carrots with pearl onions, and pecan-topped pumpkin cheesecake.

Sterling sat at the head of the table, Junior at the opposite end, Camille and Digger on one side, Angie and Paavo on the other. Junior had shaved his beard, cut his hair, and looked almost handsome.

Sterling poured Waterfield wine for everyone— the real thing, since Angie unfortunately had forgotten to refill the bottles—and then Paavo proposed a toast to Junior for taking the action that ended Kyle's stand.

"We can't drink to that," Junior said. "I know Angie has tried to convince me that shooting Kyle was the right thing. I purposefully aimed so as not to kill him. As a result, he was able to go after Angie again, despite his shoulder wound." He shook his head. "I'm sorry, Angie. I still have nightmares about it."

"Me, too," Angie and Paavo said in unison.

Camille faced Junior. "I think that was one of the most heroic acts I've ever seen. It takes strength and courage to act in a crisis. It's the sort of thing I hope to write a serious screenplay about someday."

He blushed to the roots of his hairline. "I couldn't let him hurt Angie."

Camille nodded. "That's exactly the attitude I'm talking about."

"Well," Sterling said to Camille, "If you'd like a quiet place to stay while you work on that screenplay, there's plenty of room here. I'd love to have you remain as our guest."

Junior stared at his father. "You aren't selling?"

"Frankly, I like it here," Sterling replied. "What do you say, Camille?"

She looked stunned, then gazed from Sterling to his son. "I'd like that," she said softly. "Thank you . . . both."

"To Junior," Paavo said again, raising his glass.

They all took a sip of wine this time.

Junior frowned at the wine. "If we're staying at Eagle Crest," he said to Sterling, his chin raised, "I'd like to take some classes on winemaking. What do you think?"

Now it was Sterling's turn to be astonished. "I think . . . that deserves an even bigger toast!" he cried.

"But not now," Angie shuddered and pushed her glass to the side. She reached for her water as the others chuckled.

After dinner, they gathered in the family room. All the Christmas decorations were gone except for the Little Drummer Boy, which was on a shelf beside pictures of the Waterfield family.

Angie was glad Sterling had chosen to keep him in sight. Someday the bad memories would pass, and only the happy ones would remain.

While Junior got the fire going in the big rock fireplace—a real one this time—Angie put on a CD of Christmas carols. "I was here to cook a Christmas feast, wasn't I?" she said by way of explanation. She served hot eggnog laced with brandy.

Sterling lifted it in a toast. "Thank you, Angie, for staying here these extra days and helping to make this house a happy one again."

"Joy to the cook!" Digger shouted. "And to her friend, Connie, who I wish was still here."

They laughed, cheered, and toasted Angie.

As they sipped the egg nog, jingle bells were heard in the foyer, followed by a "Ho, ho, ho."

"It sounds like Santa Claus!" Angie's eyes were bright.

"Is this a joke?" Digger asked. "*Santa Claus?*"

Paavo gave Angie a sidelong glance. She shrugged and tried to look innocent. Junior helped Camille up from the sofa.

"Let's go see," Sterling cried.

Santa stood in the living room, puffing on a pipe, smoke circling his head . . . surprisingly like a wreath, Angie thought. "Ah, here are all the good little, or should I say, *big* boys and girls. Santa doesn't usually appear this time of year," he said, "but I had a special request, and a special Christmas present for . . ."

He began rummaging around in the big sack he'd been holding on his back. He pulled out a very tiny package. "Ah, this is it. A present for"—he looked them over one by one—"for Paavo."

He waited as Angie and the others pointed to Paavo.

"Angie . . ." Paavo began, the little present in his hand, when Santa bellowed another "Ho, ho, ho," put his finger to the side of his nose and . . . walked out the front door.

Okay, Angie thought, *so he can't do everything perfectly.*

"Open it," she said to Paavo.

Inside the box was a car key. "You didn't," he said.

She grabbed his hand and pulled him to the front door, the others following.

In the driveway stood a shiny new black Corvette. Paavo said, "I can't—"

"It's your Christmas present a few months early," Angie explained.

"It's not Christmas, Angie."

"Sure it is." She extended her arms to take in him, the lovely house, the rich land, and the warm friends, old and new, surrounding them. "Christmas is more than a date on a calendar. It's a time of joy and faith, of love and giving. It's what we have with each other every day of our lives."

He opened his mouth to protest, and she held up her hand, stopping him. "Now, I'm giving. I will not worry myself sick over you driving around in that rattletrap of a car."

"The gift is too much," Paavo said.

"Don't you know it's back luck to say 'No' to Santa Claus?" she asked.

"It is bad luck, Paavo," Digger agreed. "It makes her happy to give it to you. Don't be a grinch, man. You almost lost her. Don't let something like this get between you. It's not worth it. Ask me, I know."

Paavo's gaze jumped from Digger to the car to Angie. It settled there and softened. He drew her close and she tilted her face to his. "Thank you," he said, "for the car, for being you, and for the spirit of Christmas all year long."

Tears of joy filled her eyes. Then he kissed her.

In the family room, the Little Drummer Boy smiled.

From the Kitchen of Angelina Amalfi

 ANGIE'S CHOCOLATE-DIPPED COCONUT SNOWBALLS

This is a pretty and fun Christmas cookie.

⅓ cup butter, softened
²⁄₃ cup packed brown sugar
¼ tsp. baking powder
¼ tsp. baking soda
¼ tsp. salt
1 egg
½ tsp. vanilla
1⅓ cups all-purpose flour
4 oz. sweet baking chocolate, finely grated
½ cup finely shredded coconut
½ cup finely chopped pecans, toasted
12 oz. bittersweet chocolate, chopped
4 tsp. shortening
2½ cups finely shredded coconut, toasted

Preheat oven to 350°. Put softened butter, brown sugar, baking powder, baking soda, and salt in a bowl and beat to combine. Add egg and vanilla; beat to combine. Gradually add flour mixture and beat (when mixture becomes too thick for electric mixer, stir in remaining flour with spoon). Add *finely grated* sweet chocolate, ½ cup shredded coconut and pecans.

Shape dough into 1-inch balls. Place balls 2 inches

apart on ungreased cookie sheets. Bake 10 minutes or until edges are browned. Remove and cool.

In saucepan, melt bittersweet chocolate and shortening over low heat. Stir until smooth. Dip cooled cookies in melted chocolate. Allow excess to drip off. Transfer to a cookie sheet lined with waxed paper. Sprinkle with toasted coconut. Chill about 1 hour until firm. Makes 4 dozen cookies.

SEREFINA'S ZABAGLIONE

Zabaglione is a traditional Italian dessert usually served warm, spooned into glasses or over sliced fruit or with plain cake. The following recipe presents it served over whipped cream with a garnish of chocolate.

6 egg yolks
¾ cup sugar
1 cup Marsala wine
1 cup heavy cream
1 oz. semisweet chocolate

First prepare whipped cream: beat cream until it forms stiff peaks. Refrigerate.

In top of double boiler (not over heat), stir egg yolks and sugar until soft and foamy, about 3–5 minutes.

Slowly add Marsala, stirring constantly.

Place the double boiler over gently simmering (not boiling) water. Whisk continuously as custard mixture cooks. It will foam then swell into a soft mass. When it thickens to retain a slight peak when whisk is withdrawn (about 5–8 minutes), remove from heat.

Spoon a little cold whipped cream onto bottom of

stemmed glasses. Top with hot zabaglione. Garnish with semisweet chocolate curls. Makes 6–8 servings.

PEAR, ONION, AND CHEESE STRUDEL

A delicious wintertime appetizer.

6 tablespoons (¾ stick) unsalted butter
1 white onion, chopped fine
1 pear, peeled, cored, and sliced
¾ cup grated Fontina (or cheddar or jack) cheese
3 tsp. Dijon mustard
½ tsp. salt
4 sheets frozen phyllo pastry, thawed

Preheat oven to 375°. Melt 2 tablespoons butter in heavy skillet over medium heat. Add onion and sauté until brown. Add pear and sauté about 3 minutes. Transfer mixture to bowl. Cool slightly, then add cheese, mustard, and salt.

Melt remaining 4 tablespoons butter. Place 1 phyllo sheet on work surface. Quickly brush with melted butter, and top with second phyllo sheet. (Cover remaining 2 phyllo sheets with plastic wrap and damp kitchen towel.) Arrange half of pear mixture in log along one short side of phyllo, leaving 1-inch border at each end. Fold in sides and roll up tightly into log. Brush all over with butter. Transfer to large baking sheet. Repeat with remaining phyllo, butter, and pear mixture.

Bake about 18 minutes or until golden brown. Cool 5 minutes. Transfer to cutting board and cut on diagonal into 12 pieces per log.

Enter the Delicious World of Joanne Pence's Angie Amalfi Series

From the kitchen to the deck of a cruise ship, Joanne Pence's mysteries are always a delight. Starring career-challenged Angie Amalfi and her handsome homicide-detective boyfriend Paavo Smith, Joanne Pence serves up a mystery feast complete with humor, a dead body or two, and delicious recipes.

Enjoy the pages that follow, which give a glimpse into Angie and Paavo's world.

For sassy and single food writer Angie Amalfi, life's a banquet—until the man who's been contributing unusual recipes for her food column is found dead. But in SOMETHING'S COOKING, *Angie is hardly one to simper in fear—so instead she simmers over the delectable homicide detective assigned to the case.*

A while passed before she looked up again. When she did, she saw a dark-haired man standing in the doorway to her apartment, surveying the scene. Tall and broad shouldered, his stance was aloof and forceful as he made a cold assessment of all that he saw.

If you're going to gawk, she thought, come in with the rest of the busybodies.

He looked directly at her, and her grip tightened on the chair. His expression was hard, his pale blue eyes icy. He was a stranger, of that she was certain. His wasn't the type of face or demeanor she'd easily forget. And someone, it seemed, had just sent her a bomb. Who? Why? What if this stranger. . .

As he approached with bold strides, her nerves tightened. Since she was without her high heels, the top of her head barely reached his chin.

The man appeared to be in his mid-thirties. His face was fairly thin, with high cheekbones and a pronounced, aquiline nose with a jog in the middle that made it look as if it had been broken at least once.

Thick, dark brown hair spanned his high forehead, and his penetrating, deep-set eyes and dark eyebrows gave him a cold, no-nonsense appearance. His gaze didn't leave hers, and yet he seemed aware of everything around them.

"Your apartment?" he asked.

"The tour's that way." She did her best to give a nonchalant wave of her thumb toward the kitchen.

She froze as he reached into his breast pocket. "Police." He pulled out a billfold and dropped open one flap to reveal his identification: Inspector Paavo Smith, Homicide.

In TOO MANY COOKS, *Angie's talked her way into a job on a pompous, third-rate chef's radio call-in show. But when a successful and much envied restaurateur is poisoned, Angie finds the case far more interesting than trying to make her pretentious boss sound good.*

Angie glanced up from the monitor. She'd been debating whether or not to try to take the next call, if and when one came in, when her attention was caught by the caller's strange voice. It was oddly muffled. Angie couldn't tell if the caller was a man or a woman.

"I didn't catch your name," Henry said.

"Pat."

Angie's eyebrows rose. A neuter-sounding Pat? What was this, a *Saturday Night Live* routine?

"Well, Pat, what can I do for you?"

"I was concerned about the restaurant killer in your city."

Henry's eye caught Angie's. "Thank you. I'm sure the police will capture the person responsible in no time."

"I'm glad you think so, because—you're next."

Henry jumped up and slapped the disconnect button. "And now," he said, his voice quivering, "a word from our sponsor."

326

Angie Amalfi's latest job, developing the menu for a new inn, sounds enticing—especially since it means spending a week in scenic northern California with her homicide-detective boyfriend. But once she arrives at the soon-to-be-opened Hill Haven Inn, she's not so sure anymore. In COOKING UP TROUBLE, *the added ingredients of an ominous threat, a missing person, and a woman making eyes at her man, leave Angie convinced that the only recipe in this inn's kitchen is one for disaster.*

 She placed her hand over his large strong one, scarcely able to believe that they were here, in this strange yet lovely room, alone. "But I am real, Paavo."

"Are you?" He bent to kiss her lightly, his eyes intent, his hand moving from her chin to the back of her head to intertwine with the curls of her hair. The mystical aura of the room, the patter of the rain, the solitude of the setting stole over him and made him think of things he didn't want to ponder—things like being together with Angie forever, like never being alone again. He tried to mentally break the spell. He needed time—cold, logical time. "There's no way a woman like you should be in my life," he said finally. "Sometimes I think you can't be any more real than the Sempler ghosts. That I'll close my eyes and you'll disappear. Or that I'm just imagining you."

"Inspector," she said, returning his kiss with one that seared, "there's no way you could imagine me."

Cold logic melted in the midst of her fire, and all his careful resolve went with it. His heart filled, and the solemnity of his expression broke. "I know," he said softly, "and that's the best part."

As his lips met hers, a bolt of lightning lit their room for just a moment. Then a scream filled the darkness.

Food columnist Angie Amalfi has it all. But in COOKING MOST DEADLY, *while she's wondering if it's time to cut the wedding cake with her boyfriend, Paavo, he becomes obsessed with a grisly homicide that has claimed two female victims.*

"You've got to keep City Hall out of this case. As far as the press knows, she was a typist. Nothing more. Mumble when you say where she worked." Lieutenant Hollins got up from behind his desk, walked around to the front of it, and leaned against the edge. Paavo and Yosh sat facing him. They'd just completed briefing him on the Tiffany Rogers investigation. Hollins made it a point not to get involved in his men's investigations unless political heat was turned on. In this case, the heat was on high.

"Her friends and coworkers are at City Hall, and there's a good chance the guy she's been seeing is there as well," Paavo said.

"It's our only lead, Chief," Yosh added. "So far, the CSI unit can't even find a suspicious fingerprint to lift. The crime scene is clean as a whistle. She always met her boyfriend away from her apartment. We aren't sure where yet. We've got a few leads we're still checking."

"So you've got nothing except for a dead woman lying in her own blood on the floor of her own living room!" Hollins added.

"We have to follow wherever the leads take us," Paavo said.

"I'm not saying not to, all I'm saying is keep the press away." Hollins paced back and forth in front of his desk. "The mayor and the Board of Supervisors want this murderer caught right now. This isn't the kind of publicity they want for themselves or the city. I mean, if someone who works for them isn't safe, who is?"

"Aw heck, Paavo." Yosh turned to his partner. "The supervisors said they want us to catch this murderer fast. Here I'd planned to take my sweet time with this case."

Paavo couldn't help but grin.

"Cut the comedy, Yoshiwara." Hollins stuck an unlit cigar in his mouth and chewed. "This case is number one for you both, got it?"

In COOK'S NIGHT OUT, *Angie has decided to make her culinary name by creating the perfect chocolate confection: angelinas. Donating her delicious rejects to a local mission, Angie soon finds that the mission harbors more than the needy, and to save not only her life, but Paavo's as well, she's going to have to discover the truth faster than you can beat egg whites to a peak.*

Angelina Amalfi flung open the window over the kitchen sink. After two days of cooking with chocolate, the mouthwatering, luscious, inviting smell of it made her sick.

That was the price one must pay, she supposed, to become a famous chocolatier.

She found an old fan in the closet, put it on the kitchen table, and turned the dial to high. The comforting aroma of home cooking wafting out from a kitchen was one thing, but the smell of Willy Wonka's chocolate factory was quite another.

She'd been trying out intricate, elegant recipes for chocolate candies, searching for the perfect confection on which to build a business to call her own. Her kitchen was filled with truffles, nut bouchées, exotic fudges, and butter creams.

So far, she'd divulged her business plans only to Paavo, the man for whom she had plans of a very different nature. She was going to have to let someone else know soon, though, or she wouldn't have any room left in the kitchen to cook. She didn't want to start eating the calorie-oozing, waistline-expanding chocolates out of sheer enjoyment—her taste tests were another thing altogether and totally justifiable, she reasoned—and throwing the chocolates away had to be sinful.

Angie Amalfi's long-awaited vacation with her detective boyfriend has all the ingredients of a romantic getaway—a sail to Acapulco aboard a freighter, no crowds, no Homicide-department worries, and a red bikini. But in COOKS OVERBOARD, *it isn't long before Angie's* Love Boat *fantasies are headed for stormy seas—the cook tries to jump off the ship, Paavo is acting mighty strange, and someone's added murder to the menu . . .*

Paavo became aware, in a semi-asleep state, that the storm was much worse than anyone had expected it would be. The best thing to do was to try to sleep through it, to ignore the roar of the sea, the banging of rain against the windows, the almost human cry of the wind through the ship.

He reached out to Angie. She wasn't there. She must have gotten up to use the bathroom. Maybe her getting up was what had awakened him. He rolled over to go back to sleep.

When he awoke again, the sun was peeking over the horizon. He turned over to check on Angie, but she still wasn't beside him. Was she up already? That wasn't like her. He remembered a terrible storm last night. He sat up, suddenly wide awake. Where was Angie?

He got out of bed and hurried to the sitting area. Empty. The bathroom door was open. Empty.

The wall bed was down. What was that supposed to mean? Had she tried sleeping on it? Had she grown so out of sorts with him that she didn't want to sleep with him anymore? Things had seemed okay between them last night. He remembered her talking . . . she was talking about writing a cookbook again . . . and he remembered getting more and more sleepy . . . he must have . . . oh, hell.

Angie Amalfi has a way with food and people, but her newest business idea is turning out to be shakier than a fruit-filled gelatin mold. In A COOK IN TIME, *Her first—and only—clients for "Fantasy Dinners" are none other than a group of UFO chasers and government conspiracy fanatics. But when it seems that the group has a hidden agenda greater than anything on the X-Files, Angie's determined to find out the truth before it takes her out of this world—for good.*

The nude body was that of a male Caucasian, early forties or so, about 5'10", 160 pounds. The skin was an opaque white. Lips, nose, and ears had been removed, and the entire area from approximately the pubis to the sigmoid colon had been cored out, leaving a clean, bloodless cavity. No postmortem lividity appeared on the part of the body pressed against the ground. The whole thing had a tidy, almost surreal appearance. No blood spattered the area. No blood was anywhere; apparently, not even in the victim. A gutted, empty shell.

The man's hair was neatly razor-cut; his hands were free of calluses or stains, the skin soft, the nails manicured; his toenails were short and square-cut, and his feet without bunions or other effects of ill-fitting shoes. In short, all signs of a comfortable life. Until now.

Between her latest "sure-fire" foray into the food industry—video restaurant reviews—and her concern over Paavo's depressed state, Angie's plate is full to overflowing. Paavo has never come to terms with the fact that his mother abandoned him when he was four, leaving behind only a mysterious present. But when the token disappears in TO CATCH A COOK, Angie discovers a lethal goulash of intrigue, betrayal, and mayhem that may spell disaster for her and Paavo.

 The bedroom had also been torn apart and the mattress slashed. This was far, far more frightening than what had happened to her own apartment. There was anger here, perhaps hatred.

"What is going on?" she cried. "Why would anyone destroy your things?"

"It looks like a search, followed by frustration."

As she wandered through the little house, she realized he was right. It wasn't random destruction as she had first thought, but where the search to her apartment had appeared slow and meticulous, here it was hurried and frenzied.

"Hercules!" he called. "Herc? Come on, boy, are you all right?"

Angie's breath caught. His cat . . . He loved that cat.

"Do you see him?" she asked, standing in the bedroom doorway.

"No. They better not have hurt my cat," he muttered, his jaw clenched. They looked under the bed, in the closets, and throughout the backyard.

She was afraid—and for Hercules, more afraid that they'd find the cat than that they wouldn't. If he had run and was hiding, scared, he should return home eventually, but if he was nearby, and unable to come when called . . .

They couldn't find him.

Finally, back in the living room, Paavo bleakly took in the damage, the ugliness before him. "Who's doing this, Angie, and why?

For once Angie's newest culinary venture, "Comical Cakes," seems to be a roaring success! But in BELL, COOK, AND CANDLE, *there's nothing funny about her boyfriend Paavo's latest case—a series of baffling murders that may be rooted in satanic ritual. And it gets harder to focus on pastry alone when strange "accidents" and desecrations to her baked creations begin occurring with frightening regularity—leaving Angie to wonder whether she may end up as devil's food of a different kind.*

Angie was beside herself. She'd been called to go to a house to discuss baking cakes for a party of twenty, and yet no one was there when she arrived. This was the second time that had happened to her. Was someone playing tricks, or were people really so careless as to make appointments and then not keep them?

She really didn't have time for this. But at least she was getting smart. She'd brought a cake with her that had to be delivered to a horse's birthday party not far from her appointment. She never thought she'd be baking cakes for a horse, but Heidi was being boarded some forty miles outside the city, and the owner visited her on weekends only. That was why the owner wanted a Comical Cake of the mare.

Angie couldn't imagine eating something that

looked like a beloved pet or animal. She was meeting real ding-a-lings in this line of work.

Still muttering to herself about the thoughtlessness of the public, she got into her new car. A vaguely familiar yet disquieting smell hit her. A stain smeared the bottom of the cake box. She peered closer. The smell was stronger, and the bottom of the box was wet.

She opened the driver's side door, ready to jump out of the car as her hand slowly reached for the box top. Thoughts of flies and toads pounded her. What now?

She flipped back the lid and shrank away from it.

Nothing moved. Nothing jumped out.

Poor Heidi was now a bright-red color, but it wasn't frosting. The familiar smell was blood, and it had been poured on her cake. Shifting the box, she saw that it had seeped through onto the leather seat and was dripping to the floor mat.